KIND
OF A
BIG
DEAL

ALSO BY SHANNON HALE

Real Friends

Best Friends

Diana: Princess of the Amazons

Rapunzel's Revenge

Calamity Jack

The Unbeatable Squirrel Girl

The Unbeatable Squirrel Girl: 2 Fuzzy, 2 Furious

Book of a Thousand Days

Dangerous

Austenland

Midnight in Austenland

The Actor and the Housewife

The Books of Bayern series

The Princess Academy series

The Ever After High series

The Princess in Black series

KIND
OF A
BIG
DEAL

SHANNON HALE

ROARING BROOK PRESS
New York

Published by Roaring Brook Press
Roaring Brook Press is a division of Holtzbrinck Publishing
Holdings Limited Partnership
120 Broadway, New York, NY 10271 • fiercereads.com

ISBN 978-1-250-20623-7
Library of Congress Control Number 2020908622

Our books may be purchased in bulk for promotional, educational,
or business use. Please contact your local bookseller or the Macmillan
Corporate and Premium Sales Department at (800) 221-7945 ext. 5442
or by email at MacmillanSpecialMarkets@macmillan.com.

First edition, 2020
Book design by Aurora Parlagreco
Printed in the United States of America

1 3 5 7 9 10 8 6 4 2

For Rebecca and Jennifer,
my books- and musicals-loving kindred spirits.
Les adoro para siempre.

CHAPTER 1

It began, predictably, with a dream.

Josie was walking down the busy hall in her old high school, and everyone was shouting, "Hi, Josie! Hey, Josie!" just the way they used to. After all, she had been a big deal.

I'm such a cliché, she thought. *Dreaming about high school. Just like people always do.*

"Hi, Josie!"

Josie waved and wondered why, despite the glorious and sincere adoration of her classmates, she felt only dread.

Wait, was this going to be an anxiety dream? She looked down to see if she was naked, but nope: fully clothed. She entered a classroom, expecting to have to take a test she hadn't studied for—but the teacher just greeted her with a smile.

The teacher did look like a purple, toothy octopus, but it was, after all, a dream. And judging by the fear knotting up in her gut, it was going to be a bad one.

"Something is about to happen," she said to herself. "It's going to be a big deal. And I won't be prepared for it."

She sat at a desk, facing the closed classroom door, and waited for whatever would come in.

"I'm already here," said Justin, sitting to her left.

"Oh good," said Josie. She reached out, and he took her hand.

"Me too," said Nina, squeezing her other hand.

Josie smiled at Nina. What could possibly go wrong as long as she had her safety net, Justin and Nina?

"I'm here too!" said the octopus, wagging furry octopus eyebrows and waving gorgeous purple tentacles.

Josie gave the octopus a big thumbs-up. She didn't want to offend and risk a bad grade. What class was this anyway? She meant to turn to ask Justin, but her focus kept pulling to the door. A bright light, as if from a single bulb, was shining behind the frosted glass window. The light got brighter, piercing through the edges of the door. And then, a shadow. A figure. Somebody.

Something. About to happen. Energy pulsed behind that thought, pushing forward, the way a speeding car gets louder as it zooms near—building, screeching, screaming . . .

And, predictably, Josie woke up.

A second or two creaked by before she remembered she was not home in Arizona. She also wasn't on her old futon bed in Queens. She was, randomly, in Montana, sleeping in a foldout couch in the spare room.

Josie groaned and rolled over, the springs grinding beneath her, and she bumped into something both hard and furry. A robotic voice said, "*I want to be your pal.*"

Josie sat upright, her heart sputtering. She tore back the covers.

The hard, furry thing was just Mia's talking bear toy. Its mouth moved up and down with a labored creaking.

"*Read me a story.*"

Mia sometimes had nightmares. Since her mom was out of town, she'd probably crept into Josie's room for a post-nightmare restorative snuggle and then left the bear behind.

Josie fumbled for her cell phone from the side table. It was 7:32 a.m. She hesitated to bother Justin when he was probably getting ready for school but then went ahead and texted a photo of the bear.

JOSIE
I don't remember going to bed with this guy last night but I woke up to him this morning

She stared at the phone. Its blank screen just stared back at her all blankly, so she checked her email while she was waiting for Justin to respond.

FROM: York Bank Account Services
TO: Josie Sergakis
SUBJECT: account past due

No, no, no . . . Josie's stomach folded in on itself in a way that made her glad she hadn't eaten yet. If she missed a payment, the bank might notify her mother, who'd cosigned on her credit card. And then her mother would know—*no, no, no . . .*

The bulk of Josie's nanny salary went directly to her credit-card balance. April's payment should have gone out a couple of weeks ago. Maybe there was a bank error.

She tried to log in on the bank's mobile site, but it insisted on a password her phone no longer remembered, so she dialed the bank's number.

"All of our customer-service agents are taking other calls. You are TWENTY-FIRST in line."

Josie set the phone to speaker and got dressed to the hold music—a synthesized cover of "Welcome to New York." The T-shirt and sweats she'd slept in were practically clothing, so she brushed her teeth. Washed her face. Pulled her hair into a ponytail. Called it good.

The clock read 7:43 a.m. Mia was always up by now.

Josie carefully opened her bedroom door into the family room of the condo.

"Mia?" she whispered.

Except for the tinny music squeaking out of her phone, the condo was a monolith of silence. And brownness. Brown granite kitchen countertop. Brown sofa. Brown carpet. If a deer broke in and held really still, Josie wasn't sure she'd notice.

She hesitated outside Mia's door. Josie didn't want to wake her, but she'd been Mia's nanny for months and had never known the girl to sleep in. Josie carefully turned the knob to avoid a clicking sound and eased the door open.

The bed was empty. Her heart started to pound.

"Mia?" She ran into Mia's mom's bedroom. And there, curled up in the center of the king-sized bed, was the five-year-old, her curly black hair over her face.

The girl roused. "Mommy?" she said.

"No, it's Josie. Your mom is still in Nairobi. She'll be back tomorrow."

"Okay," said Mia. And that word sounded so brave, it broke Josie's broken heart a little more.

"I'm here. I'm not leaving you, I promise," said Josie.

"Okay," said Mia, and both the tightness in her voice and her grip on Josie's arm lifted.

"Did you have bad dreams?"

Mia nodded. "Are you listening to music?"

"Um . . . yeah." Josie held up her phone. "Do you like it?"

"No," said Mia.

"Yeah, me neither."

They ate cold cereal at the kitchen counter. The four-chair square table was covered in a week's worth of crayons and paper, clay creations, used-up watercolors, and dried-up snacks. Josie reminded herself that she'd better clean up before Victoria returned and keep up the facade that she was a responsible girl—woman?—who had her act together.

Josie had been Mia's nanny in New York City, coming into the little girl's life just in time to have a front-row seat to the dissolution of her parents' marriage. She barely knew Mia's dad, a *my-work-is-sooo-important* lawyer at some Manhattan firm. When the divorce was final, Mia's mom, Victoria, suddenly decided to move with Mia to their summer condo in Missoula, Montana.

"Montana! A clean start!" Victoria had said. "I'll raise Mia in the fresh air!" Victoria begged Josie to come with them. Mia was already attached to her, and Victoria would need a live-in nanny now. She was having to take back up her international business work, with all its travel.

Josie had figured, *Sure, why not move to Montana, where I know nobody and have zero prospects or any future whatsoever? In this life, you either make it or you don't.* And Josie hadn't made it. Montana seemed like as good a place as any to waste some time.

"Nope, nope, nope," Mia said, spooning gobs of sugary cereal from one bowl to the other.

Mia had two cereal bowls—yellow for eating and red for overflow. Sometimes she had too much cereal. Too Much Cereal had to go to time-out in the red bowl until Mia was prepared to acknowledge it.

Josie was tidying to the beat of a synthesized "Smells Like Teen Spirit" when her phone buzzed. A text!

JUSTIN
ha!

Ha? That was it? Well, her text hadn't been jaw-droppingly witty or anything, but maybe it deserved more than a *ha*? She was trying to come up with something clever to text back when a voice droned on the speaker: "All of our customer-service agents are taking other calls. You are TWENTIETH in line."

"Nooooo," said Josie.

She tried to strangle her cell but accidentally hung up instead. What if the bank had already contacted Mom? What if Mom knew that at age eighteen, her daughter was already buried under an obscene amount of useless debt? What if the bank forced Mom to get a second mortgage?

"Uggghh," said Josie.

"You're noisy today," said Mia.

Josie raised an eyebrow. She really didn't need a five-year-old adding color commentary. Mia stared back in that creepy, dead-eyed way she had.

In robotic teddy voice, Josie said, *"Take me with you."*

"I want to be your pal," Mia quoted back in monotone. Her imitation of the toy bear was uncanny. Josie laughed.

"Play with me, Mia, or I will eat your brains."

Mia squealed and hopped off her stool, running

away. But slowly. Stopping to look back, to make sure Josie was still chasing.

Josie dutifully shamble-chased Mia around and around the coffee table. Mia giggled, half terrified, half excited, and then finally allowed Josie to grab her.

Mia wrapped her arms around Josie and squeezed.

"Aw," said Josie, surprised how sweet it felt to receive this little girl's hug. She hadn't realized that her chest had been feeling a little emptied out, her heart kind of shrunken and rattling around loose in there, till Mia's affection helped to fill it back up. Josie squeezed her back, wanting in turn to relieve any sadness Mia must be feeling with her mom away.

The hug lasted about 1.5 seconds, till Mia had had more than enough affection, thank you, and wriggled away.

Josie's phone buzzed.

NINA
Sorry I didn't call back last night. Busy now.
Finance class, church choir, then work. Later?

JOSIE
Yes please

Nothing to report anyway. Josie's routine was identical day after day, while her best friend was at the University of Chicago, attending fascinating lectures and dating interesting people. And apparently working somewhere?

Josie hadn't known she'd gotten a job or what the deal was with church choir. As far as Josie knew, Nina didn't attend any church. Well, she'd get the details later and would just have to hold on emotionally till Nina's voice could sustain her.

"What are we doing today?" Mia asked, putting her cereal bowls in the sink.

"Something fun," said Josie.

Mia gasped. "School?" She clasped her hands, her eyes glistening, as if she'd stolen the expression from an old movie about a pure-hearted orphan.

"Uh . . . no, not today." Victoria had signed Mia up for preschool three mornings a week, but for friend-hungry Mia, it wasn't nearly enough. "I thought we could check out that park by the river!"

Josie hoped that Mia would be entertained on a playground long enough for Josie to get to caller number one and fix this before her financial house of cards toppled.

Judging by Mia's dead-eyed expression, *park* did not even approach the grandeur of *school*. In her robotic teddy voice, she said, "*Mia is bored. Mia wants friends.*"

"Yes. Friends. There will be friends at the park. Even better friends than you play with in preschool." Josie slipped into a posh New England accent. "Dah-ling, you shall make the most mah-velous friends."

"More," said Mia.

So Josie chattered in a Russian accent, in an American Southern accent, and in her grandmother's Greek accent as they slipped on shoes. They automatically went for their coats before Josie remembered, once again, with rapturous joy, that it was May. Boldly, she stepped out the front door with nothing more than a zip-up hoodie.

A hoodie in May. The Arizona girl inside Josie shook her head in disbelief.

They crossed the street and headed toward Missoula's cozy downtown. Josie's familiarity with Missoula was mostly limited to the stretch between the condo and the grocery store. Josie didn't have a driver's license, so when Victoria was out of town, she had to do all errands on foot. And why do any excessive errands in tiny, two-horse Missoula when she could curl up in bed instead and obsessively read Broadway news and scan through old text-message chains?

But May . . . Josie reluctantly had to admit that May in Montana wasn't half bad. Air so clean you could drink it like water. That famously big sky arching its back, stretching wide and strong. Everywhere, life was just about to happen.

Their pace was slow enough to allow Mia her frequent need to hop over cracks, and Josie found herself singing not unhappily as they passed a Methodist church, a bar, a vegan restaurant, a yoga studio, another bar, an art gallery, a bar . . .

A small storefront scrunched between two buildings advertised:

COFFEE

YOUR ENTIRELY PUN-FREE SOURCE OF HOT BEVERAGES

The man out front setting up sidewalk tables was wearing all denim: shirt, jacket, and pants tucked into cowboy boots. He had golden brown skin and a head so bald it was shiny.

"Good morning, songbird!" he said.

Josie startled, briefly forgetting that outside New York City, strangers spoke to each other. There was so much room in Montana, people didn't have to pretend to be alone in public. Here, privacy leaked from the rocks and fertilized the wildflowers and sang like wind chimes in the breeze: *All the privacy you want! And all you don't want! Isolation for free, free, free!*

"You have a lovely singing voice," he said.

"Oh, thanks." Embarrassed, she looked down from his face. The name tag pinned to his collar said BRUCE. "I'm not a professional or anything, though I was going to be, and actually I was kind of a big deal in high school . . ."

Had she really just said that? Josie swallowed.

"Uh . . ." She pointed at the sign, desperate to change the subject. "No puns, huh?"

"We take our coffee seriously."

"So you named your shop Coffee when you could've named it something like, uh . . . Brewed Awakening."

"Brew-Ha-Ha," he offered.

"Thanks a Latte," she said, trying to remember past coffee shops. "Espresso Yourself."

"Java the Hut. They are pretty funny . . ." He gave her a mirthless expression. "For five minutes. I plan to stay in business longer than that."

Josie offered a polite laugh.

"So, can I get you anything?" Bruce asked.

"Um . . ." After her awkward lingering, she knew she should get something, but money talk made Josie sweaty. After dropping out of high school, she'd survived in New York City by paying all her expenses with her now-shredded credit card. If she kept putting almost all of her nanny salary toward the balance, she could pay it off in a little over a year. But Mia would start kindergarten this fall. Surely Victoria wouldn't keep Josie on full-time if Mia was in school half the day. Josie was just treading water.

She glanced at the laminated menu affixed to the front door. Civility demanded she purchase something after all the lingering.

"A . . . small tea."

"Lemon? Cream? Sugar?" he asked.

"Do they cost extra?"

He came back with a recyclable to-go cup of hot water and a peppermint tea bag, a packet of sugar balanced atop. "It's on the house."

"Thank you, Bruce!"

He winked. Not in a creepy way. But like he knew. Like he'd also once run away from his supposedly bright prospects and into an unknown place to play hide-and-seek with himself too. Or something.

"Look, a bookstore," said Mia, tugging Josie toward the shop next door. The front window display held books on wires as if they were birds in flight. "It's bad luck to see a bookstore and not go in."

Mia had a long list of bad-luck things, and when they were unavoidable, she had to do a great deal of hopping to protect herself and Josie from the bad luck.

"I've never heard that one."

"That's how it *feels*," said Mia, tugging harder.

A little bell rang as they opened the door. A flush of warm air rushed out, plucking at Josie's hair. Her breath caught; her arms prickled with goose bumps. There, on the threshold of the bookstore, she felt an unexpected lightning bolt of certainty, as she had in her cliché of a dream: Something was about to change.

CHAPTER 2

Natural light from the shop's windows slashed across wooden bookcases, the beams dancing with dust specks. Exposed wood rafters still boasted their bark. A quote was painted high on a wall in silver-outlined yellow:

"Our truest life is when we are in dreams awake."
~Thoreau

Customers wandered from book to book like honeybees over flowering sage. Josie marveled that everyone seemed at home, as if the labyrinth of bookcases created a clear pattern, as if the thousands of different book covers weren't at all intimidating.

"Mia, why don't we go—" Josie started.

But Mia had spotted a toy-train table in the kids' section and run off.

"May I help you find something?" The bookseller

wore a red apron embroidered with the name WALK-ING SHADOW BOOKS. That was as high as Josie's glance reached. She was afraid if she made eye contact, he would detect that she didn't belong there.

"No thanks, just browsing," Josie said, turning away so he wouldn't try to be helpful again. She walked with purpose to the nearest shelf and took out a book, scanning the back cover and nodding thoughtfully in what she hoped was a convincing manner. Her acting was a little rusty. Josie hadn't performed so much as an audition monologue since coming to Montana. And she hadn't read a novel for fun since sophomore year.

Slowly, Josie became aware of a conversation two women were having on the other side of the bookcase.

"You aren't going to believe it. It's like Tom all over again."

"What happened?"

"So first Brittany tells me Kevin's been working late."

"Uh-oh."

"Uh, *yeah*. And he suddenly has business trips every other weekend."

"Uh-oh."

"Uh, *yeah*. And when he *is* home, Brittany says he's distracted and distant."

By now Josie was listening very, very hard, a book titled *The Energy Diet: How to Chant Away Twenty Pounds!* frozen in her hand.

"Uh. Oh." This second woman didn't say those

words like *no, that's terrible news* so much as *pass the popcorn, extra butter.*

"Exactly," said the first woman. "And I wasn't going to say anything, because you know me, but then she went and asked me, 'How could this happen to us? We were high school sweethearts!' And I was like, 'Brittany, that was the whole problem. Everybody knows that relationships that start in high school never last—'"

And suddenly Josie fell flat on her back.

She'd been leaning closer and closer, resting her hand on what she thought was a wooden bookshelf—but no. It was one of those wobbly cardboard displays. The books it had held now lay scattered around her. A final one slipped out of the slanting display. She read its title—*Acute Love Triangle*—the split second before it pegged her on the forehead.

And then the two women were standing over her.

"You okay?" asked the first. The blonder one.

"Um . . ."

There was something Trophy Wife about them: big hair heavily sprayed, big breasts in blouses buttoned low to welcome the spring, big diamonds on wedding rings, dangling from spray-on-brown hands. When they pulled Josie to her feet, they were standing so close she was inside the atmosphere of their gardenia perfume.

"You're not okay, are you?" said the Blonder Trophy Wife. And then she held out her long-nailed hands and pulled Josie into an embrace.

Josie was so startled she just stood there, dizzy in the perfume cloud and uncomfortably aware of the woman's enormous breasts pressing against her chest.

For a moment, the unexpected kindness of the hug lodged in Josie's throat, ramming into her already-lodged fears about Justin and threatening to make her cry. But, quickly, awkwardness set in.

"It's just been . . . a weird day," said Josie, before remembering it was still morning. "I mean, already. I mean, lately."

Blonder Trophy Wife was now petting Josie's hair. "Boy trouble, am I right?"

"Uh . . . sort of . . . but not a big deal or anything. But thank you," Josie mumbled, and tried to extricate herself in a polite way, which involved patting the woman's back with one hand while disentangling her other hand, smiling gratefully while stepping back.

The Trophy Wives smiled at her, pity and perhaps understanding in their eyes.

"You're worth gold, you hear me?" said the less-blond one. "Gold."

"I'm okay," said Josie. "Really. I just . . . fell. But I'm fine. I'm new in the state, from Arizona originally, and actually I was kind of a big—"

No. No way was she just about to say that again. Josie felt her cheeks go fire hot and hoped the women hadn't filled in the blank.

"Nerd," Josie blurted. "I was a big nerd. In high school. Never mind, I don't know what I'm saying."

Even though her brain told her it was stupid and immature and ridiculous, she still yearned to communicate it somehow to these women who had only seen her in a clumsy and vulnerable position. That she was somebody. That she *had been* somebody.

Josie turned away quickly and bumped directly into someone's chest. That red apron again. Her legs wobbled, perhaps from the book blow to the head but, she admitted, probably more from the shock of the Trophy Wives' conversation. *Everybody knows that relationships that start in high school . . .* Justin had always loved her so much, she didn't just feel it in her belly but all the way down into her knees. But he had been distant lately, slow to answer texts, calling less frequently. Was he phasing her out?

The bookseller was still standing there. Josie forced her gaze to leave his apron and scan up.

He was excessively handsome, the kind of guy she imagined trophy wives would hire to be the pool boy, if they lived in a state where pools were a thing. He had a deep olive skin tone, wore his black hair a little long, a little unruly, in that *let's pretend I woke up like this* way, and he sported thick-framed, geek-chic glasses.

"Can I help you?" he asked, pushing up his glasses

with one finger in a manner that reminded her of Clark Kent.

After knocking over the display and everything, she felt she'd better buy something. She handed him the nearest thing: a bright pink *Play Princess!* magazine from a rack.

"Who is this for?" The magazine opened in his hand, revealing a vertical poster of a princess riding a sparkly unicorn. "Ooh, check out that centerfold."

"I only read it for the articles," said Josie.

"Can't I get something for *you*?" he asked. "Everyone needs to escape into a book, and I'm guessing it's been a while for you."

"How did you know?"

He smiled and shrugged. "I'm a professional."

Josie raised her eyebrow—he looked no older than college age, so she assumed he was a part-time, minimum-wage worker.

"I was practically raised in bookstores," he clarified. "And if I know anything, it's that you're never too old to develop your imagination." He gestured grandly to a poster on a bookcase end: DEVELOP YOUR IMAGINATION: READ!

Josie laughed. "Okay, give me something light and fun that doesn't force me to think."

"You got it."

He scanned a bookshelf and pulled out a paperback. Josie was relieved it wasn't a hardcover. It would be so awkward to explain that it was too expensive for her. She had Victoria's credit card for grocery purchases and such, so she gave him that for the princess magazine, but she used her debit card for herself.

DEBT. DEBT. DEBT. The words clanged in her skull. *I'm not ready for knee-shaking, life-altering debt. I'm still a teenager!* She had to get ahold of the bank ASAP.

Josie took the paperback from the bookseller. The title, *The Highwayman Came Riding*, was emblazoned in white, curly font across a cover in heavy greens, pinks, and golds. A pale blond woman in clothing from some previous century was swooning in the arms of a tanned man with a hard, chiseled, hairless chest. Her dress was slipping off her shoulders, and her breasts—just too large and too wild to be constrained by clothing—appeared to be fighting for the nearest exit. Josie blushed, wondering what about her made the bookseller think that this was the book for her.

She turned it to read the back cover. The words looked tiny, blurry. Had that copy of *Acute Love Triangle* hit her harder than she'd thought? She held the book back at arm's length and the words crisped up a little.

"What's the matter with me?" she muttered.

"Are you fairly new to Montana?" he asked. "Did you move from sea level?"

"Yes . . ." Josie squinted at him. "How did you know?"

"Just guessing. Here, try these." He handed her a pair of reading glasses from a drawer behind the counter.

She almost laughed and put them on just to humor him, but as soon as she did, she could clearly read the back cover. She gasped and took them off. The text was blurry again.

"I know, you're too young for reading glasses," he said. "You've never worn them before. Only grannies need them. I hear it all the time."

"You do?"

"From people whose eyes haven't adjusted to the high altitude yet. Usually it only affects them in the mornings and then goes away. You can keep the glasses. They were a free sample a supplier sent us."

Great, so his estimation of her was broke, granny-eyed, and likely to swoon in the arms of bare-chested men.

She stuffed the glasses into her purse.

"You don't have to take them off on my account," he said. "Glasses are, you know, sexy . . ."

By his tone, he might have been saying, *How about this weather we're having?*, so it took her a moment of squinting at him before she realized that he was flirting. Maybe?

"Um . . . that's okay," she said.

"Ooh, that's a good book," said another red-aproned

book clerk, eyeing Josie's purchase. She was blond, but unlike the Trophy Wives, her skin seemed to have never seen the sun: not real, fake, or sprayed on. She wore smart-girl glasses, like a ridiculously gorgeous starlet in a movie trying and failing to look nerdy. "Seriously, don't save that one for a rainy day; dive in now. You'll thank me later."

She winked.

"Okay . . . ," said Josie.

The blond book clerk wrapped the other bookseller's arms around her waist and leaned back against his chest. "Have you read that one yet?" she asked him.

"No, but if she does, I promise I will too." He smiled shyly at Josie and stepped away from Blondie. "This is my sister, Bianca. The bookstore's a family business."

"The family that works together stays together," said Bianca.

"I'm Deo, by the way," he said. *D-E-O.*

"Did you know your name is Greek?" Josie said and then immediately wished she hadn't. Trying to teach someone about their own name was just pathetic.

"Is it? Hey, will you come back and tell me what you think about the book?" asked Deo. "I've heard from other customers that it's super engrossing, and I'd love your feedback."

He smiled at her again. And her pulse snapped in her throat.

She'd been so isolated since coming to Montana,

passing most of each day alone in the condo, even when Mia was at preschool. It had been a while since she'd felt so *seen*.

A tiny, melancholy voice inside warned her she was unworthy of human attention. Josie broke eye contact first.

Mia ran up. "Mommy! That boy took the train I was playing with."

Josie laughed nervously, glancing at Deo. "I'm not your mommy, Mia."

Mia snorted in frustration at her mistake. "*Josie!* That boy stole my train!"

Josie smiled at Deo and Bianca. "I'm really not her mommy. Her mom. She just says it wrong sometimes. She's my, um, charge. Or ward. Or . . . I'm her nanny. Is what I'm trying to say. Not my kid. I'm single or whatever."

"Kids," said Deo with a head shake and a grin.

"Totally. *Kids*," said Josie.

Josie grabbed Mia and hurried out before there was any more awkward flirting or penetrating looks from dazzlingly blond sisters.

Deo called after her, "Come back soon!"

CHAPTER 3

They were heading toward the park, Mia staring in wonder at *Play Princess!*, when Josie's cell sang out the ringtone: "All That Jazz." Josie answered the video call, and Nina's face appeared on her screen. She had a long, angular face, her cheeks warm as if used to the sun, and one side of her hair was shaved away, the long ends dyed a vibrant purple.

"Wow," said Josie.

"You like?" said Nina, patting her hair. "I'm on my way to choir and only have five seconds but I wanted to show you."

"Love the hair. But I just got a pair of reading glasses, Nina. Reading glasses."

"Uh-huh," said Nina, distracted.

"I repeat, reading glasses."

Nina's gaze snapped back to her phone's camera. "Oh, wait, what? That doesn't seem right."

"I know! Maybe there's something wrong with me."

"You mean, besides the fact that your favorite drink is root beer mixed with heavy cream?"

"I call it a root beer melt and it's delicious and the cream cuts the sweetness and someday you will agree with me. But no, I mean wrong with me *medically*."

"Heeeyy!" Nina called out to someone, and she smiled that smile Josie knew to be genuine. "Sorry, I gotta run. We need to talk later, okay?"

"Yes, please call back."

Josie blew a kiss. And wondered who Nina was smiling at like that.

She'd only just hung up when her phone buzzed with a text.

ROXANNE

Hey Jos! It's been forever. Guess what . . . I'm coming to New York this summer!!! I want to see you. What are you in again? Can you get me tix?

Josie quickly deleted the text. *Live with what you've got. Expect no more. Pull life's blanket over your head and shut it all off . . .*

She took deep, cleansing breaths and looked at the sky.

Missoula sat in a valley surrounded by bare hills, its bluish-greenness nourished by melting snow. The Clark Fork River tumbled through Hellgate Canyon and split Missoula in half. Josie was aiming for a park in a crook of the river she'd found by examining satellite images on her phone. As they neared, the air smelled increasingly springy, and Josie wrinkled her nose at the heavy scents of pollen and tree sap.

In the fifty-five-degree weather, college students were out in shorts and bare feet. Josie passed a dark-haired guy and a girl who were playing Frisbee. On a bench behind them, a white guy in a cowboy hat and boots was plucking out chords on a guitar. Another guy, with blond dreadlocks wafting the scent of patchouli, asked to join the game, and the college girl tossed the Frisbee in his direction. He caught it in a neat swipe behind his back. The scene looked ready-made for a brochure snapshot: *Visit Missoula, Montana!*

The only things Josie really knew about Missoula was from her online research: it was a college town just south of the Flathead Reservation and full of a mix of people from retired loggers to literati to environmentalists to sovereign citizens. And second-home Californians, but it was clear that everybody hated them equally.

Josie smiled at the Frisbee players in a way she hoped looked nothing like a second-home Californian.

Beyond the grass where Frisbee was happening, a playground sprouted out of a sandy circle. Several children around Mia's age climbed, ran, screamed, tossed, and fell, and Mia immediately ran to join in.

The only non-children near the playground squished together on a single bench, but they looked too young to be parents. Fellow nannies? Josie's pulse sped up; she was way more excited at the prospect of peers than she'd anticipated. She hadn't quite realized until now just how much she'd been isolating herself.

Besides, Josie had made a promise to hook Mia up with some friends. Which meant playdates. Which meant Josie had to score some phone numbers today or face tiny-girl wrath.

The probable nannies—two girls and one curly-haired guy—each held a copy of the same book. There was a naturalness to their style that was unnatural. Plaid shirts beneath V-neck sweaters, sleeves cuffed just so. Makeup so light you might be fooled into thinking their cheeks were naturally blushing and their lips always this glossy pink.

Josie inched closer, hoping the trio would notice her and invite her into their conversation.

". . . the point-of-view shift allows the reader to empathize with the narwhal," the guy was saying.

"But at what cost?" said one of the girls, who looked South Asian. "The juxtaposition of the slight—even anemic—prose with the more romantic passages—"

"Is brilliant," interrupted the blond white girl.

The other two nodded solemnly, absorbing the thought.

"The narwhal's narrative cuts through the superfluous prose like a warm knife through cheese," the blond girl continued.

"Brilliant," said the curly-haired guy.

"So deft," said the other girl.

"Hey . . . there . . . ," said Josie.

The three looked up. Josie wasn't sure if they were squinting in the sunlight or scowling at the interruption. She reminded herself that she'd already binge-watched her way through two streaming services and, imagining a future with Montana friends to hang out with, took a breath and went on.

"Hey, how are you? I'm Josie. Josie Pie."

The two looked to the blond girl, allowing her the first reaction to this newcomer. So many blondes in Montana! And they all seemed to wield such power!

The blonde smiled coolly and said, "Josie Pie? What a unique name."

The other two laughed. Josie joined them, though she wasn't sure why. She cleared her throat.

"So, I moved to Missoula a month ago."

"Welcome to the neighborhood," said the blonde. "I'm Misty."

"Hey, Misty." Josie exhaled. Introductions! This conversation was improving.

"This is Meaghan, and this is Marcus," she said, indicating her bench mates. "We were in the same lit course at U of M last year, and when we discovered we were all also nannies—"

"Misty said, we should have a nanny book club!" said Meaghan. "Do you go to U of M too?"

"No," said Josie. "But I *am* a nanny!"

"Cool." Misty tilted her head. "So, do you want to tell us your real name?"

Josie blushed. How did they know? Pie was Justin's last name, but she'd liked how it sounded with her first name so she'd adopted it when she moved to New York. So memorable, she'd thought. A perfect stage name!

"What do you mean?"

"How do you spell your last name?" Misty asked.

"P-I-E," said Josie.

"Oh. It's just . . ." Misty glanced at Meaghan and Marcus, her gestures contrite. "Josie Pye—*P-Y-E*—that's the name of a character from *Anne of Green Gables*? That classic of Canadian literature? You've read it?"

Josie had. She felt her face drain of blood. Josie Pye! That mean girl who always teased Anne! She'd read the books in middle school, before she'd met Justin, but how had she never realized? A quick conversation changer—

"Um . . . did you know that in the US there is an average of eighty-seven people per square mile, but in Montana there are only six people per square mile? I've had a lot of free time, been googling information about my new state, as one does." Josie expected them to laugh, so when they didn't, she did for them. "Six people per square mile! Must be why it's been so hard for me to meet new people here! So few of you! Spread out so far! I have to hunt you down!"

"I hunt," said Misty. "Mostly deer. Sometimes fowl—pheasant, duck, goose . . ."

Meaghan and Marcus nodded.

"Humans are carnivores by nature," said Misty, "but how much more humane to consume an animal taken in the wild than one raised in a cage, don't you agree?"

"Um . . . that's Mia on the slide," said Josie. "The girl I nanny."

"Mine is Ahab," said Misty, indicating a toddler in a sweater vest over a collared shirt, digging in the sand.

"There's my Atticus," said Marcus. His charge was about four years old and wearing a navy-blue jumpsuit with white piping.

"Agamemnon is over there," said Meaghan, pointing to a boy in an oversized wool sweater and corduroys.

"They're adorable!" said Josie. "I promised Mia I'd find her new friends today. So, do you come here often? Um, that came out wrong . . ."

"Every morning," said Misty.

"For book club," said Meaghan, holding up a novel titled *Depression, Death, and Narwhals.*

"No way, what a coincidence!" said Josie.

"Oh, you've read it?" asked Meaghan.

"That? No. I meant that you're having a book club, because I have a book! With me right now! I'm not much of a reader usually—"

Josie noticed their expressions darken.

"I mean, I totally used to be! Like in junior high! And high school too, at first anyway. I read a ton of books, and not just for class, but actually for fun."

Expressions got even darker.

Josie dug through her purse for her new book. "It just feels like serendipity, is what I'm trying to say, that on the day I decide to get back into reading I would meet three nannies who are readers and watch kids the same age as Mia." She proudly held up *The Highwayman Came Riding*.

"Serendipity, right?" she said again.

No one responded.

"Am I using that word correctly?" she whispered.

Meaghan glanced at Misty before speaking. "Um, Josie?" she said in a patient, helpful kind of tone. "That book you're holding. It's a tawdry romance. And a tawdry romance is not the sort of book one would bring to a book club."

"Oh."

Misty smiled an equally patient, helpful kind of smile. "You are what you read, you know."

Josie nodded. She didn't dare say anything else. Especially as she still wasn't certain she'd used *serendipity* correctly.

A silence followed that was only slightly more awkward than the conversation had been. And then Misty said, "Let's take a look at the passage on page forty-seven, where the narrator describes the orphan girl with such brutalizing detail one fears her bones might break under the weight of our scrutiny."

The trio opened their books, and Misty began to

read aloud. Something about their posture, their intensity, reminded Josie of the Three Fates, perhaps from a painting she'd seen somewhere. She walked away before they could decide *her* fate.

A surge of anger tingled in her toes and rushed up through her middle, into her face, bringing both a hot flush to her cheeks and a feeling that, if she were a cartoon, her eyes would be blazing red. *Don't they know who I am?* came the sincere but also instantly ridiculous thought.

No, Josie Pie, they don't know who you are, because you aren't Millennial High School's precious rising star Josie Sergakis here. Or anywhere, anymore.

She waved to Mia out of guilt for having failed to secure playdates. But the little girl didn't notice, busy trying to recruit Agamemnon to play pirates by shouting, "Come here, scurvy wench!"

Agamemnon started to cry.

Josie pretended not to notice, busying herself by scouting out a place to sit. The trio had taken the only bench in the shade of the cottonwood trees, but after a month of cold-weather house arrest, Josie was open to sunshine. She spotted a bench conveniently far away from the trio.

The bench was weather-beaten—ancient wooden slats cracked and peeling, metal joints rusted orange, the weeds beneath it tall, their heads nosing up through the slats. One overachieving bush had sprouted up beside it, stretching its arms over most of the bench as if aggressively saving a seat for someone who was clearly very late. Josie scooted the bush over the side and sat down, crunching dead weeds beneath her.

She dialed the bank again.

"All of our customer-service agents are taking other calls. You are FIFTY-SEVENTH in line."

The hold music started up, and Josie's head started to pound. *Nope, can't do it right now.* She ended the call, leaned back, and breathed.

The sun was warm on her dark hair, the sound of the river at her back soothingly peaceful. There was nothing to distract her, and her brain began to mull. Mull fiercely over one particular thing.

Everybody knows that relationships that start in high school . . .

She'd worried before that she might be naive. After all, who stays with their high school boyfriend forever? But the way he used to look at her . . . how could someone who'd loved her marrow-deep suddenly just stop?

Well, what did she think would happen after she practically ran away from him across state borders, not once but twice? A weird, sharp laugh coughed out of her throat.

The trio glanced at her. She saw herself through their eyes—an oddly named, slouchy-dressed, anxious nanny not in college like them, sitting alone on a bench and laughing crazily to herself. Josie quickly picked up her book and opened it.

The words on the page were blurry. She shoved on the wretched glasses and hoped the trio didn't look at her. And then kinda hoped they did—maybe reading glasses made her look more mature and intelligent.

Or sexy.

She snorted a laugh and began to read.

───────────── 📖 ─────────────

CHAPTER 1:
An Alarming Turn of Events

Lady Fontaine pressed her gloved fingertips to the carriage window as if she could touch the jade-green woods on the other side. She had grown up in the tame countryside of southern France, vineyards and pleasant parks, wandering no farther from home than a walk to the church or a picnic by the tame little stream. And now to leave Ville de Marguerite for the first time, and under such strange circumstances! A hurried letter from her father: *Come to me in Paris at once. Bring only your most trusted servants. Tell no one where you are going. Travel safely and hurry.*

His words awoke something inside her. Perhaps she had been half asleep most of her life, only now realizing there was so much more to the world than a walk to church. Like secrets. And danger. And dark, mysterious woods that hid who-knew-what. It almost made her want to open the carriage door and . . .

No. Desires for wild landscapes and mysteries were uncouth and uncivil. She was Lady Fontaine de Marguerite. She was the daughter of the Marquis de Marguerite, a high-ranking nobleman in the French aristocracy. And a lady's place was not to think and dream but to sit quietly, look pretty, and be ready to serve her father. And, someday, her husband.

She sighed, her bosom swelling in the confines of her corset.

She did not know how beautiful she was. Whenever she caught sight of the carriage driver or footman eyeing her, she assumed there was something amiss. A lock of hair fallen out. A stain on her dress. She could not guess that the men were drinking in the sight of their employer's daughter and perhaps wishing . . .

Josie was already so engrossed in the words that it took her a moment to realize the colors were changing— the white page had a tinge of blue; the space around the book was spitting beams of yellow and orange. Instinctively, she let go of the book to grab the bench for stability, but nothing fell from her hand. The book was gone. And so, it seemed, was her eyesight. Was she actually going blind? The colors of the park, greens and browns and grays, were blurs in her shaking vision, swirls like the kaleidoscopic shapes that light took when she shut her eyes tight. She held her breath and waited for the world to come back into focus. Or for death, whichever came first.

CHAPTER 4

A few dizzy moments later, the colors and motion did resolve themselves, but not back into the park. Not into Missoula, Montana.

Josie was sitting on something soft. She brushed it with her fingertips. Velvet. A window revealed green woods lurching past. The window was in a door. She was inside a car. No, more like an old-timey carriage.

Josie Pie was riding in a carriage.

"What a wretched span of road," said a voice beside her, in a French accent.

Josie turned to see Misty, the blond book club leader, though gone was the flyaway hair and cable-knit sweater. Now her tresses were piled high in a tremendous updo, way beyond prom night and a few black streaks away from Frankenstein's bride. Pearls draped around the peak of her hair and from her ears and long white neck. She was dressed in a pink gown with huge skirts and gigantic hips that took up half the carriage.

Clearly eighteenth century. Was Misty performing in a production of *The Scarlet Pimpernel* or something? But just moments ago she'd been in the park, dressed as if for a Patagonia catalog shoot.

Facing Josie and Misty on the carriage's opposite bench sat Marcus and Meaghan, equally outfitted in eighteenth-century costumes, though less resplendently.

"Misty, what's happening?" Josie said.

Misty kept staring out the window. "It is *hardly* misty out. Clear for miles. Not that there is anything worth viewing in this godforsaken landscape."

"What are you wearing?" Josie tried.

Misty looked down at her gown. "What is the matter? Did that impudent wench at the last inn spill some of her ghastly excuse for breakfast on my gown? Clean it at once!"

Meaghan and Marcus leaned forward, inspecting the skirts of her gown.

"It looks fine, milady," said Meaghan.

"Fine?" Misty asked with a raised eyebrow. "Just fine?"

"It looks magnificent," amended Marcus. "Absolutely spectacular. And not a spot on it."

Josie had been dumbly looking around, still waiting for the world to resolve itself. But with each second that ticked by, panic tightened her ribs. She fought for a deep breath but couldn't seem to breathe. Due to her tight corset, perhaps? Because she was indeed wearing a corset. She could feel it binding her beneath a river-blue servant woman's dress. Gone were her sweats. Gone, apparently, were her wits. She tried again for a deep breath and began hyperventilating.

Marcus and Meaghan looked at each other and giggled.

"Milady, your waiting woman has taken to hysterics," said Meaghan.

"Oh yeah, I have," said Josie between gasps. "I'm definitely . . . having some kind . . . of a 'sode." She pulled on the glass window, sliding it halfway open, and shouted, "Help! I'm hallucinating! Is Mia okay? Someone call 911!"

Misty scooted as far away from Josie as her hips would allow, which was a good centimeter.

"Regurgitate your breakfast on my gown and there will be a beheading," she said.

Josie grabbed at her neck to loosen her dress so she could breathe, but there was nothing there. Her neck and upper chest were bare, her dress so low-cut she was surprised her breasts didn't just pop out. That corset must be really tight.

A corset that she hadn't put on. Yet she was somehow wearing. Was she having another stress dream—without having fallen asleep? Hallucinations couldn't feel this real, could they? Had she been so upset about Justin that her sanity had instantly snapped? Or maybe the park had been gassed with a hallucinogenic chemical. In that case, Mia might be affected too.

"Mia!" she shouted. "Mia!"

"Oh, for the love of the Mother, shut up," said Misty.

Meaghan and Marcus giggled again.

Josie looked at them hard, her stare accusing them of drugging her, dressing her in a costume, and stuffing her in a carriage. For a prank this elaborate, she must be on video.

She looked out the window for the cameras. But all she saw was wild woods. And then, coming up from behind, a man on a galloping horse.

Thump. An arrow lodged into the carriage beside the window. Josie startled. Misty screamed.

More buzzing as arrows swarmed past them. Frightened neighs of the horses. And then they heard the carriage driver shout, "Highwaymen!"

"Highwaymen!" said Misty with terror.

"Highwaymen!" said Meaghan and Marcus with glee.

"Highwaymen?" said Josie. "What *are* high—"

A face appeared in her window: a man dressed like an old-time bandit with a scarf tied over his nose and mouth. He was riding a horse, keeping pace with the speeding, lurching carriage. He grabbed onto the open window and leaped from his horse onto the door of the carriage.

40

Josie punched him in the face.

"Sorry!" she said as he fell off the carriage. "It was instinct! I . . . I don't know what's happening!"

Her knuckles throbbed. She rubbed them and looked around to see if anyone was mad at her for punching one of these odd cosplayers. Maybe she'd get arrested for assault? But Misty was just staring straight ahead at nothing, literally clutching her strand of pearls. Meaghan and Marcus shoved each other, each trying to see whatever was happening outside the other window.

A thump on the roof of the carriage. The wheels squeaked; the carriage lurched. More shouts. The carriage shuddered and stopped.

Muffled voices. A cry for help. Laughter. Josie held her breath.

Her door opened.

Standing there, fists on hips, was a guy with a black scarf around his lower face. He was otherwise dashingly dressed in a tricorn hat, long black leather coat, green silk shirt, tight brown pants, and knee-high riding boots.

This wasn't the same guy she had punched. Though all she could see of his face were his eyes, they arrested her. Dark brown, under rust-colored brows.

"Justin?" she said.

But his attention was on someone else.

"My Lady Fontaine!" he said. "I had no idea you were riding inside this wheeled tea cake. How unexpectedly adventurous of you."

Lady Fontaine? And highwaymen. From the book. The book! Josie looked around her, but it was nowhere in sight.

The highwayman with Justin's eyes offered the lady a bow both deep and extravagant, with one arm across his chest and the other behind him. As he rose, he lowered the scarf, revealing his Justin-like face. Misty and Josie gasped in unison.

"Justin!" said Josie.

"Marquis de Sainte-Marie!" said Misty.

"My lady, that name is no longer my property, nor are the house and lands that go with it, as you well know. Now you may address me as His Highness the Bandit King."

He reached out his hand, and Josie lifted her own, thinking he was reaching for her, but he went right past, leaning against her leg to get to Misty. He took the hand of "Lady Fontaine" and kissed it. Josie pressed herself against the seat, trying to get out of their way.

He looked like Justin, but it clearly wasn't Justin. Justin was a boy who knew her better than anyone, and who looked at her like he loved her. He'd loved her.

Misty slapped his cheek. It was a nice, loud crack of a slap, not a fake stage hit.

"Rob us quickly and then let us go, you insufferable refuse."

He rubbed his cheek thoughtfully. "Allow me a moment to consider your kind request."

He stepped away from the carriage.

Misty was fanning herself. Meaghan and Marcus were holding hands, at once terrified and delighted.

"This is all from that book," Josie said. "The tawdry romance, you know? *The Highwayman Came Riding*. There was a Lady Fontaine—that's you!—riding in a carriage. And here I am . . ."

Where am I?

Josie felt strangely calm. She'd heard that this was what it was like to drown. First you panicked and fought the water, but just before losing consciousness, everything became eerily peaceful. Josie's head felt light as a bubble, and she looked around in wonder, drowning and marveling at the sensation.

"Hey, is it weird that you three all have M-names? Like, what are the odds, right?" She held her hand in front of her face. "It sure looks like my hand, but it can't be real, because . . . I think I'm in a book. Isn't that strange?"

A voice outside the carriage shouted, *"En avant!"*

A bandit grabbed Josie around her waist, hoisted her over his shoulder, and ran off.

CHAPTER 5

Josie squirmed and kicked but could not dislodge herself from the bandit's shoulder. Blond dreadlocks escaped from under his hat. Hadn't she seen someone with blond dreadlocks recently?

The bandit lowered her to her feet. They were in a forest clearing. Tree houses nestled up high in the canopy, with dangling ropes providing the only way up. The visible sky was deepening into night, though it had been morning in Montana only a few minutes ago. In the dimness, the orange campfires were excruciatingly bright.

A couple dozen bandits milled around the fires, gnawing on turkey legs and hunks of bread and laughing. Both men and women, they were dressed in cheap clothing worn to rags, topped with fine garments likely liberated from wealthy victims.

I'm in the book, Josie thought again, dizzy with the idea.

Her kidnapper tipped his hat politely as he walked

away. Blond dreadlocks, she noticed again. Like one of those college students playing Frisbee in the park! She scanned the bandits, and all their faces looked familiar, as if she'd just seen them in the park or the bookstore. Two bandit women strolled past, wearing ladies' fine gowns with mud-splattered boots, their long blond hair full of thin braids and snarls, decorated with jeweled pins. The Trophy Wives.

". . . and then she said, he hasn't robbed a carriage all week."

"Uh-oh," said the second.

"Uh, *yeah*," said the first.

"Justin?" Josie wandered through the camp, feeling as strange and unmoored as if her head had turned into dandelion fluff. If only she could find Justin . . .

She turned and recognized a tall woman in fitted breeches, a man's coat so long it hung like a dress, and a feathered-and-flowered cap.

"I know you!" said Josie.

"All who ride these woods burdened with too much gold will know the Bandit King's crew soon enough," said Nina.

"You're my best friend," said Josie.

Nina patted Josie's cheek and smiled. Nina would never trick her. Josie's stomach sank with the certainty: *This isn't real. None of this is real.*

Josie clung to Nina's arm. "Stay with me. Please? I need a friend. I need you."

Nina smiled politely. "Of course. Of course I'll stay with you."

"Always," Josie said. She tried to let herself feel calm and safe and pretend this was real Nina.

"Beware!" said an old woman, suddenly in Josie's face.

"Aah!" Josie yelled in surprise.

"Aah!" said Nina, a couple of seconds later. "Sorry, delayed reaction."

The bandit woman was perhaps seventy, with a freckled face and silver hair, her eyebrows auburn. Josie wondered where her brain had come up with this unfamiliar woman's face. Had she been in the bookstore or park and Josie hadn't noticed?

The woman came even closer, her breath hot on Josie's face. "They get you here and they never let you go! Never!"

Josie startled, bumping into a guy's chest for the third time that day—if it was the same day. It was certainly the same guy. No red apron now—he was dressed in bandity tight pants and a pirate shirt—but he had that same too-handsome face and warm Mediterranean skin tone. He was even still wearing glasses, though they had thin wire frames now.

"You!" she said, stalling while she remembered his name. "Deo!"

"Don't worry about Grandma Lovey." Deo tilted his head in the direction of the older woman. "She's just cranky. The Bandit King's crew is not such a bad lot, and no one has ever stayed on with us who didn't want to."

Josie grabbed the front of his shirt.

"You've got to get me out of here. You sold me a book, and then the story swallowed me."

"Book?"

"What if I got a brain injury when those books fell on my head and right now I'm unconscious in the back of an ambulance? Mia must be so scared! I promised I'd never leave her alone. I have to wake up!"

Deo put his hand to Josie's forehead as if testing for fever. His fingers were surprisingly cool, and she felt her body lean into them. His touch seemed more tangible than the spongy forest ground beneath her feet.

"Don't be scared," he whispered. "I won't let anyone hurt you."

She was still clutching his shirt and was now aware of his hard, muscly chest. Probably hairless. Undoubtedly chiseled. Josie remembered she was in a tawdry romance and quickly let go.

Hey, she was in a romance. Was something about to happen? With her?

She looked up at Deo.

With her and *him*? The idea wasn't unwelcome.

"Heyyy," she said, feeling it out.

His smile was a little surprised, but he said "Hey" back, with great warmth.

"Hey," said Nina, standing beside them, smiling innocently.

No, this was too weird. Josie stepped away and looked around again for that Bandit King with Justin's face, finally spotting him walking Misty into camp.

"Please welcome the Lady Fontaine to our enlightened civilization!" he declared.

"Huzzah!" shouted the bandits.

Justin the Bandit King led Misty to a throne built from barrels and crates and draped with cloaks. He leaned in and whispered something in her ear. She flung the contents of a mug in his face. The entire camp gasped. Even the forest seemed to hold its breath.

The Bandit King tightened his hands into fists and marched away, storming right between Josie and Deo.

Josie stumbled backward. "Rude!" she was about to yell when he tore off his wet shirt.

"Oh, hello," she said, confronted with his bare chest. "Okay, then."

This Justin was looking incredibly fit. Maybe he'd joined a gym since she left Arizona . . . *no.* She had to remind herself again that this was a fake Justin. Real Justin was the exact same height as Josie. Other shorter-than-average guys Josie had known wore thick-soled shoes and threw hateful glances at anyone who mentioned their height. But Justin had never seemed to notice or mind, not even when she wore heels.

This taller, protein-enriched Justin threw down the

wet shirt and riffled through stacked crates, finally pulling out a blousy white shirt. He shoved it over his head, leaving the front undone, his chest exposed. It was indeed hard, chiseled, and hairless, though his skin was a lot paler than the guy on the book's cover.

"Your lady is in a foul mood." His eyes on Misty across the camp, he spoke to Josie. "You know, we ran together as children. When we were six, we married each other in that way that children do, all innocence beneath the flowered bower in the shady shoulder of her fraudulent father's magnificent manor."

"*Admirable alliteration,*" Nina whispered to Josie.

"I just wanted her to *see* me again," the Bandit King was saying. "To see the boy she loved, not the disgraced nobleman."

"Yeah, well, these kinds of stories always require romantic tension," said Josie. "Obvious compatibility masked by a misunderstanding or an old feud or something. With Shakespeare, the story is a comedy if they end up together and a tragedy if they don't."

Josie thought she'd contributed an idea to the conversation worthy of an *aha!* or even a thoughtful *hmm*. But the Bandit King was still gazing longingly at Lady Fontaine. Maybe he wasn't really Justin, but still, seeing him ogle another girl made her feel simultaneously furious and forgotten.

"Typical." Josie put her hands on her hips. "She's rotten to you, and yet you're going to fall in love with her anyway, right? Because she's beautiful? And unattainable? And isn't a broken girl who you're sick of already? You want the drama and excitement of falling for someone you can't have, so the story supplies an ice queen—a cold, independent woman who will eventually melt under your touch. Classic sexist cliché."

"I beg your—" Not-Justin started to say, but he was interrupted by screams.

Meaghan and Marcus were trussed up in ropes and dangling from a pulley that was attached high in a tree. Beneath their dangling feet, a campfire crackled. Two bandits held the end of the rope—a middle-aged black man and young blond woman. Out of context, it took Josie a moment to recognize them as Bruce the coffee-shop guy and Deo's sister, Bianca.

"Here we go, lads and lasses!" said Bruce. "We'll roast the loudmouths tender slow!"

"You'll kill them!" said Josie. "What genre is this story anyway?"

She turned to Nina, expecting some flippant commentary like old times.

"Baroque comedy? Classical tragedy?" Nina broke a leaf off a tree, raised her eyebrow, and said, "Pastoral?"

This version of Nina seemed to be a mix of a story bandit and the real Nina, who Josie had first met in drama class, where they'd sat in the back row and whispered running commentary, always trying to make each other laugh.

Bruce let a little rope out, dropping them lower. Marcus and Meaghan screamed again, tucking their legs up away from the flames.

"Stop!" Josie yelled.

The laughing and shouting silenced. Everyone was staring at Josie, and she experienced that same sickening drop in her middle she got during an actor's nightmare: opening night, standing in a spotlight, and no memory of rehearsals or what to say next.

She shrugged. "I mean, I wouldn't be surprised if they were being obnoxious, but that's not justification for, you know, *murder*."

"We're just wanting a little entertainment," said Bianca.

"I know, *mon amour*," Nina said sweetly. "But we talked about this. There *are* other forms of entertainment besides burning people alive. Right?" She looked at Josie, as if double-checking the truth of that statement.

Josie smiled. They had each other's back—forever and ever—even in this weird fever dream.

Bruce let the rope slip an inch more, and Meaghan and Marcus screamed once more.

Josie said, "STOP!"

Again, everyone stopped. And stared.

She added, "In the name of love . . ."

She glanced over at Not-Justin, a tiny hope flaring

inside her that he really was himself here, and that he remembered. She'd sung the Supremes song "Stop in the Name of Love" for freshman-year talent show, the night they'd met.

At the time, Josie had been locked in an awkward roiling of hormones and was crushing on a new guy every week. Age fourteen had been as painful as an orthodontist visit, her emotions constantly rewired and tightened, rewired and tightened. It was all tension and discomfort, and yet sometimes that could feel good, like the weirdly addictive pain of pressing a fingernail into her gums. She'd fall for a guy, achingly hard, and then, if he seemed remotely interested, she ran away before he had the chance to abandon her first. But with Justin, it had been different from the start. She'd known she could trust him with her vulnerability.

She could still see him, waiting outside the school auditorium doors, the folded paper program rolled up in his hands.

"You were so great," he'd said, his eyes shining. "Really great."

"No, I messed up that one part," she'd lied, having bought into the idea that girls who acknowledged their own talent were brats just asking for the universe to smack them in the face.

But Justin hadn't let her duck the compliment. "No," he'd said gently but emphatically, "you were amazing. You made it hard for me to *breathe*."

At that, she'd lost her own breath. His eyes were wide, taking her in, appreciating her—and not just her singing, but *her*. Never before had she felt so seen. And he'd kept seeing her. None of her flaws scared him off— not her insecurity, nor her confidence, nor even her tendency to snort like a pig when surprised by a laugh. And knowing her better had somehow made him like her more. It felt like a miracle.

Bandit King Justin was still staring at Misty. In this story, Lady Fontaine was the protagonist, not Josie. Josie was certain that real Justin would never have fallen for her—wouldn't even have noticed Josie—if she hadn't been the star of the talent show.

Well. There was something she could do about that.

She broke into "Stop in the Name of Love," singing till he looked at her. And then she kept on singing, like she was Broadway star Idina Menzel. Like she was multiple Tony Award winner Audra McDonald. Like she lived in a world where you could just sing out your true feelings as easy as moon pie.

She cast a surreptitious glance at Bandit Justin. All his attention was pinned on her now. The bandits and captives were also rapt. Even Meaghan and Marcus, slowly swinging back and forth above the fire, stared, mouths agape. If she were in a musical, everyone would be like, *Oh cool, that girl is singing, why don't we all join in and dance down Main Street together?* Musicals were more perfect than life.

Josie reached the end of the first verse. She took a breath and whispered, *"Be a musical."*

Nina Bandit lifted a mug and said, "By George, that maid can sing!"

Deo knelt over a barrel and began to play it like a drum.

"'Tis the right idea," said Nina. With a tin spoon against her mug, she added to the beat.

Josie began to sway, and she caught the second verse.

She walked around as she sang, smiling at the bandit crew, getting them to clap their hands as she teased out the curves and swells in the song. But always, always, she stayed aware of the Bandit King and his gaze on her.

The song ended, but Josie curled back around to the first verse again. She sang, and she imagined more instruments to round out the sound. As if on command, bandits pulled out carved wooden flutes; others added to the percussion on barrels and crates.

The treetops vibrated with the rhythm; the forest breeze danced in it; the campfire flames snapped and twisted with it. The drumming grew bolder and faster, a dance-club remix. Still dangling, Meaghan and Marcus were swinging back and forth to the rhythm.

"Dance break!" said Josie, envisioning a big tap number like "Anything Goes." And the bandits complied. No stage, no tap shoes, but in unison they shuffled and ball-changed and buffaloed on the pine-needle-strewn forest floor.

"Ha-ha!" Josie crowed.

Grapevine, pivot, jazz hands, jazz hands.

It had been so long since she'd really sung out, with her chin lifted, that she'd forgotten how the notes felt warm and bright rising from her middle, straight up her throat, and into the sky—not even touching her, just moving through her. She'd forgotten how her voice could snap at the words or flow over them like water around rocks, sometimes grounding the notes, and other times setting them free.

She'd forgotten how when she sang, the sounds connected her to other people, sending out silver-fine filaments that came back again, linking them in the same web. Loneliness was a distant idea, solitude unthinkable.

She'd forgotten how Justin used to look at her, as if she were the world itself.

Josie put out her arms and made the last note so big and vibrato-y she would have been booed off a normal stage for her reckless Ethel Merman parody. But who cared? She bit the note off and shook earnest jazz hands.

The camp erupted into cheers, the bandits toasting with their mugs, laughing, kissing one another, and generally celebrating.

Bruce and Bianca lowered Meaghan and Marcus onto nice, nonflammable ground.

"That was amazing," said Marcus.

Josie felt out of breath and warm all over. The Bandit King approached her, and she hoped she wasn't stinky sweaty. If she was wearing a corset, it wasn't likely she'd had access to deodorant.

He looked at her as if at a magical creature that might disappear if he blinked. "Who are you?"

"Who am I?" she said. "I'm Josie Pie."

"You tamed my wild band with music, Josie Pie. You are a song sorceress."

"That was nothing. You should have seen me when I was really a star—" She'd just spotted two bandits drinking from mugs and snuggling together beneath a tree. She squinted at their faces. "Mom? Dad?"

"Cheers!" the bandit that looked like her dad said—or slurred. Drunk here, as he often was when she used to see him at home. But her real parents hadn't snuggled together ever, as far as she knew, and definitely not in the ten years since their divorce.

She was about to go to them, but the Bandit King put his arm around her waist and signaled to someone in the treetops. She hadn't noticed that he'd put his foot into the end loop of a rope until suddenly they were rising into the cool air. A bandit on the other end of the rope and pulley passed them on the way down, waving congenially.

Josie's stomach seemed left behind on the forest floor, and she squealed.

"I've got you," the Bandit King said reassuringly.

They rose two stories, alighting on the railing of a tree house. The Bandit King released the rope, hopped off the railing, and, holding her by the waist, lifted her down beside him. He smiled at her in such an open, honest way, she couldn't help but whisper, "Justin."

"Shall I take you back down?" asked the Bandit King. "Or . . ."

He gestured to the tree house settled solidly in the arms of a massive tree high above the bandit camp. They stood on a little balcony. Under a thatched roof, the one-room house boasted a low bed spilling pillows onto the floor. Besides silk scarves hanging like kites from the ceiling, the main decor was coffers overflowing with gold and jewels.

She imagined the Bandit King telling an interior designer, *I'm in the market for a bandit love lair.*

Wonderful, the decorator would say. *Are you picturing it in an I just robbed the king's treasury style or something more subtle?*

And he'd reply, *I do not know what this word* subtle *means.*

Josie put her hand into one of the coffers, lifted a handful of gold coins.

She thought, *With this I could pay off my credit card.*

The thought was so dismayingly mundane, so *adult,* she cringed. When Mia was playing a pirate discovering buried treasure, she never said, "*Arr!* Now I can discharge my unsecured debt—plus that *scurrrvy* interest!"

The Bandit King sat back on the bed and watched her. And she looked back at him like he was an ice cream sundae. In a good way. Also in a bad way. In several ways at once. She shook herself.

"You are a singer," he said.

"I was." She sat beside him and imagined he really was that safe, warm, kind person who knew her better than anyone. It was easy to do. For one thing, her adrenaline and general confidence were still spiking after the impromptu musical number, and anything felt possible. "I was going to play in big theaters, entertain thousands, sing out till I heard my voice echo back from the far wall . . ."

"And then?" he prompted.

She hesitated. This past year, she had begun to hold back some things from Justin, hiding her more embarrassing feelings. "I dreamed of splashy shows, rousing musicals that end with a big dance number and a kiss. But the only New York shows I've ever done were in basements that smelled like standing water and rusty pipes—sad and small, and they made me feel sad and small too. You thought I was a star, Justin. But I'm not. I'm nothing."

He kept looking at her, expressionless, as if still waiting for her to speak. So much for the big emotional reveal. So she sighed and tried to step into whatever role she was supposed to be playing.

"I have no family, no wealth, nothing to recommend me in this world but my voice and my hands. And since it isn't proper for a lady to make a living with her voice, I'll use my hands and be a maid."

He sat upright. "Your words try to dissuade me, but I hear your voice echo from the back of my heart. I do not understand my own feelings, Josie Pie, but I am taken with you. I am a mouse seized in your talons. I am a fallen leaf breaking in your wind."

She snorted. "Breaking wind . . ."

He gestured grandly to the artistically placed treasure chests. "For you, all the spoils of my labors! If only you will trust me with one secret—how I might win your heart."

He was on his feet at once, and he pulled her into his arms. His mouth was on her neck, and her knees went soft. She'd forgotten how good she felt with him, how good their bodies felt close.

Be real, be Justin.

But Josie was also interested in this here charming Bandit King. He seemed like the type of guy who was impetuous enough to run after his true love and competitive enough to fight for her.

His mouth was at her ear. He whispered, "Be my bandit queen. Help me knock that tyrant King Phillip off his throne of blood."

A marriage proposal? "Well, that escalated quickly," she said.

She put her hand up, resting it on his chest but not pushing him away. He felt as solid as reality—and his chest, as aforementioned, was hard, chiseled, and hairless. Her thumb touched a cluster of freckles visible through the opening in his shirt. They made him seem vulnerable and real. She met his eyes, and only a breath separated them.

Music drifted up from the camp. A rustic waltz. He put a hand on her back, his other hand sought hers, and he led her in a slow, close dance.

It had been like this with Justin at first. Just his nearness had made her heart beat faster. His heat. His breath never smelled bad to her; his skin even after a workout was delicious. She'd read a magazine article about pheromones, those scented hormones that attracted creatures to each other, and figured that his were a good match for hers. But the pheromones couldn't predict if he'd fall out of love with her. If his feelings would cool once she was no longer a star.

He dipped her. And then, right on cue, the shoulder of her dress slipped off.

"The sound of your song stole my breath," he said, his mouth just above hers. "Lest I suffocate, allow me to share yours?"

"Um . . . yeah," she said.

And then, an explosion—intense heat and brilliant light.

That was not a metaphor. The tree house around them was literally in flames. Josie threw her arms over her head as burning branches fell. She ran onto the balcony.

"The law!" came a shout from below. "The law is upon us!"

Screams and shouts, the sounds of steel swords meeting swords. Fiery arrows whisking by, lodging into trees.

"Help, help!" Lady Fontaine called out. "He kidnapped me and made my waiting woman sing like a tavern hussy!"

"Hussy?" said Josie. "She is beyond—"

A trapdoor opened in the floor, and three men came leaping up, swords out.

"Behind me, my lady!" shouted the Bandit King. He drew his sword and fought all three at once, parrying and thrusting and doing all those sword-fighting moves that Josie didn't know the words for. He tripped one swordsman right over the balcony, shoved another back through the trapdoor, and knocked a third unconscious with the hilt of his sword.

"Oh my!" said Josie. She was tempted to look down at herself to see if her bosom was heaving.

The Bandit King grabbed the only rope not currently on fire, wrapped it around his forearm, and grabbed it with his fist. It stretched out into the dark night. With his other hand, he reached back to Josie. He raised his eyebrows: a question. Would she trust him?

Burning wood crackled around her. Ash fell. Shouts rose up. She took his hand, and he put his arm around her waist as they climbed onto the railing.

She kissed his cheek and said, "For luck," because tonight was a night full of why-nots.

As the tree house collapsed behind them, he jumped, swinging them into the darkness.

The motion stole her breath. She gasped.

They landed on another tree-house platform, and the Bandit King began to untie a second rope. The night smelled of wood smoke, pine trees, the mineral scents of water nearby. And Josie thought, *My dreams aren't usually scented*. After the heat of the fires, the night forest air felt freezing, raising goose bumps on her arms. The Bandit King gripped her closer and swung again.

And again. And again. She had her arms around his neck, clinging for life. She learned to exhale as they jumped to prevent that suffocating slap of air. The night didn't feel as cold anymore.

At last they stopped on a small wooden platform hidden in a high tree, their arms still around each other. She could no longer hear the shouting at the camp, only the night breeze as it sifted through the leaves. And his rapid breathing. And her own heartbeat, speeding up like drums at the end of a song.

No firelight here, just the moon, impossibly big and round above them—a spotlight on two lovers center stage.

Her corseted chest fought for breath, her bosom indeed heaving now, as appropriate for the genre. She leaned back against the tree's trunk. He leaned with her, against her, his lips on her neck. Her eyes shut.

"Josie Pie," the Bandit King whispered. "Conquer the world with me. Be my bandit queen."

She smiled in the dark. Bandit queen sounded like a pretty good gig.

The moon lit his face. He was looking at her

longingly, his gaze starting at her eyes and drifting to her lips. Josie's eyelids fluttered. Her back arched, her mouth lifted to his. Her entire body seemed to be emptied out and filled with ache.

Finally, this tawdry romance was paying off.

"Yes," she said, though she couldn't remember if there'd been a question.

They kissed, and all she wanted was to stay here forever with him. With Justin. She'd missed him so much. She'd missed this person, who was always on her side, who always believed the best in her. And she'd missed this guy whose kisses made her feel both as fiery as a tree house in flames and as calm as a stream . . .

Wait, I can't be a bandit queen. I already promised I'd be Mia's nanny.

"Mia . . ."

She pulled away, and the Bandit King looked at her in surprise. Looked at her with Justin's achingly familiar face, but the colors of him were fading into the forest night like too-watery watercolors.

"Wait," she said, not ready to let go of him. But she blinked and he was gone. So was the tree; so was the sky. She was nowhere.

And then, suddenly, she *was* again.

Park bench beneath her, sunny May morning above, the open book in her hands.

CHAPTER 6

Josie bolted to her feet, dropping the book as if she'd discovered herself holding a snake. She couldn't see and pushed the glasses up onto her head.

"Mia!" Josie called out.

Mia was going down the slide. She waved distractedly.

Josie ran to her, grabbed her from the bottom of the slide, and squeezed her tight.

"Are you okay?"

"No hugs, Josie!" said Mia, squirming.

"Come on, we should go home."

"But we just got here!" Mia wiggled free and ran up the stairs for another go at the slide.

Josie fumbled for her phone and checked the time. They'd only been at the park for a couple of minutes. She felt her head for lumps or other signs of traumatic brain injury.

The trio was still on their bench, Misty reading aloud

a passage from their book, all dressed Montana preppy, nothing eighteenth-century about them. Josie hobbled over. She felt stiff, like she'd been sitting for hours.

"What just . . . did you . . . were you there?" she asked.

The trio looked up with triplet expressions of annoyance.

"What are you talking about?" asked Misty.

Josie pointed back to the bench and mimed swinging on ropes and masked bandits and heaving bosoms and rousing choreographed musical numbers.

"My book! With the highwaymen . . . and we were in it? With the . . . and it was all . . . no?"

Almost in exact unison, Misty, Marcus, and Meaghan narrowed their eyes.

Misty shook her head and whispered, "Tawdry romances . . ."

"Sorry," said Josie.

She hobbled back to her weather-beaten bench but didn't dare sit down in case whatever had just happened might happen again. Instead she paced, occasionally calling out, "We should go, Mia!" to which Mia would reply, "Five more minutes!"

Again Josie probed her cranium. Not so much as a bruise! Yet the images of the story stayed strong and intact in her head, not softening into wispy images the way dreams did upon waking. Had someone slipped her a powerful hallucinogenic? But surely drugs would wear off slowly, not all at once like that.

Still, she felt kind of amazing, like she'd just finished a perfect opening night of a high school show. Like she was about to exit the stage door and find Justin waiting, his face glowing, full of her.

Why couldn't it still be like that?

Maybe it could. Maybe it was. Maybe she'd left too quickly.

Boldly, she dialed Justin. With each ring, her heart beat faster. Justin. He could be hers again. He'd climb a tree for her and fight the law for her and kiss her against a tree and—

"Hey you've reached Justin Pie, I'm—"

Josie hung up, not ready to leave a voicemail. Not sure what words she could even say.

Her phone buzzed, and her heart flip-flopped.

JUSTIN
Hey I missed your call. What are you doing?

JOSIE
At the park with Mia

JUSTIN
I only have five minutes on the family phone.
What are you doing this week?

Justin's old phone was frequently dying, but there was a family cell phone that was shared among his eight brothers and sisters. The key was not to say anything personal, because every text was freely scrutinized by curious siblings.

JOSIE
The usual stuff. Victoria will be back tomorrow so I'll be more free to talk

JUSTIN
Ok I'll try you later

She stared at his texts, trying to squeeze out every drop of meaning, read them like tarot cards that would declare the everlasting fate of their relationship. They were so mundane, while every emotion pulsing in her body was extraordinary. *We just escaped a burning tree house!* she wanted to text. *And we kissed! Really good kisses! And we loved each other again! Can't you feel that?*

She scrolled through his old texts and realized that lately it had been just a text or two each day, no long threads, mostly like:

JUSTIN
What are you up to?

JOSIE
Nothing much

She had to go back to February, weeks before she left New York, to find a conversation.

JUSTIN
Today I saw a sign on a gas station advertising World Famous Chicken

JOSIE
Did you get any?

JUSTIN
I tried obviously but they'd sold out. It is world famous after all.

JOSIE
I don't think we're world famous chicken people

JUSTIN
That is above our pay grade

JOSIE
We're basic people. Chicken-chicken people

JUSTIN
We only consume Obscure Chicken

JOSIE
On principle. Who else will think of the little chickens? The simple chickens?

JUSTIN
Down with Big Chicken!

Lately, Josie felt more obscure than Obscure Chicken. It felt like a different life when she was capable of being somebody's World Famous Chicken.

Josie felt dizzy. She started to sit, stopped herself an inch before her backside touched that freaky bench, and jolted back up.

"Mia!" she called, and finally the little girl came running.

"Did you get phone numbers?" Mia asked. "Can you text them for playdates? I like Memmon," Mia said, pointing to Agamemnon. "Text his nanny."

She'd spoken in her little-girl yell-talk voice. Surely the trio had overheard, but they were studiously looking down at their books. Josie didn't have the heart to explain to Mia the weirdo social dynamics that awaited her in the future.

"We'll come back another time, okay?" Josie whispered. "We'll play here at the park again, and hopefully Agamemnon will be here."

Josie held Mia's hand and speed-walked down the main street and into the bookstore, a whole musical of emotions still tap-dancing inside her chest. Mia deftly squirmed just right to get away and ran again to the train table.

"Oh, hi!" said Bianca, seeming very surprised to see Josie.

"Hey, sorry, I know I was just here . . . ," said Josie. She'd spotted Bianca's brother, Deo.

"Oh, hi, Josie!" he said with surprise, sounding exactly like his sister had. Despite his movie-star face, Deo looked all innocence in that collared shirt, buttoned all the way to the top, and those thick-framed glasses. "I didn't expect to see you again so soon."

"What did you sell me?" Josie asked, brandishing the paperback.

"Is there something wrong with the book?" he asked.

Josie leaned in. "I don't know, was there?"

Deo widened his eyes and leaned back slightly. Josie was certain she was wild-eyed herself, and she warned herself to shut up, but she was pacing now, all cagey energy.

"I was in the story! In a . . . like a wench gown with the push-up bra thingy—a corset! And you were there. All sexy bandit or something."

Deo raised his eyebrows and his cheeks flushed.

"I . . . I mean—" Josie stammered. "Have you heard of cursed books? Or magic books or . . . I don't know what it was, but I was reading, and it was so intense. It was like I was actually there in the story . . ."

Deo pointed to a poster that said EXPLORE NEW WORLDS: READ!

"Let me guess," he said, "you haven't read a novel since high school?"

"Well, no, but—"

"*The Scarlet Letter* did you in?"

"Actually, yeah, but—"

"Reading a good book can feel immersive and amazing. It's okay to get lost in a story."

"Lost?" He didn't get what she was trying to say. To be fair, neither did she. Immediately she regretted admitting any of this to anyone, especially a stranger.

Deo carefully arranged his arm against the GRAPHIC NOVELS bookcase and said in a low tone, "I could be your reading tutor."

This guy even leans cute, she thought. And then, belatedly: *Oh! He's flirting with me!*

Now Josie felt her cheeks warm. In Arizona, everyone knew she and Justin were a thing. In New York, she'd been too laser-focused on Broadway to notice guys. She'd honestly forgotten that meeting a guy and flirting with him was a possible event in an otherwise normalish day.

She smiled.

She winced.

She looked at her shoes. She thought of Justin, and her heart hurt. She tried to think of some polite way to kind of flirt back and yet not make any commitments so he wouldn't feel bad, but her heart was full of having just kissed Not-Justin, and her mind was exhausted from all that develop-your-imagination-ing, so she just turned, gathered Mia, and fled.

"Or not!" he called after her. "I could just hook you up with more books or whatever . . ."

Without turning around, she waved in thanks and

pushed through the door, the dangling bell celebrating her departure.

When they got home, Josie called Justin on both of his phones, but this time she was relieved when he didn't answer either. Her heart was still beating hard, but with an upside-down feeling, hollow instead of full. What if things had changed so much between them that when she told him about the book and the bench, he didn't believe her?

Maybe she had to face reality: Justin was part of a different life. Where she'd been a star. Where her future was coffers full of potential and he was her audience, front-row center.

CHAPTER 7

Josie was that rare bird who peaked in high school.

It had been such an improvement over childhood, after all—alcoholic father, divorced parents, distant mother, angry older sister. Lila, five years Josie's senior, had warned her sister: "High school is a hellscape beyond your imagination."

So imagine Josie's surprise when, instead, it was a wonderland.

As a little girl, Josie had had a cute singing voice. But as a teenager, her voice strengthened, roughened in interesting ways. She joined the high school choir for frivolous reasons—a cute boy (baritone). By October, the baritone was forgotten but something else discovered. The choir director, Mr. Camoin, cast Josie as the lead in the winter musical. She was only a freshman. And in her school, musicals were cool.

Mr. Camoin came alive with the hope of her potential. He'd been on Broadway himself, singing chorus in two separate productions, and his eyes still sparkled when he reminisced about those days on the Great White Way.

"You have star power, Josie," he said, those French blue eyes a-sparkling. "Your range is incredible; your instincts are spot on; your stage presence radiates. You will invade Broadway, you will set it afire, and they will never, ever forget you."

Josie's heart fluttered.

She lived, breathed, dreamed, and woke to daydreams of Broadway. She took online math and science in the evenings so she could fill her school schedule with dance, choir, and drama. She borrowed stacks of Mr. Camoin's scripts and read them aloud in her bedroom. Her walls disappeared; her window became a proscenium arch. Every movement she made, every word she spoke, she envisioned a rapt audience.

The Muses are always watching, Mr. Camoin had told her.

"For you," Josie whispered to the air, as if addressing the Muses of theater, music, and art. "I perform for you."

Her junior year, Mr. Camoin scored the rights to put on *Wicked* and didn't even audition her.

"Do you want to be Elphaba or Glinda?" he asked.

Elphaba, of course.

Sometimes younger students stopped Josie in the halls to ask for her autograph.

"In a few years, this signature is going to be worth a lot of money," said a freshman girl with a sincere smile.

Josie laughed the laugh of a confident upperclassman and thought, *Yeah, it probably will be.*

She didn't think she was being vain. After all, she performed to standing ovations. She got recognized around town. And then, the summer before her senior year, she traveled to Washington, DC, to compete against the top teens in the country in the Jimmy Awards and won the Rising Star for her solo: "As Long As He Needs Me" from *Oliver!*

The Rising Star award! Josie felt more than just happy. All those long years she'd spent alone at home bonding with the television, she'd never imagined that one day she'd really, truly *matter.*

"You matter to me," Justin said in that way he had of just saying things straight up, no self-consciousness, no worry that he was being cheesy.

They were sitting in her quiet house on the couch, her feet on his lap. Though they had completely different families, they'd discovered how much they had in common. He'd rarely been alone yet had felt it all the same. With eleven family members in a four-bedroom house, his parents got one bedroom, his two sisters got another, leaving two bedrooms to split between seven brothers. For a book- and music-loving introvert, there were no quiet corners to think deep thoughts. It was all action—chores and carpet wrestling, homework to the tune of the TV, big dinners and big cleanups and rowdy games of backyard soccer. And always that suspicion that he didn't quite fit in.

Josie knew his family and could see how much Justin adored them, and how universally liked he was. But in a family like that, no one had time to sit down, look him in the eyes, and ask, really, "How are you?"

Josie saw Justin, and he saw her. They noticed each other, listened to each other, cared about and for each other in a way neither had ever known. And at the time it had felt so exquisitely perfect that even with her robust imagination she wasn't capable of conceiving of it ending.

"I matter to you," she said, "but maybe I could matter to the entire world!"

And then they kissed. A lot.

In the fall of her senior year, Mr. Camoin showed up at Josie's house on a Saturday and sat at the laminate-top kitchen table with Josie and her mom. Though it was the first time he'd visited them at home, Josie found his presence natural. *He's more my dad than my father is,* she thought. It wasn't the first time she'd wished she'd grown up with this stocky, bearded, swollen-nosed man, that he'd whispered hope to her in her crib, met her fierce toddler tantrums with patience, beamed at her for her tiny childhood successes, and always promised there would be more, more.

Mr. Camoin was barely able to sit still on his kitchen

chair. "I have an old friend who works in casting in New York. On *Broadway*," he added emphatically. "We were in an acting class together a lifetime ago—two gay French guys in the same workshop, what are the odds? Anyway, we keep in touch, and you'll never guess what show he's working on now. The revival of *Oliver!* at the Winter Garden Theatre."

"Oh!" said Josie, because she'd already started to hope. Back then, hope had been as close as a tattoo on her skin.

Mr. Camoin was already nodding. He was speaking to her mother, but his sparkling eyes never left Josie. "I told him about Josie, the Jimmy Awards, her ridiculous talent, and . . . he agreed to get Josie an audition!"

Josie stood up. Just stood straight up, the chair squeaking against the linoleum as it pushed out from under her. So many zings and zips of joy and anxiety and anticipation inside her, there wasn't room in her body to hold it, and she had to expand, expand.

"When?" she asked when she could speak again.

"Three weeks," he said.

And then they both started screaming. They held hands and screamed and hopped around the kitchen till Josie's mom, Lorna, shushed them.

"Are you both crazy? She's still in high school!" was Lorna's response, which hurt Josie more than she'd ever admit. It wasn't enough that the entire school worshipped her if her own mother didn't think she was talented enough to make it.

"Well, she might be too young to land the part of Nancy—or any *lead* role," said Mr. Camoin, "but perhaps a spot in the chorus, a way to get her foot in the door."

Lorna started to cast her stones of doubt again, but Josie and Mr. Camoin were already shimmying around the kitchen singing "Everything's Coming Up Roses."

After Mr. Camoin left, Josie hopped on her bike and rode to Justin's house. Her mom's negativity had sent little earthquakes of doubt through her core, and she needed his unwavering support.

But even Justin, after his initial shout of excitement and celebratory hug, said, "Broadway? Already? Are you sure?"

"Well, Mr. Camoin thinks I can do it."

"But . . . what about school?"

"It's just for a couple of weeks," said Josie. "And if I get cast, maybe they'll get me a tutor or something?"

Justin's questions sent parallel cracks alongside her mother's doubt, but they went even deeper, into her foundation. She couldn't have Justin doubt her. Proving herself to him felt like life and death.

And Mr. Camoin remained so certain: "You're a star, Josie! Anyone can see that."

Online she found a youth hostel in Harlem for a cheap daily fee, and, miracle of miracles, her dad answered his phone and even agreed to pay for her one-way plane ticket.

Three weeks later, Josie exited the subway and jogged up the steps through a crowd of strangers as if she did this all the time, no biggie.

New York City! Her heart beat in her throat; her feet seemed to have wings. Seventeen years old and feeling every day of it, she strode down Forty-Sixth Street, breathing in exhaust and the acidic body odor the warm early autumn picked out of the Manhattan pavement. It smelled like heaven.

The auditions were held around the corner from the strobe and thump of Times Square, in an unassuming structure apparently playing the part of a depressed office building. She'd been expecting an actual theater, but she supposed Broadway stages were too busy being razzly-dazzly to waste time on auditions. The elevator was wide enough for nearly two whole people, if they squished. The doors opened and spilled Josie out into a tiny lobby on the sixteenth floor. A crowd of twenty-somethings lounged on 1990s surplus office chairs, studying their music and humming to themselves, a dozen different tunes in beautiful cacophony.

This was no open call, with herds of cattle-like hopefuls waiting in line around the block. Mr. Camoin's friend had gotten her a slot on the day the real pros auditioned, even though she was a nonunion newbie and had no agent. Many were in pairs or groups, chatting at the low volume of a hospital waiting room. Josie smiled with a *hey!* expression, as if she totally knew everyone there.

She checked in with a purple-haired, emo-eyed woman at a desk. She was two hours early for her audition slot, so she waited against a wall, smiling so hard her cheeks creaked as if about to crack.

At last the woman called her name—sadly, as if all hope in the world had died, but it was probably nothing personal.

Josie followed her into a dance studio: hardwood floors rubbed dry of polish, walls of mirrors, an upright piano. Behind an entirely unglamorous folding table sat four white men and one white woman.

Josie gave her music to the pianist, took her position front and center, and smiled, confidence heating her feet and shooting up her spine. She wished she'd brought a resume to give them, just to have something to do with her hands, but they hadn't requested one. Pros were such pros they didn't even need a stinkin' resume.

"Josie . . . Pie," said the woman. "Great name. Um, so, we don't know you, do we? What do you do?"

"Anything," said Josie. "I mean, whatever you want me to do." Was that the right answer? Or was she supposed to list her, like, special skills or something? Should she mention that she could juggle three oranges?

"What are you singing?"

"'As Long As He Needs Me,'" said Josie, glad to have

a question she knew how to answer. And then slightly less glad when her response seemed to evoke an eye roll from one of the folding-table men.

She didn't have time to dwell on it; the piano player started the introduction. With the first note Josie sang, she knew she would nail all sixteen bars. Nail them to the mirrored wall.

Except, by her fifth bar, none of the people were even looking at her. A couple of the men sorted through papers. The woman checked her phone. Josie hadn't even finished her twelfth bar when one of the men said, "Thank you." He had spent her entire audition unwrapping a piece of gum. Maybe it was a really, really good piece of gum. Like, life-changingly good. It had better be.

"Thank *you*," said Josie. Smiling. Waiting for a delayed case of gasps or applause, a tardy *Forget the chorus—you're our new Nancy!* that was taking longer than expected to gestate in their mouths.

The gum chewer glanced up at last. "That's all we need," he said.

And with those words, a shard of ice seemed to shoot right through her chest.

She'd never been that's-all-we-needed before. Josie bowed her head and shuffled out of the room.

She leaned against a wall in the hallway for another hour, her hands folded in front of her, till at last a French-looking bearded man passed by.

"Excuse me, Mr. Bourdain? I'm Josie Pie. I'm Enzo Camoin's student."

"Yes, how do you do?" he said in a British accent growly with French. He kept walking, and she followed, speaking rapidly.

"Thank you so much for arranging this audition," she said.

"Uh-huh."

"Do you, uh, know if I'll be asked to come back?"

He stopped, his mouth set in an expression of reluctant patience. "What did they say?"

She swallowed. "They said, 'That's all we need.'"

"Then, no."

"Do you think—" she said quickly before he could walk away again. "Could you ask them to have me back? I'm sure if I had the chance—"

"Darling." He looked at her dead in the eyes now. "That *was* your chance."

He said it kindly—with compassion, even—which somehow made it hurt so much worse. That icicle that had shot through her chest was bleeding cold all through her, and when he walked away this time, she couldn't follow.

But . . . I can do anything, she wanted to say. To scream.

It took a couple of minutes before her legs warmed enough to walk her to the elevator.

She called Mr. Camoin from the sidewalk. Mr.

Camoin, who had said, "When I look back on my decades of teaching, *you* will be the reason it was all worth it."

She told him all of it. For too long he was silent.

And then, quietly: "I think I made a mistake."

Josie had enough money for two weeks of youth hostel and cheap eating, staying in New York City just in case she got that callback. After all, she'd won a Jimmy Award—*a Jimmy Award!*—for singing a song from that very same musical. It had to be fate.

Everyone back home knew where she was and what she'd come to do. She couldn't just return to high school with a *Welp, guess I'm not as talented as you all thought!* She had *grit*. She would outlast any obstacles.

When talking to Justin, she tried to keep her voice peppy and confident. "Oh yeah, this is just all part of the process. Now that I have a connection, I just need to keep working at it."

Her emotional calls went to Nina, who was a year older than her and already a freshman at the University of Chicago: "I'm nobody," Josie said after her second or third attempt at an open audition. "I can't believe I used to think I was somebody."

It was a dramatic shift, with Nina now the emotional bedrock of their friendship, comforting and encouraging Josie day after day. "You've got this. You can do this."

Josie's desperate calls she saved for Mr. Camoin. "What do I do? What do I do?"

"I'm sorry," he'd say. "I'm so, so sorry."

After her money was almost gone, she still stayed at the youth hostel, sleeping in empty rooms and the occasional broom closet. By the time she was found out, she'd answered Victoria's ad for a nanny, started watching Mia part-time, and found roommates at a five-story walkup in Queens. And begged her mother to cosign that fateful credit card.

Victoria's schedule was flexible enough for Josie to go on the cattle calls. She'd show up hours before the posted time, a line already to the end of the block. Early on a New York morning, the sunlight was grayish blue, the streets already busy with cars and speed-walking pedestrians. She wrapped herself in her Salvation Army coat and stared down at the sidewalk that countless Broadway stars before her had walked. With so many discarded wads of gum, the cement looked purposefully polka-dotted. For a long time, she found this charming.

Josie waited her turn. She went into the dance studio with a group of thirty other hopefuls and stood there while the casting director looked them over. If Josie had the look they wanted—if she wasn't "typed out" and instantly dismissed—then she got to sing her sixteen bars.

Then, inevitably, someone behind the Folding Table of Authority said, "Thank you, that's all we need."

Week after week, Josie felt more like a wad of chewed gum, spat out on the cement, identical to thousands of other gum wads.

At first she and Justin spoke every day. Her six-roommates-in-a-two-bedroom-apartment was too public, so she'd take his calls on the street, where the foot and taxi traffic felt more private.

"It's not happening instantly," said Josie.

"But I didn't expect it to," lied Josie.

Maybe that was the first atom of distance that lodged between them: when Josie couldn't quite get herself to confess to Justin her fears of failure. If she made it—if she mattered to the whole world—then surely she would always matter to Justin. Surely he would never abandon her.

Justin, who scored a 35 on the ACT and had been planning on enrolling at the University of Arizona, had started to apply to colleges in New York City and came to visit over the holidays. Despite the straight-to-her-marrow cold of winter, Christmas in New York felt like all the sparkly hope in the world. Justin loved it, especially the subway, because he said he never knew who would get on and what they would do. He loved surprises. Each of her birthdays since they'd been together he'd thrown a surprise party for her.

She hated surprises. But he loved planning the parties, so she'd never confessed.

He was going to move to New York for her. And

she'd moved there for Broadway. She had to prove his move and his faith in her were worth it.

On days when Victoria didn't need her and she had no auditions, Josie would skulk to the TKTS booth in Times Square to purchase a same day, highly discounted ticket to a Broadway show. She sat in the upper balcony, half obscured by a pillar, watched the spectacle down below, and yearned. Yearned so hard, surely those actors could feel it, her yearning pulling at them, ghost hands on their thickly made-up faces, tugging on their wigs and professionally laundered costumes.

Sitting in the dark at the back of the house, she could almost feel the warm spotlight on her face, hear the rustle of crew members in the wings at her sides, sense the percolating energy of the audience before her. The boards beneath her feet, warmed by the ghost feet of thousands of performers who had come before her.

Mr. Camoin believed that if you really felt your character strongly enough, you became them—just for an instant sometimes, and never for longer than the performance lasted, but you were changed for certain.

"Dramatic transubstantiation," he called it. He was Catholic, but believed in the Theater more than he believed in the Church.

At the back of the theater, in a pillar-obstructed seat, Josie wondered if the dramatic transubstantiation could work in another way. If she yearned hard enough, if she believed she herself was on the stage, could it happen? Would the Muses of theater—or whatever power gave life to art—pluck her out of the upper balcony and place her down on the stage? Warm her with the spotlight. Take her disappointed husk and breathe into her mouth. Make her real again.

In the spring, she asked Mr. Camoin for the hundredth time, "What should I do?"

But this time he said, "Josie, my therapist has advised me not to talk to you anymore."

"What?"

"She says your failure is bringing back my own . . . um, failures, and I'm having panic attacks again, and my husband says he'll take away my phone if I don't stop talking to you, so . . . break a leg. And all that."

That night, Josie huddled on her futon bed, trying to sob quietly into her pillow so her five roommates wouldn't hear. She never called Mr. Camoin again.

She'd left Yasmine, Arizona, a local celebrity, a star that would only shoot up, up, up! Slouching back like a deflated balloon was as impossible as staying in New York City, where nearby Broadway dazzled, beautiful and indifferent. Her skin, rubbed raw by rejection, had begun to sting at the thought of staying in New York a day longer.

And then, the exact same day Victoria invited her to go to Montana, Josie got an email:

Hi Josie! I'm sure you know that I've taken up
duties as drama-club prez since you left. And
I have awesome news! We sold enough tix
and concessions and those nasty protein bars
to fund a trip to NYC! Mr. Camoin says you're
killing it in your role! Which show is it? And
could you arrange to get us group discount tix
or even comps? We can't wait to see it and
give you a standing O!!!

There is nothing worse than peaking in high school.
And no one knew that better than Josie Pie. Eighteen
years old and already a flop.

She texted Justin from the airport, telling him that she
was moving to Montana for the time being, so he should
not feel obligated to go to college in New York on her
account, since she didn't know where she'd end up.

She glanced out the airplane window just as the
postcard-perfect Manhattan skyline disappeared from
view, and promised she'd return. But even then she'd
had a strange, ticklish feeling in her stomach. *Will you,
though?* If her life were a novel like the kind she'd studied in English class, she'd have called it foreshadowing. But this was reality, so she figured it must just be
nerves.

If she stayed far away, perhaps Justin wouldn't notice
what she really was. Perhaps he'd still see her the way
he had that night after the school talent show. As a star.

CHAPTER 8

"When will Mama be back?" Mia asked as they ate mac and cheese at the kitchen counter.

She asked every day.

Josie smiled and said, "Tomorrow!" But just minutes later, she got a call—

"I'm so sorry," said Victoria. "I have to stay in Nairobi a few more days."

"Oh, that's okay."

"Thank you so much, Josie. You're saving our lives! This whole single-parent thing and this job, it's all harder to juggle than I thought it'd be. It's such a relief to know that Mia is safe with you."

"And loved!" said Josie. "I mean, I know you love her too. She knows that. Just, while you're gone—" Josie cut herself off.

"Yes, safe and loved," said Victoria. "That's the best part."

Josie managed to keep the sigh out of her voice till

she gave Mia the phone so she could have a video chat with her mom. Part of Josie was still an eight-year-old kid, fresh off losing her dad, unused to a working mom away so much, sitting alone staring out the window . . . and that part ached and throbbed like a fierce, new wound.

After she hung up, Josie helped Mia complete her nighttime ritual: toothbrushing, bathroom using, hand washing, one game of Candy Land, one book, and then a song. Which Mia sang.

"I could sing you a song, if you like," Josie said.

"Nope," said Mia.

Josie wasn't going to lie to herself—that smarted a little. *Even a kid doesn't want to hear me sing.*

Still, Josie couldn't help grinning as Mia paced back and forth in her room, gesturing wildly as she ad-libbed tonight's aria: "You are bad bad bad when you kick a treeeee!" She was such a weird little thing, so many opinions stuffed into such a tiny frame. Josie was shocked to feel how much she loved her—like, jump-in-front-of-a-speeding-bus-to-save-her kind of love.

"I love you the whole world," said Mia, settling under her fluffy purple comforter.

"I love you too, chicken nugget," said Josie.

"Mommy usually says, 'I love you the whole world and the whole moon too.' Say that."

"You want me to say your mama's part when she's gone?"

Mia nodded. So Josie complied. Mia endured a hug and then rolled onto her side, her head sinking lower into her pillow, ready to be left alone now.

Josie shut off the light and carefully closed the door. She turned to face the empty house, and the forgotten smile on her lips forgot to stay put.

Her phone rang. She dived for it, slid her thumb to answer the call, and realized a second too late that it wasn't Justin.

"Oh, hey, Mom . . ."

Oh no. Oh no no no. She hadn't followed up with the bank yet. Had they called her mom?

"Do you know where I put the garlic press?" asked Lorna.

"Mom, I haven't been home in months."

"That's probably the last time I used it. I checked the nonsense drawer . . ."

"Hey, Mom? How did you know when your marriage was over with Dad?"

"How didn't I know? He smelled unfaithful. He reeked of it. Like he'd eaten a lot of unfaithful garlic and the smell oozed out his pores. Maybe he has my garlic press . . ."

"But you stayed with him for a long time, even after he—"

"Why do you want to dredge up the past? Let bones stay buried, like that woman says on the show."

"Um, what show?"

"The woman! The one I like. With the hair and the powers."

"Wonder Woman?"

"And the sad past. Ah, that poor woman! Her life has so much potential, but she's so lonely, everyone betraying her and dying around her all the time . . ."

"Meredith Grey? Miss Marple?"

"Being alone is stupid, Josie. I've been alone for twenty years. You think it's noble? Plus I've got a disease—"

"You don't have a disease, Mom . . ."

"I saw a thing: We all have rare diseases probably, only the symptoms are so small we don't notice. Like right this very second, my finger is twitching. It never twitched when I was married. Why would you want to be me? This Montana nonsense is nonsense. Nonsense in a drawer. You're acting like a child."

"According to the law I am still a child," said Josie. Wasn't she? If she was still in her teens, how could she officially be an adult?

"Don't hide behind the law!" Lorna said. "That's another thing that sad woman says."

"This is temporary," said Josie, repeating her well-crafted explanations. "New York is expensive. I'm just figuring things out."

"Speaking of, I called Justin. I thought I was calling you, but it was him and a girl answered."

"Wait, what? Are you sure you didn't call his family phone?"

"No, it was his phone. Didn't catch the girl's name. Maybe she has my garlic press. Though that doesn't explain why she was answering his phone."

"Why would a girl with Justin's phone have your garlic—"

"I'm kidding, Josie. Honestly, sometimes I think you didn't inherit my sense of humor. I have to go. My show is on."

"Kidding about what? About a girl answering Justin's phone?"

"Now why would I kid about something like that?"

"Wait—" Josie started, but her mom had clicked off, leaving her with a confusing mess of relief that she hadn't brought up the credit card, disappointment that Josie hadn't been able to tell her about the weirdness with the book, and distraction in the form of Justin's mystery. Was it possible that he thought they were over and was already dating someone new? Soprano or alto? Dancer or singer? Cheap date or the secret love of his life? *What should I do? What should I do . . .*

Josie called Nina. Nina didn't answer. She texted Nina. Several times. No immediate response. For now, she was on her own.

Josie fled the unnerving open space of the family room and shut her bedroom door.

On her bed, her purse tipped over, spilling out contents including a certain paperback. The sight of it struck her two places at once—in her gut with fear and in her heart with excited beating.

She picked it up gingerly, as if afraid it would burn her hands. Squinting, she opened to the first page and read, *Lady Fontaine pressed her gloved fingertips to the carriage window—*

She shut it, looking around for signs of forest encroaching on the condo. Nothing.

Another peek at the book. She hurriedly read the first page, her heart pounding, expecting at any moment to gallop into another reality.

Nothing.

But she flopped down on her bed and kept reading.

The story followed the two point-of-view characters: Lady Fontaine and the Bandit King. The Lady Fontaine in the book was nothing like Misty. Perhaps taking on Misty's look had changed the character's personality. Lady Fontaine's three maids were all female, and none of them punched a bandit in the face.

Josie read on to see what else had changed in her version, cautiously at first, afraid of the reality switch. Then angrily, confused why it didn't happen again. And then hungrily, completely lost in the story and aching for that moment when at last the star-crossed lovers could be together.

First she had to battle through sword fights and faintings, misunderstandings, plots by nefarious bandits and lawmen, as well as not one but three moonlight trysts explored in great detail, complete with sly names for body parts (for example, *his virility* and *her crossroads*). The first was an unexpected and swoony rendezvous in a tree-house lair, the lady swearing after to never see him again. The second was a silent *we can't help ourselves* roll in the back of a wagon, where they were hidden beneath a load of hay, trying to smuggle themselves out of the country. The third was a kind of last hurrah in a dungeon cell, sneaking together before their upcoming execution. But in the end the lovers helped overthrow the evil king and were married on the now-reinstated marquis's grand estate, culminating in a descriptive honeymoon that used more than its fair share of adverbs.

There were no musical numbers.

Though the story was different from her hallucination-or-whatever, some of the lines were eerily similar.

———————— 📖 ————————

The Bandit King stood with his back to her, almost as if he was afraid to see her response to his words. His broad shoulders and manly arms were outlined in the firelight. He bowed his head solemnly, and she could make out his strong jaw and sensuous mouth. Lady Fontaine found herself licking her lips.

"Be my bandit queen," he murmured. "And help me knock that tyrant King Phillip off his throne of blood."

"What you speak is treason," she spat. "We were friends once, Anton. Do not trap me with your pretty lies."

He turned suddenly, his strong muscles manifest in his every manly movement. "You doubt my sincerity," he intoned. "You think me a rogue."

He seized her hand, and she gasped. A new sensation crackled fervidly between them, his touch like fire, and she mere cheese to melt under his heat.

Not exactly what she'd experienced—and any non-ironic use of the word "manly" was a turnoff—but similar enough to give her goose bumps.

Sometimes when she was in New York, she and Justin used to watch the same show at night and text each other throughout, a kind of cross-country date. But lately he'd had phone trouble (or was that just an excuse?). Josie didn't wait for him to text, reading into the night until, exhausted, her head still full of the story, she fell asleep in her clothes. Which were basically pajamas anyway.

She reread the book in pieces the next day—while

Mia watched a show or played with a doll or complained about being B-O-R-E-D, and finished it for a second time that night after Mia was in bed, closing the cover with a sigh. She was still glowing with the stomach-tingling, heart-snapping, breathless moments of almost kisses and then yes kisses and carriage chases and sword fights and sensual mouths and swinging from trees and doing bold things to earn their lady's love.

The house creaked. Outside a car alarm yipped.

"Why can't I go back?" Josie asked aloud.

In the story she'd felt more herself than she had since leaving home. And at times she'd almost felt more—as if she were powerful, as if she could control the story itself. The memory of it yawned inside her, a hunger.

The whole experience reminded her of the dream ballets in musicals like *Oklahoma!* and *An American in Paris* and even *La La Land*—a sequence where the story and symbolism were amped up to eleven. Where what happened was separate from the actual plot. It wasn't real, and yet it was more real—or more honest, anyway. Where the characters could be true about how they felt, could explore romance and ambition without fear of rejection, could really *feel*.

By dancing and singing about it. Musicals were better than real life. And if Josie could make a wish, she'd live in one forever.

CHAPTER 9

The next morning, Josie had a plan. It had been a
long time since she'd had any plan beyond staying warm
and alone indoors and binge-watching something escap-
ist, and the mere presence of the plan started to loosen
the bluesy clouds that had been clogging her brain. That
made her feel both bold and vulnerable.

This was the first part of the plan: *I'm going to get a
new book.*

Followed closely by the second: *And go read it on
the bench.*

Because maybe . . . maybe . . . if she repeated those
steps, she could go into a story again. She had to wonder: Did that rarely used park bench hold some kind of
magical powers that had transported her magically into
a magical story . . . with *magic* . . . ?

Josie rolled her eyes at herself.

But still she held tight to the plan, like a skydiver

gripping the rip cord even after the parachute has failed to deploy.

While Mia was busy video-chatting with her dad, Josie showered and blow-dried her hair to get more volume, styling it with the top pulled back, the way she had as Lady Fontaine's maid. And she allowed herself some eyeliner. Lip gloss. Just a brush of blush—no more, or she'd have to admit that she cared about how she looked, and she wasn't ready to care yet.

It was a preschool morning, so Josie dropped Mia off. For a moment she was tempted to hole up in her room like usual and nap or look at her phone. But today, the plan gave her so much energy, she did the grocery shopping and put everything away before heading to the bookstore.

Bruce waved when he saw her. He wasn't wearing all denim today. Maybe that had been more of a laundry mishap than a conscious fashion choice.

"Hello there!" he said through the open door, not sounding at all like he had as a bandit.

"Hi, Bruce. Thanks for the tea the other day," she said. Had it just been the day before yesterday? Time felt off.

He held up a *wait a sec* finger, ducked back inside, and brought out a cup, a tea-bag paper hanging out. "Here's another. On the house."

The warmth of the tea in her hand plus the kindness felt so wonderful, she almost teared up.

She sipped the tea slowly, savoring it, as she entered the bookstore. The door's bell filled Josie with anticipation—not unlike Pavlov's dogs, she imagined. At least she kept from drooling.

The store was more crowded today, and the half dozen clerks in red aprons were busy helping customers while simultaneously being inordinately attractive. Were they all part of the same family or did the bookstore import models to Montana? Josie finally spotted Deo in BIOGRAPHIES. She smoothed her hair with her palm.

As she rounded the bookcase, there were the Trophy Wives, chatting him up. The blonder one was laughing, her long-nailed hands fingering a pendant that nestled in her cleavage.

Josie immediately lost her nerve and pivoted. The last she'd talked to Deo, she'd been all freaked out post-*Highwayman*. Surely he thought she was a complete weirdo. Still: the plan. Get a book. Go to the bench.

She browsed bookcases for a bit but felt overwhelmed by all the choices. She wasn't even sure what genre she wanted—maybe another romance? She was embarrassed to admit even to herself how good it had felt to get some kissing action. Several books were propped up on the OUR STAFF RECOMMENDS table, handwritten note cards bearing gushy reviews. One book titled *Valentine's Day* caught her eye.

Josie would have expected more pink and hearts on the cover with that title, but maybe the somber grays and blues hinted that it contained romance without adverbs, the kind that would make her heart pound while also allowing her to hold up her head around Misty and her literary cohorts.

Josie grabbed it.

She turned around, and bumped into Deo. Again. *I should enter some kind of chest-bumping competition,* she thought. *With this record by accident, imagine what I could do on purpose!*

"Hey, you're back!" he said. "Josie, right?"

"Yeah, Josie Pie," she said. "Hey, Deo."

He smiled, like it was an honor that she remembered. "I like your name. It's memorable."

"Right? It's my . . . my stage name, actually."

"Oh, you're an actress?"

"Yes, and a singer," she said. She did not say, *I was kind of a big deal in high school.* But she thought it.

His eyes widened as if he couldn't believe his luck. "Would you?"

"Would I what?"

"Sing something for me?"

Josie barked a laugh. "Here? Now?"

"Sure, just a little."

101

He was looking at her like he cared. So she shrugged and sang the chorus from "A Whole New World," soft and trembly. On the third line, he joined her. In harmony. She was so surprised, she stopped, but he took her hands and kept singing, gazing at her with the most sincere expression, that she couldn't deny him this moment. She caught back up, and when they reached the end of the chorus, a few book browsers applauded.

"We sounded pretty good together, actually," she said. "I mean, our voices blended well."

"Almost like they were meant to be," he said simply, seemingly without understanding his implication.

"Um, can I get this book?" said Josie, holding up a copy of *Valentine's Day*. "I could definitely use an escape. And something for a five-year-old who could also use an escape."

"Escapes are my business," he said, as he selected a chapter book about a ninja princess from a children's shelf. "Call me if you ever need one."

They looked at each other and both laughed.

"Did you work out that pickup line? Like, in advance?"

"Maybe I should start . . . hone them a bit before I try them out. Let me know if one ever works?"

Josie smiled again, this time without meaning to. He had such a harmless quality to him.

"I'm dating someone. I think," she said. "Just FYI."

"You think?"

She nodded. Then shrugged. Then nodded again. She didn't want to be unfaithful to Justin, even if she was uncertain.

"Sure." He looked down as he rang her up. "Maybe let me know if anything changes there?"

She laughed a little in case he was kidding, but she suspected that he wasn't. When she turned to go, Deo's sister Bianca was by the door, waiting.

"Hey . . ." Her beauty again seemed almost unnatural, and Josie fancied that if the girl removed her glasses and flipped her hair, every person within range would fall in love with her. Or explode. "So, my brother has taken to you."

"Really?" Josie looked over her shoulder and caught him glancing in her direction. "But we've only talked a couple of times . . ."

"He's a romantic," said Bianca. "He gets these ideas, love at first sight, those sorts of things. He's convinced that you're the one."

"The one? Like, the *one* one?"

Bianca raised her hand. "I swear on Zeus's beard, those were his very words. But I can see that you're not that into him, so I just want to say, don't mess with his head, okay? Go for it or don't, but anything in between will probably kill him."

"Um, okay. I mean, I won't. He seems like a really nice guy but—"

"He's more than nice," Bianca snapped. She stepped

in closer. "He's perfect. And I don't like to see him disappointed. We're an all-or-nothing family. What I want to know is, what are you?"

"I . . . I'm Josie Pie . . ."

"And when you commit to something—"

"I'm all in," she said quickly. She felt too startled to speak anything but absolute truth. "Obsessively. One hundred percent. But—"

"I'm not asking for your intimate details," said Bianca. "I just want to tell you, jump into the deep end or leave the pool, but don't dip in your toes to test the water, you got me?"

"Okay. Okay." Josie felt weirdly out of breath.

Josie's phone alarm vibrated, reminding her it was time to pick up Mia. She held up her phone by way of explanation and left quickly. Saved by the buzz.

Her heart was pounding the whole walk to the school, faster than her feet on the sidewalk.

"Good afternoon, Josie, how was your day?" asked Mia, so Josie guessed they must have been practicing politeness.

"Dating sucks," Josie whispered.

"What?" asked Mia.

"Just—stay little for as long as you can," Josie said.

"I will," Mia said brightly.

As soon as they crossed the street toward the park, Mia ran on ahead to join the kids on the playground.

The nearest bench was full. Josie could make out the

backs of three heads: two girls, one guy, in that western preppy style. She tiptoed behind them, stealthily making her way to the unwanted bench on the other side of the playground.

"Hi, Josie!"

Josie froze, dredged up a smile from her depths, and turned.

"Oh! Hi, Misty. Hey, Marcus, Meaghan. Out reading again?"

"Every day in good weather," said Misty.

"This long, huh? I thought you might have gone home by now. Well, I won't bug you. I'm just heading over there. To read."

"Whatcha got?" asked Marcus.

"Hmm? Oh, this?" Josie glanced at the book in her hands as if she hadn't known it was there. "I don't even know; it's probably trashy, I just . . . um, what are you reading?"

"Literature," said Misty.

Misty, Marcus, and Meaghan all lifted up their books to continue reading. Josie could make out the title on Marcus's book: *Bleeding from Our Eyeballs*.

Marcus peeked, squinting at her book as if trying to read the title.

Probably just to make fun of me, Josie thought. She'd reached the forsaken bench and was distracted by her heartbeat thudding in her ears.

It wouldn't happen again. She'd been upset about

Justin last time. She'd entered some kind of fugue state, her disturbed mind mixing with the story in the book, making the fiction seem nonfiction. Briefly.

It wasn't as if there was such a thing in the world as magic benches. Or magic at all, of any sort or object or breed.

Still, that rhythm in her ears drummed faster, drowning out the calls of the children, the swoosh of the river at her back, the breeze tapping the tree's leaves.

She opened the book. She held her breath.

She couldn't read a word.

When she held the book at arm's length, the words finally became legible again.

Josie muttered a few choice swears, dug the glasses out of her purse, and tried again.

PART 1

Melody climbed a tree. She moved cautiously, her arms testing the strength of each branch before pulling her body weight up. A fall likely meant death. A broken bone, a concussion, or even a sprain, and she'd become fodder for the hordes.

Fodder for the hordes? A fall likely meant death? Josie glanced at the cover again. No pictorial clue about the plot. The back cover didn't have a plot description, just the ambiguous tagline *No one celebrates Valentine's Day anymore* . . . and a bunch of review blurbs that included the words *romantic* and *heart-racing*, so Josie read on.

Melody reached the highest sturdy branch and looked out. Meadows. Low rolling hills. Copses of aspen and fir. She might still be in Colorado. As if borders meant anything anymore. In the distance, a thin gray line shimmered. A river? Or a road, heat shimmering over the asphalt?

She swallowed, conscious of the ache in her belly. And it wasn't only hunger for food.

A road.

The last time she'd followed a road, she'd nearly lost her life. But a road might lead to other people. The ache of emptiness in her middle rose up—

Josie leaned back. It was instinctive, like sitting heavily in the saddle of a galloping horse to slow it down. Because the bench did seem to be galloping beneath her. Or maybe it was the whole world. She shut her eyes hard and opened them again, expecting to see the park. When she saw nothing, dizziness filled her till she was just a swirling, tipsy, merry-go-round of a thing.

And then she was somewhere again. But falling. Still definitely falling *somewhere*.

CHAPTER 10

Josie landed on a prickly bush. For a split second she thought she was in the weeds under the park bench, but a quick, dizzying look around proved she was far from the park. Nothing in sight but trees.

It worked! She'd gone into a story! And then, apparently, she'd fallen out of Melody's tree.

Josie checked herself for that feared break, concussion, or sprain. She seemed whole. She had on dirty, ripped jeans and a black shirt that fit way tighter than she was used to, some sturdy hiking boots, and a backpack. Her clothing looked as if an ogre had chewed on it and then spat it out. Probably for being too dirty.

With a title like *Valentine's Day*, she'd been expecting the setting to be a romantic cafe, maybe with a couple of hunky guys: the dark-haired, flirty football player, only now realizing that true love had been hiding in the house next door, and the bespectacled best friend in an Atari

T-shirt, finally getting up the nerve to tell her that yes, he'd loved her, loved her all along.

But, no. Nobody. Just trees.

"H-hello?" said Josie.

What if she was alone in this story? Really, really alone? She started to hyperventilate again, and the edges of her vision crinkled dark like burned paper.

A crack of a broken twig startled her. She scrambled out of the bush, trying to gain her footing.

Suddenly a rough-looking guy stood before her, holding a hatchet. Reddish hair, mediumish build, longish nose. This story gave him the same-ish face as the last story had given the Bandit King. Justin's face, though not his expression—this Justin's stance was cagey, his eyes cautious.

Her heart leaped at the sight of him. "You're here too!" she exclaimed. She lurched forward to embrace him, but he took a step back.

"Do you know me?" His voice was rougher than Justin's, perhaps from lack of use.

"Um, no," said Josie quickly, catching on. "Of course not. I mean, who really knows anyone . . . anymore? In this"—she glanced around, trying to fit the puzzle pieces together—"postapocalyptic wilderness?"

The guy nodded, and Josie exhaled, relieved she'd gotten it right.

And then, on second thought, not so relieved.

Postapocalyptic wilderness? Not her best idea for a brain vacation spot. But at least there was someone here being Justinish.

"So, hi, I'm Josie," she said, then wondered if she should have introduced herself as Melody. Oh well, too late.

He just stared at her. And Josie felt those familiar gnawing nerves—the cold, empty shudders that always came with an actor's nightmare. Onstage, no rehearsal, no script, everyone but her seeming to know their parts . . .

Muses, accept my offering, she thought automatically.

"It's . . . been a long time since I spoke to another human," he said.

Obviously.

"So . . . what's your name?" she asked.

He hesitated before replying, "I'm Hatchet."

"Hatchet? Okay. Nice to meet you. Hatchet."

Wait . . . why did he say *human*? Did he talk to any nonhumans?

Maybe he talked to his hatchet.

She reached out to shake his hand. He slowly reached back, watching her hand as if expecting it to turn into a snake. When they finally touched, he sighed.

"I don't think I know how to be a human being anymore."

"It's okay," she said. "We all forget sometimes."

As she said the words, she felt as if she really were talking to Justin, and her heart kind of folded in on itself. *We all forget sometimes . . . to be human, to be decent to each other, to be in love . . .* She blinked away the sting of threatening tears. He was still holding her hand but reluctantly let it go.

"Remember how people used to worry that personal robots and virtual-reality games were isolating humans from each other?" Hatchet said.

"Yeah, I remember!" Josie said with a forced laugh. "I mean, I do, right? At least . . . I probably have amnesia."

Hatchet nodded knowingly. "From the stress."

"Exactly. From the stress. So . . . what's going on in the world?"

His serious face became seriouser, his head nodding seriously. "Nothing proved more isolating than the Zombloids."

"Zombloids?" said Josie. "You mean, like, zombies?"

"I wish," said Hatchet with a bitter exhale. "Zombies are fictional."

And overdone, Josie thought.

Hatchet sat on a log, took out a wicked-looking knife, and began to sharpen it on a stone with long, raspy strokes.

"It all started on Valentine's Day."

"Aha!" she said.

He jolted up, his knife out.

"Sorry!" said Josie. "It just . . . um, triggered a memory. Tell me more. I love exposition."

Hatchet looked around warily before sitting back down.

"I'd gone to a cafe to grab a quick sandwich—roast beef with Swiss cheese and extra pickles."

"Roasted red peppers?" she asked.

"No, they were out." He sighed heavily as if his heart were broken. "But I noticed how many couples were lunching on the patio."

So there *was* a romantic cafe in this story! Though in the less-desirable flashback portion.

"It wasn't until a man knelt before his girlfriend that I remembered it was Valentine's Day," said Hatchet. "I hadn't gotten anything for her. For . . . Rosaline. My girlfriend."

He paused and sniffled.

Oh, she's for sure dead, thought Josie.

"Rosaline and I were high school sweethearts. Even after graduation, when she went out of state, we stayed together. We just . . . *loved* each other. Back when people did things like that."

Josie squirmed. Though Rosaline was fictional, Josie couldn't help but feel a twinge of jealousy. In high school, all kinds of girls liked Justin. And guys. Everybody. At least half a dozen people considered him their best friend. It had felt like such a privilege that Josie was the one who really knew him best. She was who he'd confided in, sought out—*cherished*, even. She'd hammered that fact into the very foundation of her being, and if it was no longer true, she honestly didn't know how she'd stand up.

"It was at that moment when . . . I heard the screaming . . ." Hatchet shook his head. His knife sharpening against the stone made angry *grrrzzzzt* sounds. "I ran toward it and saw my first Zombloid. Four arms, four legs, two heads, gray skin. The Zombloid seized the man who was down on one knee and, with two mouths, bit his face."

"Yikes!" said Josie.

"The bitten man ignorantly grabbed his fiancée, as if to protect her. How could he know that, once bitten, he was her greatest threat? Their flesh merged; their skin grayed; their mouths grew wider. Where there had been two human beings, in seconds there was only one Zombloid. And the Zombloid was hungry."

Josie squirmed. What kind of book was she in, anyway?

"Millions of couples were torn apart that day— literally and figuratively—only to reunite again as the doubly deadly undead." Hatchet slumped, seeming to lose the will to sharpen his awesome knife. "No one celebrates Valentine's Day anymore."

Okay, then. But Josie still thought that *Valentine's Day* as a title was unfairly misleading.

"The virus can infect a single person without doing any harm. It needs to combine with a second person in order to activate. So the only way to survive"—he looked up mournfully—"is to be *alone*."

That was basically why Josie had run to Montana in the first place, minus the virus part. She knew it was selfish and ridiculous to expect Justin's perfect love to endure after that, but she still had. She'd still hoped.

Hatchet was silent, as if waiting for Josie to speak her line. So Josie reminded herself to embrace the melodrama and said, "I, too, have been alone for a long time. A long, lonely, lonely time."

Hatchet nodded wisely. He was good at it. He'd likely had a tremendous amount of practice. "The loneliness is sometimes . . . *unbearable*. But safer. For both of us."

Josie nodded wisely too. She was just okay at it. She needed more practice.

"So I will go now," said Hatchet.

"Wait, what?" she said.

Josie had assumed that since Hatchet had the same face as one of the main characters in the last story, he must be a main character here too. It was the *Law and Order* rule: if the cops interviewed a character played by a well-known actor, then that character was likely that episode's killer. As a TV kid, Josie had seen hundreds of hours of *Law and Order*.

But what if Hatchet did leave the story and Melody was alone for pages and pages?

"Usually in horror stories, everyone's all 'we have to stick together to survive,'" said Josie.

Hatchet looked at her with sad, puppy-dog eyes. "But this isn't a story, Josie."

So he didn't know. That it actually *was* a story, Josie.

"But Hatchet—hey, is your name really Hatchet?" she asked. She half suspected he'd forgotten his name, and that when she'd asked, he'd blurted out the first thing he saw. Like he'd almost been Tree or Rock or Elbow.

"Hatchet is all that's left of who I was," said Hatchet. He turned as if to walk away, but paused and said, "I really hope we run into each other again."

Hatchet smiled for the first time, revealing that single dimple Josie knew so well. Had the Bandit King sported a Justin dimple too? Josie hadn't noticed, distracted by the swooning and the bandit-lair interior decorating.

With adorable shyness, Hatchet lifted his hand, wanting one last chance at physical contact before he would go on his lonely, lonely, lonely way. Justin wasn't a shy person normally, but Hatchet's gesture reminded her of the first time Justin had taken her hand while they walked together to class, and she could feel his racing pulse with her fingertips.

Josie really didn't want him to go. When she'd sung in *Highwayman*, the bandits had started to dance along, as if her song were a spell and she could make things happen. If she sang again, could she change the narrative?

But this place was *so* not conducive to musical comedy. And then—

"GAAARRRRRRR!"

"ZOMBLOIDS!" yelled Hatchet.

"AAAHH!" screamed Josie.

A herd of what could only be Zombloids broke into the copse. With shiny gray skin and multiple limbs, they resembled huge, drooling, bloated spiders. They were even horribler than the horribleness she'd imagined. She simply hadn't been capable of imagining the true horribility.

But wait, she thought—isn't *all* this my imagination?

Just in case, she imagined herself to be an invincible, amazing warrior.

With a guttural battle cry, Hatchet ran at the nearest Zombloid, burying his trusty hatchet into one of its heads. He pulled the hatchet free, drippy and gooey with blackness. He struck the second head at the neck. The globby creature fell to the earth. But more Zombloids shambled over its corpse, smacking their lips hungrily.

While Hatchet showed off his mad hatchet skills, Josie fumbled open her backpack, searching for a weapon. A crossbow! Bolts ready in a neat little quiver. Josie snapped a bolt into place and was trying to figure out how to fire it when she accidentally hit the trigger. The bolt shot over her right shoulder.

She turned. There was a Zombloid, its arms out in

horror-monster pose, her bolt through one eye. It fell to its knees.

She reloaded and faced the oncoming horde.

"Die, Zombloids!" she shouted, trying out a battle cry.

"Die, Zombloids, die!" Hatchet echoed.

A Zombloid shoved her down and was nearly on top of her, its dual-mouthed breath greasy and hot on her face. Its slimy teeth were inches from her head when Hatchet hatcheted it down.

"You're always saving my life!" she said.

"What?"

"I mean . . ." She aimed and fired. Struck a Zombloid in the head. Reloaded, her fingers super quick, as if she'd done this a thousand times before. "I used to say that to my boyfriend. In high school. I . . . uh, I was a pretty lonely kid, and he made me feel . . ." She turned, aiming as she moved, and shot. Another down. "Made me feel like I had a family. Like he was my family." A Zombloid reached out with four hand-shaped append-ages. She ducked just in time, kicking low to slow it down. She rolled away, lifted her crossbow, and shot it in one of its heads.

"Eat our rage, Zombloid scum!" she said, because she was feeling awesome.

A Zombloid behind Hatchet was about to bite him. She shot that one too.

The final Zombloid slumped to the ground, gurgling and drooling till it dissolved into a puddle of gray goo. Then there was silence, just birds singing, totally unaware that a fight for life had just happened under their nests. Or maybe they knew and just didn't care. Birds could be jerks.

Josie and Hatchet leaned against each other, too tired to sit. Heads touching. She let her left hand dangle and felt his hand take hers. They were both sweaty, a little goo-stained, clutching each other, in desperate need of nearness in the near slaughter. It was, she supposed, kind of romantic?

They turned now and looked at each other. Josie let out a breath that she didn't know she'd been holding. And since people only did that in books, this was another irrefutable piece of evidence that she was, in fact, in a book.

She smiled at him. "It would be nice not to be alone . . ."

He smiled back. The world seemed to pause; the breeze held its breath. And Josie yearned for him to be real, to be Justin after all. This guy with Justin's face leaned closer, and who knew what might have happened next, but for: *footsteps.*

Into their clearing trotted a dog, followed by a tall, black-haired man. It was Bruce, but with hair.

"AAH!" Bruce said, raising a shovel.

"AAH!" said Josie, raising her crossbow.

"AAH!" said Hatchet, raising his beloved hatchet.

They all stared at one another, frozen with weapons lifted. Bruce lowered his shovel.

"'Aah'?" he said. "Not 'gaarrrr'? You're humans?"

Josie nodded.

Bruce stumbled forward and pulled both of them into an embrace. "Humans! We thought there were no more left!"

"'We'?" asked Josie. "You and . . . your dog?"

Bruce looked at her like she was crazy.

"My dog isn't human. I'm sure it's been rough for you, but try to pay attention." He rolled his eyes at his dog and, with a thumb toward Josie, whispered, "This one thinks you're human."

Hatchet said, "She has amnesia. From the stress."

"Ah." Bruce nodded in agreement. "The stress." He called out, "Good news, survivors! We're not the last!"

A small group of raggedy-dressed people traipsed into the clearing—if *traipse* meant what Josie thought it did, which she immediately second-guessed. Leading them was the bookseller Deo.

"Oh! Hi!" said Josie, surprising herself by feeling genuinely happy to see him.

Bianca still looked amazing, her clothes sporting a few artfully placed tears and just-so dirt smudges. Josie's smile turned self-conscious. Would revealing that she was happy to see Deo mistakenly lead him on and invoke his sister's wrath? No, wait—she didn't have to worry about that here. This was Make-Believe Land.

Deo noticed Josie and made straight for her. He gazed down at her face, lifting a hand as if tempted to touch her cheek. "You're real," he said with wonder.

"Yep, I'm real. So are you, complete stranger who I'm just now meeting. Yay, realness!"

Hatchet had moved closer, his unfailing hatchet ready and visible, resting on his shoulder. He stared Deo down.

Josie backed away before there could be boy-on-boy shoving and turned, suddenly face-to-face with Grandma Lovey. The old woman exhibited her ongoing talent for appearing out of nowhere, all creepy like.

"They suck your life away!" said Grandma Lovey, also exhibiting her talent for saying definitively creepy things.

Grandma Lovey was staring at Josie with those washed-out blue, wide and wild eyes. "They keep you alive and breathing but live a thousand lives in your minutes! Or years! I don't know how long it's been!"

"Yeah, I plan to avoid the Zombloids," said Josie.

"No, the . . . the . . ." Grandma Lovey gripped Josie's shirt and seemed about to say something urgent.

"Don't mind her," said Deo. "The trauma has made us all a little anxious."

Grandma Lovey blew air out through her lips. She picked up her skirts as if afraid to get the filthy rags filthier and wandered off.

"The Doctor is going to save us." Deo nodded toward Bruce. "He's our hope."

Bruce—the Doctor—was crouched down, letting the gray-brown mutt lick his face. Nothing in his manners or expressions reminded her of the actual man who'd given her free tea.

Wait . . . the tea! Both times she'd gone into a book had been after passing by his shop. Maybe the magic wasn't in the bench but in the tea? In fact, she couldn't help thinking, could he be the guilt-tea party? Thanks a latte for the spiked drink. If he thought he could mess with her mind, he was about to have a brewed awakening. By any beans necessary.

Among the survivors were other familiar faces. Deo's fellow bookstore clerks were easily identifiable, even though their skin tones and hair color varied, no physical resemblance beyond top-notch bone structure.

Also slumping onto the ground in exhaustion were the two Trophy Wives, the guy with the blond dreadlocks, the college-age Frisbee players she'd seen in the park, and the guy she now thought of as Cowboy, who was still wearing his eponymous cowboy hat.

Eponymous, Josie thought with a touch of pride. Good word. Her English teacher Ms. Lopez would be proud. Though probably not enough to forgive Josie for dropping out of high school.

And then Nina arrived.

"Yay!" Josie said, waving at Nina. "Hi!"

Not-Nina spooked and looked behind her.

"Hey, don't be nervous," said Josie.

"Ha," Nina said without humor. Her eyes were wide, and she looked like she'd been through a war. Josie squashed her instinct to give her a comforting hug.

"That guy over there—Hatchet—he and I just killed a bunch of Zombloids," said Josie. "We're pretty good at it. We'll protect you."

Nina smiled, and Josie's heart warmed. Even in real life, things with Nina had been a little awkward lately. Maybe here they could share that easy kindred-spiritedness from high school and she could play the role of Nina's protector again. Josie felt lighter, back in her element, despite the wilderness and the dead Zombloid goo at her feet. Nina was here. And all the many familiar faces she'd seen in the bandit camp. She felt she wasn't alone, like she belonged to a community. A *cast*.

Wait . . . was everyone from the bandit camp here? She winced, thinking of her parents, and thought, *Please don't be here, please no*, as she looked around. No sign of them.

"We're all gonna die," said Blond Trophy Wife.

"Don't mind her," said Nina, staying close to Josie. "She just says that sometimes."

"All the time," said Blonder Trophy Wife.

"It's like her mind got stuck on repeat," said Nina.

"We're all gonna die . . ." *Whimper.*

The survivors who were pacing had a bit of a shamble to their gait. Their skin was so dirty, it was practically gray like the Zombloids. Their clothing, too, was holey and ragged and stinky. Weak and ill and damaged, they barely seemed human at all. More a parody of monsters, their eyes full of the deaths they'd seen, half dead themselves, sure they too would die at any moment.

Was this really life? Josie wondered, sharing the thought of every hero of every survival horror story ever.

And then the adjacent thought: Had her real life really been life? Perhaps her relationship with Justin was dead along with the dream of her Broadway career, and she'd been too busy shambling along to notice.

She looked at Hatchet, wanting to share this idea with someone who looked like the person who had understood her best in the world. Then she glanced at Deo and got a chill remembering their unexpected duet. It wasn't an unpleasant feeling. If only she could have a little time alone with him here where there was no dating pressure.

The Doctor picked up the dog and announced, "Enough rest. We need to be on our way."

He started out of the grove, and those who were sitting jumped up to follow.

"Come with us," the Doctor said to Hatchet.

"We can't," said Hatchet, gazing into the distance, the perfect noble loner. "The only way to truly survive is to be—"

"Cured," the Doctor interrupted. "You don't get it, do you?"

Josie nodded. He'd spoken that line, the one people always said in books and movies but never in real life. Another sure sign she was in a story.

"I have the cure," added the Doctor. "So come on!"

The Doctor whistled for his dog and marched out of the clearing, the survivors following, except Deo.

"The Doctor is our best chance for a cure," said Deo, "so we have to protect him. I . . . I hope you'll come with us."

Deo smiled at Josie. He was so close, she could smell him, and he didn't smell stinky. In fact, he had a sweet, candy-like scent. Perhaps showers *were* an option at some point. Showers with caramel-apple shampoo and vanilla-sugar body scrubs.

"A cure, Hatchet!" Josie said. "We can help make this happen, change the story!"

Hatchet looked at her with happy amazement, in such an adoring and familiar way.

Justin. She almost spoke his name.

"I don't know how you still have so much hope left," Hatchet said.

Josie blinked hard, tried to stay in the moment. "Probably because of the amnesia."

He nodded knowingly. "From the stress."

They caught up with the Doctor's group, tromping through the countryside in the direction of the road.

124

I hope Nina walks with me, Josie thought, and immediately she did, smiling at her like they were old friends.

"Doctor, when you say *cure*, do you mean for the Zombloid virus?" Josie asked.

"What do you think I mean, the cure for boredom?" said the Doctor. "Think, girl!"

"Where is the cure?"

"In my farmhouse lab, of course. West on Route Six, take the road marked HOURGLASS RANCH. Big red house? Rooster weather vane on top? CAN'T YOU SEE THE PICTURE OF IT IN MY HEAD?"

Hatchet and Josie exchanged a look. But the Doctor continued, his voice suddenly reasonable again.

"I was in New York City, presenting my findings at a conference, that fateful Valentine's Day. It's taken me months to get this close to my farmhouse. When I started, I was with the entire Academy of Peculiar Viruses. Nearly all were bitten along the way."

"Those of us left have one job: keep the doctor alive so he can save the world," said Deo, walking alongside Josie. She felt an impulse to hold someone's hand. Deo was there. So was Justin. Or, rather, Hatchet. She twitched with indecision.

"Sai, Nancy, and Colin fell into a Zombloid trap in the wilds of St. Louis," the Doctor said. "Very foolish. As if there had been any real chance that McDonald's was open for business. Mabel and Hiroto metastasized in the suburbs of Columbus."

Impulsively Josie reached for Hatchet's hand. It was a little clammy, a little cold. But as they walked on, she felt him relax. And then he linked his fingers with hers. Just like the first time in the school hall, his touch sent cold tingles up her arm, right into her pounding heart, making her grin like the Cheshire cat. Her grin was a bit too stiff—nearly rictus, really—but, after all, she *was* having her second psychotic break in a week and, within that, a sophomoric emotional reaction to a fictional character with a familiar face. And a hot bookseller on her other side who kept glancing at her hopefully. And a best friend who seemed to look up to her again. So many emotions all at once. She was tempted to shoot them with crossbow bolts. The emotions, not the people.

"Mabel and Hiroto made a beautiful Zombloid, so perfectly proportioned," the Doctor was saying. "Heads set decently side by side, limbs mostly the same length, their shamble nice and smooth, in flawless unison. Like that one there."

"GAAARRRRR!!!" said a perfectly proportioned Zombloid, which was suddenly coming at them.

"AAH! Zombloids!" the survivors screamed.

"Die!" Hatchet yelled, lifting his namesake weapon.

But before he could strike the relatively attractive, well-formed Zombloid, another shambled into Hatchet's path, this one lumpy and bloated, with one head sprouting out a good two feet below the first. The Doctor would not approve.

Others followed. They were surrounded by a small Zombloid army.

Josie moved in front of Nina as she loaded her crossbow.

Just how, Josie suddenly wondered, *does a girl who is fleeing her life in an uncivilized, death-plagued world find a crossbow and bolts? They're not exactly sold in the corner pharmacy. A hatchet, sure, or some sharp gardening implements. But a crossbow?*

Deo was fighting with some nunchuck thingies.

Even nunchucks I can believe, Josie thought as she shot a Zombloid in each of its faces. *Maybe he raided a dojo.*

"You are like lightning with your crossbow!" Deo said, fighting beside her now.

"Thanks! You're a pro with those . . . things," she said, suddenly unsure if *nunchuck* was the right word.

"I've had a lot of practice with my danger sticks," said Deo.

Wait, danger sticks? She couldn't help snorting.

Deo cleared his throat. "That's . . . what they're really called. Sometimes."

"We're all gonna die . . . ," wailed Blond Trophy Wife.

They fought on, Josie loading and firing, loading and firing, her bolt supply apparently limitless. It didn't feel real, like playing a video game. Josie kept her eye on Nina, always protecting Nina. Soon Hatchet was at her back, and their movements synced. She felt like half of a tornado of death.

Tornado of Death would be a good band name, Josie thought.

This back-to-back fighting felt so natural, a metaphor of how they'd been in high school. Justin would identify someone who was down or friendless or teased, and he and Josie would swoop in, use the power of her popularity and his kindness to defeat all foes, defend the vulnerable, and save the day! Or something. But something good. The way she remembered it, it had been really, really good.

"There are too many!" someone yelled.

"I gotta get my family!" said Frisbee Guy. "Cynthia! Cynthia, I'm coming home, baby!"

He tried to barrel straight through the Zombloid horde. Several survivors shifted away from the Doctor, trying to stop Frisbee Guy, but he went down like a hot dog at a competitive-eating contest. And for a split second, the Doctor was vulnerable.

Immediately, the Doctor screamed. A Zombloid was gnawing on his arm.

Josie jolted forward, but Hatchet grabbed her, held her.

"It's too late! Everyone, get back! He won't turn Zombloid as long as no one gets near him!"

The survivors moved away, but the little dog ran right up.

"Shoot it!" Hatchet yelled.

The mutt was sniffing at the Doctor worriedly. Josie took aim but hesitated. Even in a fever dream, shooting a dog was too much to ask. The Doctor's flesh was already undulating, bulging, reaching out for the dog. Within seconds the Doctor's body had enveloped it like an amoeba eating a paramecium, and he became something else entirely. His skin bulged and tightened, grayed. His mouth opened wide; his teeth sharpened. And a little dog head poked out of his middle. It barked.

"GAAAARRR-BARK!" said the Doctor-dog Zombloid. "GAAARRR-BARK!"

"I'm so sorry," Josie said. "I don't like this story anymore!"

The Doctor-dog lurched, grabbed Deo with two huge gray paw-hands, and bit his face.

"No!" said Josie. *Don't be here, Nina,* she thought. *Don't be here.*

Josie spun around, but she couldn't find the girl with her friend's face. The whole group, distracted by the loss of its leader, was falling before the Zombloids, merging into gloopy gray lurching shapes. In panic, Josie tried to pull back. Pull away. Feel the park bench beneath her, the Montana sun above. For a second, the air around her started to feel as slippery as a bubble bath.

But then Hatchet grabbed Josie's hand. His hand was warm and callused, and felt real and safe. She held on. And, together, they ran.

CHAPTER 11

They ran in the same direction they'd been heading, because when being chased by a horde of undead plague victims you just want something familiar. They headed toward a long, shiny line that proved to be a road. Asphalt, two lanes. A highway sign said ROUTE 6.

"We know the location of the cure," said Josie.

"Alone, I'd never risk it. But with you . . ." He brushed a lock of hair from her forehead. It was stiff with dirt and sweat and clunked back into place. "Your hope is infectious. Not like infectious-disease infectious. Though similar. Like a virus, but not one that kills us. Though maybe it will kill us, if in the process of following this hopeful plan we get killed."

"Okay," she said, so she could contribute to the conversation.

"What I mean to say is, I like your infectious hope." He smiled at her. And she wanted to stay with him forever.

They walked for hours. To pass the time, they

conversed about safe topics, like recounting the plots of movies and books. By evening she was telling him about *The Highwayman Came Riding*.

". . . and then the Bandit King grabs the lady around her waist, seizes a rope, and swings from the tree-house hideaway just as it goes up in flames. They land in a nearby tree—"

"GAAARRRR!" said a random Zombloid, lurching out from behind a boulder. Without breaking his pace, Hatchet hatcheted it down.

"—and with the fire blazing behind them," Josie continued, "painting their faces with its gold light, the Bandit King whispers, 'I love you. I will always love you, my lady fair.'"

Hatchet laughed. "There are people who enjoy reading that?"

"Oh sure. It's a great escape, especially when your life is a postapocalyptic nightmare of shambling, bite-happy horrors. Besides, some parts of the book really get your heart beating . . ."

Hatchet looked away. The barest allusion to intimacy made him blush.

And then, for a long time, they didn't talk, quiet with their own thoughts.

It had been like this with Justin, too. After the initial months of giddy, infatuated falling-in-love-ness, there had followed a comfortable familiarity with each other. They could be cozy in silence.

Josie shot a pheasant that they startled out of the brush. Hatchet prepped it with his big scary knife. They roasted the meat over a fire and paired it with a bottle of orange soda they'd discovered in a car abandoned by the side of the road. The soda tasted exotic and forbidden. Josie felt drunk on the sugar and carbonation and was prone to giggle.

"In high school I once drank a two-liter bottle of root beer and then threw it up, but I was laughing so hard it came out my nose. It felt like sneezing bees."

Hatchet giggled with her. Everything was funny, in that way that mundane things are funny when you're sauced on soda and near-death experiences.

"How's your amnesia?" he asked.

"I still have no memory of that fateful Valentine's Day," Josie said honestly. "But I have memories of before. A different life."

"Tell me," he said. His face bright in the firelight, darkness all around.

I used to tell Justin everything, Josie thought, but just as quickly reminded herself that that wasn't completely true anymore. Since her failure in New York, she'd begun to guard herself a little, in case knowing all of her might make him not love her anymore.

But here, in make-believe land, she could say anything.

So Josie talked. About the difference between just singing a pretty song and entering a place where she was sharing a piece of her soul with the audience, and how when she managed to do that, she came away somehow more herself than before she gave herself up. And how, thanks in part to Mr. Camoin, she did feel she had to give herself up. The Muses demanded it.

She told him about New York—instead of candy-colored, feel-good musicals on big stages, she'd paid out her meager money for a chance to perform in basement theater surreal weep-fests, the kind that left you with hunched shoulders and a kink in your neck. She wasn't quite strong enough an actor to keep her character at arm's length and simply pretend, so those roles made her depressed because they were depressing. She had no boundaries.

No boundaries anywhere. In her loneliness and isolation, she tended to try to merge with whoever was nearest.

Right now, Hatchet was nearest. And he was listening in a way that a rapt audience listens, silent with intent, receiving what she offered and sending energy back in return.

The fire was just embers now. Hatchet stamped them out. Too dangerous to keep a fire burning, a signal to any Zombloids on the prowl. The loss of heat made her shiver.

She heard him settle down on the ground a respectful distance from her.

"Do you mind if I sleep beside you?" she asked. "For shared heat."

"I don't mind," he whispered.

She lay on her back, their arms touching. Both kept very still. Josie let her head shift, and her temple touched his shoulder. He put his arm around her, and his heat was welcome.

Josie wondered: If Hatchet had looked nothing like Justin, would she still be lying beside whatever random person the story had stuck her with? In this kind of story, would anybody do? Just to keep from being alone?

Maybe her relationship with Justin had been survival horror love too, not so much real as convenient. Even for Millennial High's Most Talented student, being a teenager was still, at times, a horror movie. She tended to forget about the stress—trying to keep up with classes despite all the rehearsals, feeling always one slip away from failure, the chaos of school followed by the piercing loneliness of home. Justin, too, struggled at times. While he was entirely nonjudgmental of others, he was so hard on himself, setting impossible expectations to succeed in school and be helpful to his family and friends, and just generally be everything anybody might need of him. She and Justin had stood back-to-back, fighting for each other and fighting for others, too. She'd been his constant, his safe space. And he hadn't only made her feel loved—he'd made her feel capable of being a hero.

But adults outgrow their high school relationships.

Hatchet moved closer to her. Her legs went soft; her heart pounded.

"I hope the Zombloids don't get us in our sleep," Hatchet murmured by her ear, "now that I have something to live for."

She put her hand on his cheek, and she kissed him. His arm slipped under her side, pulling her closer, and they made out like the world was ending. Her heart beat harder, and, eyes closed, she pretended she and Justin were on her couch in the real world. There was far more joy in kissing Justin than in making out with a stranger.

They kissed for hours, it seemed. Any second a Zombloid horde might rip through their campsite, but they kept kissing.

No story is too apocalypsey for a little romance.

If Josie fell asleep that night, she didn't remember it. One moment they were kissing, and then—

Snap!

She and Hatchet were walking along and laughing, though she didn't remember why.

"What's happening?" she asked.

He looked at her as if he didn't know what she meant.

Oh, she guessed. *It's like when a book moves from one day right into the middle of the next, or like in movies when they skip over stuff to have a montage.*

And sure enough—

Snap!

Now they were sitting by a fire eating roasted meat and some kind of tuber. And so it went.

It was day, and then it was night again. Nights were

always cold. Nights made sleeping next to each other a necessity. And facilitated make-out sessions.

The time shifts didn't alarm her, though in the back of her mind, buried under chocolate withdrawal and her valiant determination to pretend she couldn't smell her own scalp, she thought that they should. But, conveniently, the montage skipped over the boring parts. It was all money scenes. Laughing. Clever conversation. Snuggled sleeping. And so, so much making out.

One moment: Josie was describing for Hatchet the movie *All About Eve* when he suddenly yanked out his scary knife and threw it in her direction. It sailed just above her head and struck something in a tree behind her. *Thump*—a knife-skewered raccoon fell at her feet. Josie smiled. Dinner!

Another: Freezing at the sounds of rustling in the bushes, weapons ready, sweating palms and anxious breathing, they expected a Zombloid attack, only to spot an adorable bunny, which hopped away. Hatchet and Josie looked at each other and laughed. *WUT?*

Yet another: They came across an empty house and scoured it for food and supplies, then rode a mattress down the stairs, just 'cause. Sometimes postapocalyptic worlds could be fun!

Then she woke up on her side with him spooning behind her. He was larger, so the fact that he was the big spoon felt like practical utensil management. She rolled over, seeking more of his warmth.

The morning light picked out his freckles and made his blond eyelashes look gold. Her heart ached for this warm, strong guy with his sunburned nose and lips exhaling onto hers. Ached as though he was already gone. Why did she feel like he was gone?

Hatchet moved in his sleep, his arms remembering her, and he pulled her in. His head adjusted, and his mouth pressed to her forehead.

"Melody?" he said. "You awake?"

"Mm-hmm . . ." She just wanted to lie on top of him and twine her arms around him. Maybe morphing into a single Zombloid with him wouldn't be such a bad fate.

She pulled back. "What did you call me?"

He squeaked open his eyes. "Um . . . Josie?"

"Oh. Okay."

No, wait. Hatchet had called her Melody. And she'd responded, like it was her name.

Another name exploded in her brain: *Mia*.

In all the montagey days, she hadn't thought about Mia at all. Or Nina. Or Broadway. Or the real world. *Beware, beware,* her pulse thrummed in her throat. Forgetting herself, believing she was Melody, seemed like a good way to get so lost in the story that she never woke up. She'd already been in this one much longer than the first.

And here was a guy lying beside her looking like Justin. That already-gone feeling expanded inside her.

Josie rolled away, waking Hatchet fully. He sat up and grabbed his precious hatchet.

"Is there danger?" he asked, his eyes wild.

"No danger," she said.

Except the danger of falling in love.

That line popped into Josie's mind so quickly, she wondered if it was from the real book.

"Josie?"

"Yeah?"

He swallowed. "Hatchet isn't my real name."

"I kinda figured."

"I used to run with a crew of survivors. They called me Hatchet," he said. "Because of my hatchet."

Josie nodded solemnly. The hatchet always invoked solemnity.

"I never told them my true name, because by then I felt more like a weapon than a human anyway. But I want to tell you."

She stood up, listening, her whole body full of expectation. Would she still feel the same about him if his name was Rufus? Ashley? Excalibur?

Wait . . . what if his name was Justin?

Hatchet exhaled. "My . . . my name is—"

"ZOMBLOIDS!!!" said Josie.

With Doctor-doggie in the lead, the Zombloid army crashed through the trees. In an instant, Hatchet was at Josie's back, and they fell into their fighting pattern, slowly turning, Josie shooting, Hatchet hatcheting, Zombloids dissolving into burbling gray goo at their feet.

Then, from above, a crack of a branch. Josie looked up. And a Zombloid dropped onto her.

They rolled through the undergrowth, Josie fighting to get her crossbow pointed at her attacker. But just as she was able to pull it from her body, she felt a bite on her leg. She shot the Zombloid in the gray fleshy mid-section. It spasmed and rolled off her. Josie scrambled back and grabbed her leg. The pant leg was torn. And darkening with blood.

"NOOO!!!" Hatchet exclaimed. He tried to hack his way to her.

"Run!" she said, scooting back. "It's too late! You'll stay human as long as you stay away from me!"

"I'm not leaving you!" he said. Crazed with grief, he axed madly, getting closer.

Josie crawled to her feet and, hobbling on her wounded leg, broke into a limping run. She heard foot beats behind her. Not Zombloids.

Hatchet had hatcheted his way free of the Zombloids and was fast approaching. She tried to run faster and reliably tripped, just like so many heroines in horror stories.

Hatchet stopped. Right on cue, from behind him Zombloids approached, groaning.

"I'll fight them, keep them off you," he said.

"Don't come back for me," she said. "Don't look for me. The best thing I can do for you is to stay far away."

Hatchet looked heartbroken, glancing between Josie

and the Zombloids. His face set with decision, and his shoulders slumped with the weight of it.

"I love you," he said desperately. "I will always love you, my lady fair!"

He ran at the Zombloids, hatchet raised heroically.

Josie reached toward the sky with dramatic, outstretched hands.

"Why?" she asked the sky. "WHYYYYYY?"

Honestly, it felt immensely satisfying.

For a minute, anyway. She tried shouting "WHY?" a few more times as she limped away, but it quickly lost any fulfillment. And she was alone. Completely and absolutely. This, for Josie, was the real horror story.

She hobbled along and wished she would montage again, no matter the risks, but the time just crawled by. For hours. And hours. Did normal days honestly have this many hours?

She stayed off the road, heading in the direction the plot seemed to want her to go, until at last she crested a small hill and glimpsed a red farmhouse. With a rooster weather vane.

And a Zombloid army.

Dozens of Zombloids surrounded the farmhouse, clawing at walls, elbowing in the windows. Their bulbous bodies were never still, limbs sliding, relocating to other sides of the body. Even from a distance, Josie could hear their groans and the creaking and clacking of their bones adjusting. Their misshapen gray noses sniffled at the air; their mouths dripped with saliva.

Clearly they smelled someone inside.

Josie gasped. It could be Hatchet inside the farmhouse. Maybe he'd gotten there before her, holed up when the Zombloids attacked, but now was utterly outnumbered.

"Justin . . . ," said Josie.

She limped-ran down the hill, shooting Zombloids with her endless supply of crossbow bolts the moment she was within range.

A few Zombloids broke off their assault of the farmhouse to come at her. And she shot and shot again with undeadly accuracy. She was kicking such serious butt she briefly considered changing her name to Crossbow. But the rest of the Zombloids were still clawing at walls, breaking windows.

"Let him go!" she shouted. "Come on, you slobbering cowards! Fight me instead!"

And then, at her command, they did. All of them.

Scores of Zombloids surrounded her, hands outstretched, crooked fingers reaching, repositioning, reaching again. Josie started to fire but suddenly she was out of bolts. What terrible timing!

They were almost upon her, gooey mouths open to eat her alive.

Josie yelled, "Stop!"

They stopped.

"Oh!" said Josie. She remembered the feeling of singing to the bandits, the heat in her fingertips, the way her thoughts had run ahead of her, excited and agile, imagining a group dance number.

Josie smiled. She didn't have to go along with the story. She did have some power to alter it.

So Josie Pie sang the Spice Girls.

The year her parents divorced and her mom went back to work, Josie had briefly had a thirtysomething nanny who would sit at her laptop watching Spice Girls videos and silently crying. Josie had realized there were things about being a woman she didn't understand yet, but that the Spice Girls would help. The Spice Girls weren't afraid, they weren't ashamed, they loved being girls, and they let you know it constantly.

That was how she felt now as she faced the Zombloid hordes: Unashamed. Unafraid. Spicy. Girly.

"Stop!" had led her to the Spice Girls song of that name, and she sang it out like a soundtrack to her kick-buttery. The song stunned the Zombloids. Some just stood there, swaying slightly, as if patiently waiting for her to kick them.

So she did. Kicked and sang, spun and sang. While the musical interlude in the historical romance had turned into a beer-hall revelry, in this genre it slid neatly into a dance-fighting sequence.

Josie hadn't danced in some time, but she imagined that she was really good at it, and her body seemed to respond. Any Zombloid that came too near was getting the Rockette treatment: high kick to the face, knee to the groin. Or groin area. On a Zombloid, you never knew where their body parts had gotten to.

She sang, and noticed there was music backing her up as if broadcast from the sky itself: keyboard, guitar, bass, drums, horns, strings.

"GAAAARRR!" said the Zombloids.

"Die, Zombloids, die!" she yelled.

Here she was again, she realized, singing ensemble songs as if they were solos. She yearned for a cast, a community. A crew of girls. Hope tickled her stomach, like magic percolating in her middle till it expanded, made her hopes reality. She paused mid-kick to look up at the hill. A figure stood there, quickly followed by three more. Reinforcements. Down the hill they came running, Nina in the lead followed by the Trophy Wives and Frisbee Girl.

"Hey, lady," said Nina, high-kicking in unison.

"Oh, Nina, I know you've always got my back," said Josie. "Just not too close to my back, because FYI, I'm infected."

Josie broke into a whole Spice Girls medley, and her reinforcements sang their parts, both musical and kickbuttical. They fought with keen energy during "Say You'll Be There," their moves more rhythmic with some hip action while she sang "Spice Up Your Life," and then they ripped into what was clearly the climax with "Wannabe."

The music made Josie feel anything was possible. She jumped and seemed to float there as she kicked. Her punches became blurry-fast. She knocked the last Zombloid across both its jaws, and it seemed to fall in slow motion. In the middle of this bizarro dream sequence, Josie felt more like herself than she had in ages.

In mounds at their feet, the entire Zombloid army lay still, slowly dissolving into goo.

"Yes!" said Nina.

Josie lifted her hand to high-five Nina before remembering she couldn't touch her. Instead, she struck a heroic pose, fist up.

"Eat our Spice Girls, Zombloid scum!"

"Yeah!" echoed her girl crew.

The Zombloids didn't respond. They'd already eaten their Spice Girls. They were dissolving into sludge.

"We'll go look for more Zombloids around back," said Nina, and the four of them jogged away before Josie could react.

Well, the book was probably over anyway. Josie gazed mournfully at the farmhouse. At least she'd been able to save Hatchet. But to truly save him, she had to get far away.

She turned her back to the farmhouse and slowly walked toward the hills, a dramatic closure for the shockingly mistitled survival horror story. She expected to wake up in the park at any moment, but as she passed by an old, rusted tractor, it suddenly tipped over, pinning her solidly to the ground.

"Help?" she said.

A figure stood above her, the sun behind it. She squinted, trying to make it out.

The tractor-tipper was no ordinary Zombloid. It was a Zombloid trio. Three googly-eyed heads gargled and spat at her, and despite the glassy gray skin and bloated, bubbling faces, she recognized Misty, Marcus, and Meaghan, combined into a grotesque mutated book club.

They crouched over her, and her skin twitched and burned, ready to merge into a quadruplet Zombloid.

Josie screamed and tried to imagine she was free, but the tractor was so heavy, and the Zombloid trio was so scary and so close—

Then, a hatchet. It rose, glinting heroically in the sunlight, before chopping down.

The Zombloid trio fell dead. Or dead again. Extra undead. And where they'd stood, Hatchet now posed with his hatchet, as golden as a Greek god in the sunlight.

"Get back!" Josie yelled. "Staying apart is the only thing keeping us human!"

He rolled the tractor off her and knelt beside her, reaching out with one hand, as if asking her to take it. Like he had at their first meeting, hesitant yet yearning.

"The only thing that keeps me human"—he paused for a beat—"is being with you."

"No," Josie said, trying to scoot away. "I must save you."

"You already have," he said.

These lines were so good! She was serving it up to him, and he was spiking it.

His hand remained outstretched, steady and sure. "I've got you."

Something in her melted. She reached back, and he clasped her hand.

Josie watched in horror as their skin started to merge. But he was holding something in his other hand, and it wasn't his faithful hatchet.

A syringe. A very special syringe with two needles, as if made for lovers.

He thrust it, piercing both of their hands simultaneously.

"The cure . . . ," Josie whispered.

"It's working," said Hatchet.

Their hands unmerged. Yet they still clutched each other. Two separate appendages, not forced to combine but choosing to touch.

"We can save everyone," he said.

"Change the world," she said.

"Start over," he said. "Together."

Hatchet put his other arm beneath her, helping her to sit up. They were so close. Even sweaty and dirty, Josie felt beautiful. And deliciously human.

"Happy Valentine's Day," said Josie.

And so Josie/Melody learned an important truth. What is left behind when all of civilization is stripped away? Love. Love remains.

Hatchet leaned in. And they kissed. Melody and Hatchet. Josie and Justin. She wouldn't mind getting stuck in a make-out montage.

But she hesitated. Shouldn't this be over now? Shouldn't she get out and get back to . . .

To . . .

Hatchet's thumb touched her lips.

What did she need to do again?

Um . . . Mia. She needed to take care of Mia.

She leaned back. *Mia!*

Her whole body vibrated, as if it had been asleep and now blood was rushing everywhere, heating and tingling away the numbness. Josie winced. This would be the part when she'd come to and didn't necessarily want to come to. Not yet. Hatchet's hand was in her hair. His mouth exhaled on hers. She tried to lift her chin, to meet him halfway.

But she hesitated again, and now she was fully gone.

CHAPTER 12

Josie jolted to her feet. She was gripping her copy of *Valentine's Day* in the same hand she'd been gripping Hatchet's hand.

She looked around, taking off her reading glasses to see more clearly. The park. Missoula. The real world was so beautiful! The sun shone shinier; the air was crisper. She ran her fingers through her clean hair. She put her fist in the air, striking that *I defeated the Zombloid army* pose, and said, "Yeah!"

Misty, Meaghan, and Marcus (who were not a Zombloid, though still a trio) glared at her from their bench. Josie didn't even care. She felt so full, so large. Had she been hunkered down inside herself? Because suddenly she felt like she could stretch, fill up that emptiness, reclaim her space.

"Yeah!" Josie said again.

"What is the matter with you?" Misty said. "Your kid has been calling your name for like two minutes."

Josie checked the time on her phone. She estimated that she'd been in the story for about five minutes this time.

"Must be a pretty engrossing book," said Marcus with one eyebrow perfectly arched.

"You know, ignoring a child can cause excessive-attachment disorder," said Meaghan. "I heard that on a podcast."

"Josie!" Josie heard Mia now. "Josie!"

Josie rushed onto the playground, sand shooting out from beneath her heels. "What happened? Are you okay? Are you hurt?"

"Josie, can you swing me?" said Mia, sitting on an immobile swing, her little legs pumping uselessly.

"Can I swing you?" She'd taken down an entire Zombloid army! While singing the Spice Girls! She could do *anything*.

Josie pushed Mia so high the swing's chains were nearly parallel with the earth. Mia laughed.

"Josie!" she said. Now it sounded like a battle cry. "Josie!"

Josie and Mia played together at the park for another hour: hide-and-seek, princess castle, and monkey-bar dangle. As the trio got up from their bench, Meaghan passed by Josie, who was hiding inside the playhouse. "Do you always have this much energy?"

"Not really," said Josie. "Just when I'm feeling awesome."

"Yeah . . ." Meaghan frowned. "It's sweet, though, how you play with her."

Before Josie could respond, Meaghan hurried after Misty.

At the condo, Josie still felt a mile high. She made Mia her favorite snack of peanut butter and jelly in a cone, followed by a dance party. Later they visited the library and sat in the kids' section reading book after book. None of them came alive around her.

I was powerful, Josie thought. *I was capable. I wasn't washed up.*

And, she realized, she'd been fighting—literally fighting—*for* Justin. Or pseudo-Justin. And that had felt right.

She called him again. Still no answer. But the hot core of her was beating out a tune of possibility. Could she fight for him in real life? Out here, where she had no power to control the narrative? Because at times, inside the story, she thought she could affect it, bend it to her will. Call to Nina. Save her.

JOSIE
I miss you. I don't know who I am without you.
And without Justin. And without New York and
the impossible dream and all of it.

NINA
Hey you

JOSIE

I had like a dream I was living in a postapocalyptic story, and the guy in it looked like Justin but wasn't

NINA

Good dream or bad dream

JOSIE

I defeated this undead army with a crossbow, high kicks and spice girls songs

NINA

Spice girls???

JOSIE

Hells yes the spice girls

NINA

Hells yes the spice girls

JOSIE

I love you

NINA

Love you too but I've gotta go

Josie stared at her phone, her face scrunched in a hurt frown. Usually Nina made time for her when she needed to talk, and she'd been hoping to tell Nina about the books and the bench and the tea and everything. Busy Nina was kind of a letdown.

While Mia was absorbed with a board book, Josie sat at a library computer. It opened to the local newspaper's website. Top stories:

Two Missoulians Succumb to Comas
No known injury, disease, or connection to each other
Spring Has Sprung!
Enjoy a week of balmy 50 degrees F
Mystery of the Missing Nuts Solved:
It was squirrels!

Josie started to search some terms.

psychotic break:

Now that she read about it, this didn't fit the bill.

fugue state:

Maybe, but still not quite right.

drug-induced hallucination:

Naw . . .

She got tired of trying to self-diagnose. Besides, she still felt too fearsome and formidable to worry.

While humming "Wannabe," she found herself typing:

community theater missoula montana

There was one within walking distance. And the next monthly audition for their repertory company was actually this week. Talk about fate. Talk about a sign. Talk about earning the favor of the Muses.

Still . . . *community theater*. Mr. Camoin had spoken those words like one might say *overflowing sewer*. It had always been Broadway or bust. And Josie had gone bust.

A head full of playground sand necessitated a bath night for Mia, which meant two hours of cajoling before she finally got into the tub. She refused to sit, standing in knee-deep water with her hands above her head because raisiny fingertips horrified her. Josie washed her as fast as she could, rinsing her with cups of water and rescuing her from the tub before her fingerprints had time to wrinkle. After, Josie held Mia for half an hour while she cried.

"I don't get it, Mia. It's just water."

"I don't . . . like . . . raisin fingers," she said through sobs.

Josie didn't know if it was normal or not for a

five-year-old to require so much love and assurance just to get through each day. She remembered her own younger self, the way she'd insisted on keeping her room exactly the way she liked, exerting control over her own little world to combat the chaos in the rest of the house.

When Mia's panicked breaths slowed, she pressed her cheek against Josie's and said, "I love you the whole world. But the world is bigger than you. How do I love you more than a bigger thing?"

Mia's five-year-old logic seemed sound. After all, the biggest cookie on the plate was clearly the best one. Broadway trumped community theater. Surely New York City trounced Missoula.

"I don't know," said Josie. "Isn't that weird?"

Mia's cheek was soft against her own.

"It is weird." Then Mia whispered, "*I love you more than ice cream.*"

Josie kissed Mia's head. It was a big thing, to be loved more than ice cream. A beautiful thing, but marred by a tiny worry that Mia should be saying this to her parents, not to a nanny. Not to someone who could leave.

Then Mia said, "I miss Mommy. And Daddy. But mostly Mommy."

"I know."

"Is Mommy going to forget me?"

"Of course not," said Josie. "She'll be back soon."

"But she always leaves."

And just like that, Josie felt eight again. Dad gone. Mom working. Lila slamming her bedroom door. Josie sitting alone in front of the TV.

After Mia was asleep, Josie picked up her phone to call Victoria before remembering that it was too late in Kenya to call.

Phone in hand, she hesitated to call Justin again. If only happiness and fulfillment could be won by physically defeating an undead army instead of through *conversation*.

She scrolled through old text messages, reading one from December, just before Justin visited her in New York.

JOSIE
What day will you get here? I want to make sure you get tickets to my show

JUSTIN
I need a ticket? I thought it was a class

JOSIE
It is. I think the ticket thing is to make us feel like it's a real show? FYI prepare yourself, I'll be wearing a full stocking mask. You'll know which one I am by my stop sign hat

JUSTIN
Um

JOSIE
Yeah

JUSTIN
So

JOSIE
Stop. Sign. Hat.

JUSTIN
I'm not laughing

JOSIE
Maybe you should be

JUSTIN
I'm laughing a little. But laughing WITH you

JOSIE
How do you know I'm laughing?

JUSTIN
My phone is shaking. I bet you're adorable in a stop sign hat

JOSIE
And full stocking mask

She smiled to herself and dialed his unreliable personal phone. This time he picked up.

"Hey, Justin."

"Hey, Josie!"

"What's that noise?"

"Oh! Uh . . . I'm in the car."

"Car? What car?" He was one of nine brothers and sisters; he didn't have his own car.

"My friend's car. The last month of senior year is kind of a joke, so we're taking a few days off to drive across the state and visit . . . their friends."

Singular *they*. Was the friend nonbinary? Or was the friend female and Justin was using *their* to obfuscate the gender?

Josie was only 80 percent sure she knew what *obfuscate* meant, so she didn't say it aloud.

"Hey Joz, I shouldn't talk while driving. Call you later?"

It was only eight o'clock. Josie usually stayed awake till midnight, and tonight her fingertips were still buzzing with Zombloid-fighting adrenaline. Josie steeled her spine and paced while calling her mom.

"Do we have family history of mental illness? I mean, besides Grandma's PTSD. And whatever Dad's deal is."

"Probably," said Lorna. "Who doesn't? I think I have the bipolar."

"You're not bipolar, Mom."

"Yesterday I cooked four batches of snickerdoodles. Today I don't feel like cooking a thing."

"Mom, bipolar is a real thing. It's not just being motivated one day and not the next."

"You don't know me."

Josie briefly shut her eyes and tried again. "Look, I've been having, like, waking dreams? Like it's a full-fledged dream but inside a book I was just reading? Maybe I'm psychotic."

"You're not psychotic. You're depressed because you're not as special as you thought and your life's a mess and you're looking for excuses."

"Thanks, Mom."

"Depressive states can make you think about things you never would. I should know. I haven't cooked a thing all day."

"But Mom, this was weird. Like, really weird. So weird that I was . . ." Josie chuckled to show she wasn't taking it *completely* seriously. "I wondered if the book I was reading was magic. Honestly—magic! That's how bad it got."

Lorna coughed disapprovingly. "So quick to dismiss magic, are you? Think you know all the things?"

"You are telling me to believe in magic. *You* are."

"I'm studying to be an energy worker."

"You are not. You're kidding."

"I'm kidding."

"I knew you were kidding."

"I'm not kidding."

"Mom . . ."

"You have a silver sheen around you with—"

"What does that mean?"

"How should I know? I'm new at this. I told you I just started studying. You have a silverness and a yellow center and you're bound to attract the attention of certain forces. Your energy stands out like a lantern on a moonless night."

"You're still kidding. You're waiting for me to believe what you're saying and then you'll shout, 'Aha!'"

"All silvery but burning yellow. Very eye-catching, probably, for those who are into that sort of thing. Bound to notice you."

"What? Who? Who would notice me?"

"How should I know? I started the internet course last week and the video was so boring I fell asleep. Sitting up. That's how boring."

"When I told you how onstage I could feel the energy of the audience, you laughed at me. In sixth grade, you wouldn't come see me in *Cinderella* because you said fairy tales are just setting up children for a lifetime of disappointment."

"You need to learn to let things go. Like all that negative energy you're holding in your solar plexus."

"You don't believe in negative energy!"

"If I can get through that boring video, I'll find out. Maybe if I watch it while marching in place I won't fall asleep."

"Family history, Mom. Of mental illness. Anything I should know about?"

"I dropped you on your head when you were a baby."

"Mom!"

"No, wait, that was Lila. Don't tell her."

"So, you have nothing to say to me?" Josie asked. No mention of the credit card. Had the bank still not informed her? All this waiting for the other shoe to drop was giving Josie an ache in her wincing muscles.

"I have to go. There's a dust storm coming and I want to bring in my babies." She meant the pair of terra-cotta deer "grazing" on the gravel in her backyard. She oiled the deer regularly. She'd named them Clio and Calliope because those were two of the names she wanted for her children, but their dad had vetoed all her choices.

"Nice Greek names!" Lorna always said. "But no, your father turned his back on his heritage just like he eventually turned his back on us!"

Josie thought about calling her dad to ask about family mental-health history, but she wasn't feeling *that* brave. Still brave enough to close her eyes and imagine new plans.

The first step to making something happen was to see it in her mind. Mr. Camoin had taught her that. She imagined Justin running to her with open arms . . . and then cringed. No. She couldn't allow herself to wish for that. That hurt. This was not a fantasy where anything could happen. She had to be practical.

She imagined her friendship with Nina as it had been in high school, when Josie wasn't such a deadweight. She imagined landing those lead roles and performing to standing ovations in high school. And being popular again. In high school.

Josie, she quietly whispered to herself, *maybe it's time to let go of high school?*

All her imaginings involved going backward. What was forward? Broadway. That had been the plan. Well, at least for now, she could imagine an imaginary Broadway, out there somewhere, waiting for her to discover it.

And while she was at it, she imagined all the negative energy uncurling from her solar plexus and floating away into the cosmos. Just in case.

She was still pacing, putting off something. The book was sitting there in her bag, waiting for her, full of promise and threats. And she honestly didn't know what she hoped would happen.

But she couldn't put it off forever. She sat on the floor and opened up *Valentine.* In her mind, she'd started abbreviating the book titles to a single word, the way theater people did with shows. *The Phantom of the Opera* was *Phantom,* and *Fiddler on the Roof* was *Fiddler.* Likewise, *The Highwayman Came Riding* became *Highwayman,* and *Valentine's Day* was just *Valentine.* Abbreviations were as much a part of theater culture as humiliating vocal warm-ups and jazz hands.

Josie held the book, closed, at arm's length. Her

heartbeat ticked in her ears. Part of her yearned to jump into the story again, meet up with Hatchet and pretend-fall-in-love. Feel his warmth beside her. And take down a Zombloid army in an act of terrifying courage and skill mixed with spicy-girly goodness. Not to worry about dating and insecurities and failures and auditions, but just truly get lost in a story.

Another part of her really didn't want to be unshowered anymore.

She squinted and read the first page. And the second. She didn't fall out of the tree. She was still in the Missoula condo. Her clothes still smelled springtime fresh.

The flashback-heavy narrative slowly revealed Melody's troubled past alongside the current action. At last the crossbow was explained: Melody's grandfather had been a conspiracy-loving old coot who had a cabin stocked with all kinds of end-of-the-world supplies, including a crossbow. Hatchet's real name wasn't Justin. It was Gus Bankowski, and he was the son of the scientist whose genetic meddling had produced the Zombloid virus.

The story varied wildly from Josie's dream/hallucination/whatever. The final confrontation occurred not outside a farmhouse but at the eerily abandoned Mall of America. The Spice Girls weren't involved.

But there were also too many similarities to be mere coincidence—like running across other survivors, including a doctor with the secret to the cure, and a mutated multiple Zombloid that sucked in everyone who got near.

By the end of the book, Josie was pacing again, arguing with herself.

There has to be a reasonable explanation.

Maybe, she told herself, *you read that book years ago and forgot, but parts of the story were stored in your subconscious and worked themselves into your medically explainable hallucination.*

Or, she thought with a wince, the bench or the tea was . . . was . . . *magic.*

Josie had scanned the whole book through and then started to read in earnest from the beginning when a knock at the front door startled her.

She frowned as she walked to the door. Not a friend stopping by, as she didn't have any in Missoula. If Victoria had returned home after all, she would use her key to get in. A neighbor wanting to borrow an egg? A doorbell ditch? A police officer come to tell her that her boyfriend-possibly-ex-boyfriend had been found in Arizona naked and dead, murdered by his successful-singer girlfriend?

Josie opened the door.

Nina put out her arms and said, "Ta-da!"

CHAPTER 13

"Nina!" said Josie.

"I know!" said Nina, pleased with herself.

"You're here!" said Josie.

"I know! I know!" said Nina.

Josie attacked her with a hug. She had to stand on her toes. Nina was over six feet tall, striking in a coral jumpsuit and that newly purple-tipped hair, wearing high heels because she liked them, thanks. Nina entered a room and filled it up. And yet, when Nina was around, Josie didn't feel less. She felt more.

"I got a cheap flight last-minute out of O'Hare. It took all my cash but I did it! Surprise!"

Nina peeked in on sleeping Mia, let Josie give her the grand tour of the condo, and caught her up.

"I'm not dating anyone right now. Romance takes so much energy, and school is too fun."

"Did you end up auditioning for that play?"

"Naw, I'm not really interested in theater anymore.

There's this summer internship I'm waiting to hear about; it'd lead to a good job next summer. Like, a seriously sweet salary. And it's right downtown. I love the city and the noise, and being an adult at last. Don't you love being an adult?"

Josie didn't answer.

"I am literally the only mature person in our apartment," said Nina. "So much insecurity masked as meanness."

"Like drama club my sophomore year when Cyndee Rasmussen was president?"

"Um, yeah, sure. Anyway, I've got to be back tomorrow afternoon, but I'm staying the night. So we can talk."

"Yes, please. I need to talk to you so bad my fingernails actually hurt. Is that possible? Can fingernails hurt?"

Nina tilted her head.

"I feel like I'm going crazy, Nina. Sometimes when I'm reading a book, I have this full-blown hallucination that I'm the main character. And the other characters look like people I've seen recently. Even you."

"You're hallucinating about me?"

"It's hard to explain, 'cause it was all in my head but time didn't pass. Do you think I should, I don't know, commit myself somewhere?"

"Um . . . did you rob a bank? Join the mafia? Murder a neighbor and hide the body inside the walls?"

"I read a book. And it was way more intense than—never mind. I don't know what happened." Josie was pacing now. "Time is weird. It feels like we should still be sitting in the back row of drama whispering to each other, and suddenly . . . Do you ever feel like you're in the wrong story? How did I end up in Missoula, Montana? And without Justin?"

"A little distance is probably good, right? I mean, it's not normal how fast you two became inseparable."

"You know he's the only guy I've ever even kissed. Except for stage kisses, which don't count."

Nina sat on the sofa and leaned her head back, eyes closed. She slowly breathed out.

"Are you tired?"

"Yeah," said Nina. "You know how travel is. It was tricky to get here, and I'm worried about missing classes."

"I'm so glad you did, though. This is perfect timing . . ." Josie took a deep breath and looked down at her hands. Speaking it aloud would make it real. But this was Nina. "Justin doesn't love me anymore."

"That can't be right," said Nina.

Josie nodded, trying not to cry.

"Not possible!" said Nina.

And then Josie full-on ugly-cried.

"Come here, baby," Nina said, reaching out.

Josie plopped down on the couch beside her. She let Nina pull her close, lay her head against her shoulder, and stroke her hair, the way Josie always wanted to do for Mia, if Mia would let her.

"I feel like trash," said Josie.

"Did he say the words, 'Josie, I don't love you anymore'?"

"Well, no."

"Josie." Nina pulled away to give her a stern look. "This is Justin we're talking about. How's about not jumping to conclusions before—"

"Because it hurts! I can't keep hoping for another thing that's going to go belly-up or I'll die, and I'm not being dramatic about this, I will literally die."

"Maybe it wouldn't be a bad idea to talk to someone. Like, a therapist."

"Are you serious?" Josie couldn't tell. Nina had talked to a school counselor at age fourteen, before she transitioned, when she was terrified of puberty, hating all the ways her body was becoming more like a man's when she knew she was supposed to be a woman. The counselor had made her feel like she was crazy. Nina hadn't cared for therapists ever since.

"I'm seeing a therapist in Chicago," said Nina.

"Really?" said Josie. "I mean, that's great! I'm just surprised. There was a time I knew everything about you."

"You never knew everything about me, Josie. No one does."

"Oh, sure." Josie hopped up, then started picking up

stuffed animals and doll clothes, tossing them into the toy basket. "Who ever really knows anyone, right? I just thought . . . we're kindred spirits. We're platonic soul mates, right?"

Nina frowned at her, considering. "I feel like this friendship-talk thing isn't in the cards tonight. Would it help the funk you're in if I took you out to distract you?"

"I doubt it, but I can't leave Mia anyway."

Nina took Josie by the shoulders and looked her in the eyes. "You are adorable. Justin was lucky to get you. Anybody would be lucky to be with you."

"Thank you. Hey, listen, what I wanted to call you about—you know there's a university in Missoula? It's a pretty good one, I've heard."

"Yeah? Are you thinking of enrolling?"

"Or you could," said Josie. "You could transfer here! Josie and Nina, just like old times!"

Nina pulled out her phone and started browsing. "You know what? I'm gonna call a babysitting service. You need a night out."

"This isn't Chicago or New York. There isn't going to be a babysitting service in Missoula. But . . ."

"What?" said Nina.

"Mia's preschool did give me a list of teachers' aides who are available for after-hours sitting, and Victoria said to call them if I ever needed a fill-in . . ."

"So call already! Stop finding reasons to say no to everything."

Nina helped her pick out some non-sweatshirt tops and non-sweatpants bottoms and did her hair and makeup. And by the time the sitter arrived, Josie was feeling a little more like a girl and a little less like a notebook left on the porch in the rain.

Nina had come in a cab from the airport, so they walked toward downtown.

"Why are you here again?" asked Nina as they passed all the closed little shops and the occasional horse post. Josie figured the posts were ornamental. Probably.

"Space. Change. Impulsivity."

"But New York City is your jam. And this place is just *small*."

"Maybe I'm small too," said Josie.

"Baby, you're not small."

"I feel small."

Josie had left New York feeling like a cartoon character who gets clubbed over the head and goes accordion, compact enough to fit inside their hat. If she went back to New York, would she find where she'd left Josie Pie?

Wait, if she and Justin broke up for real, would she stop using that last name? Josie Pie had always sounded so memorable . . . because of *Anne of Green Gables*?

Josie rubbed at sudden goose bumps. Had her subconscious tricked her into believing she belonged with Justin Pie based on the name in a forgotten book? Maybe they'd never been compatible. Maybe only their names had been.

Josie linked her arm through Nina's. "It feels so good to be with you again. We're like Anne and Diana."

"Who?"

"From *Anne of Green Gables*?"

"Never read it. I'm not really into bonnet books."

"What about corset books?" asked Josie, having recently been deeply into a corset book.

"I could might maybe make an exception for corsets . . ."

As they walked down the sidewalk, Nina nodded her head in greeting to a couple in matching cowboy hats, and suddenly Josie was flashing back to high school and braving those halls with Nina. Only then, Josie had been the one walking tall with that unmistakable air of confidence.

Hey, Josie! Hi, Josie! How you doin', Josie? Hey, Josie. Josie! 'Sup, Josie. Hey . . . Nina.

That had been during the height of Josie's high school stardom. Star of the winter musical and the spring one. Lead singer for the school's coolest band, Deviant Yodel. (Justin played bass—or at least plucked at the strings in a concentrated manner.) Who gets voted Most Likely to Succeed *and* Most Talented when they're only a junior? Josie Sergakis, that's who.

Josie had sometimes worried Nina might feel relegated to a sidekick position next to Josie's sparkly princess power. But Nina had never complained, had auditioned for the chorus in all the shows Josie starred in to spend more time with her, and more than once had theorized that Josie's superpowerdom was sheltering her from some of the fallout of her transition. Some.

After Nina had come out as transgender, five boys attacked her, dragging her into the boys' bathroom and pulling out a chunk of her hair. The memory of that day and the weeks after hit Josie like a punched gut—the stress, the panic, the worry for Nina. And she hadn't been the one threatened. How much worse it had been for her friend, Josie couldn't even comprehend.

She'd rearranged her schedule so they shared four classes, and when the classes they didn't share ended, Josie would run to Nina's side to walk her down the hall. Whether or not the bullies cared about Josie Sergakis's singing prowess, everyone in Millennial High School knew her. Fame had real power. Anything done around Josie was done in the glare of her natural spotlight. No one near Josie was able to hide in the dark.

The lampposts in Missoula flickered on above them, hovering ghosts of light. Nina followed a map on her phone to a pub on Main Street, the front door plastered in flyers advertising a poetry slam, an art show, and TESTY FESTY: THE ANNUAL TESTICLE FESTIVAL IN CLINTON, MT with a big red CANCELED stamped over it.

Inside was warm, humid, and a little funky, overstuffed with electronic slot machines and cracked pleather chairs, baroquely decorated with beer signs.

A man in brown camouflage passed by them in the

doorway. Nina raised her hand in greeting and said, "Thank you for your service."

He frowned as he left.

"He was a hunter, Nina," said Josie. "It's a thing they do here."

"In a karaoke bar?" asked Nina, eyeing the taxidermied moose head hanging on a wall.

"They just like to be prepared in case they need to go hunting on a moment's notice," said Josie. "I think. I haven't figured it out yet."

As they sidled through the crowd, several people, both men and women, gave Nina that familiar full-body sweep. Their expressions ranged from curiosity to apprehension and, at least once, disgust. Josie's adrenaline spiked, tiny lightning bolts zapping her chest and wrists.

"Nina . . . ," Josie started.

"I'm cool," said Nina.

"Should we leave?" Josie whispered.

"Everything's cool," said Nina.

Everything's cool, her posture said too. As did her smile. Loose and easy. This was not the same Nina who had shuffled down their high school's halls. This Nina acted as carefree as if the world were a tree for her to lean against.

Josie didn't know Missoula well enough to guess if there might be someone just mean, drunk, or angry enough to challenge Nina's confidence. She wished for the power of her high school stardom to grab on to. For anything. She was nobody here.

What good was she to Nina unless she was a star?

They seized newly vacated stools and ordered sodas. Josie was too tense to talk, hyperaware of everyone nearby, eyeing their body language. But minutes ticked by, and no one approached Nina.

"Everything's cool," Nina said again.

"Josie?"

Josie whipped around. Deo had lost the red apron and unbuttoned a couple buttons of his button-down, gracefully revealing a hint of—yep, hard, chiseled, hairless chest. Josie quickly raised her gaze to his face.

"Hey! Um . . . Deo! Hey there, this is my friend Nina."

"Hi," said Nina, waving.

Deo nodded in greeting, but his attention immediately returned to Josie. "I was hoping you'd come back to the store for another book."

"Oh! Um, yeah, I'm sure I will."

"Really?" He smiled, and the effect on his perfect face was uncanny.

"Totally."

"Oh good. Wow, you look amazing."

Josie blushed. "Um . . ."

"Was that rude?" he said. "I hope that wasn't demeaning. I mean, you're so much more than how you look. I just . . ." He grimaced. "I should just shut up."

Josie laughed. "No, really, it's okay. Thank you."

"Okay, well, I hope to see you soon, Josie! Nice to meet you, Nina."

"Bye," said Nina, watching him as he walked out. She turned to Josie. "What's the story about Adonis there?"

"Nothing. He's . . . just this guy who works in a bookstore—"

"He is unreal. Who looks like that? Seriously, he should be in movies."

"I think he's too shy for that."

Nina raised her eyebrows. "Oh. I see . . ."

"What?"

Nina sipped from her straw and looked sideways.

Josie laughed. "He's kinda flirty? I guess? But there's nothing there."

"Hmm," said Nina.

Across the room, three women on the karaoke stage were screeching, "I Will Survive."

Nina gestured toward them with her chin. "You're going up there."

"No . . ."

"Josie Pie à la Mode, you think I didn't choose a karaoke bar on purpose? You're going to show this scrubby little town Millennial High School's Most Talented student."

"Nina . . ."

"*And* show Justin, wherever his nasty self is, the kind of girl he's messing with. If he is. Which fact is unconfirmed."

"Right. You're right." Josie finished off her drink in one gulp. "I'll do it. I am a song sorceress."

After all, she wasn't *that* rusty. She'd sorta performed for a whole bandit camp a couple of days ago, and she'd killed that Spice Girls medley while killing Zombloids as Melody.

Josie put in her song request and waited by the stage, bouncing on the balls of her feet while a middle-aged cowboy finished up a Carrie Underwood. She shook her hands by her sides and did some mouth warm-up exercises. *Aaa Eee Iii Ooo Uuu. Waaa waaa waaa. Ppbbbb.*

Instinctively she whispered, "Muses, I perform for you." An old habit, written so deeply in her by Mr. Camoin that it had probably altered her DNA.

Mr. Camoin had talked about theater as if it weren't entertainment but survival. "We are performing for the Muses," he'd told them. "If you value your life, do not displease them."

"I thought the Muses inspired artists to create," Josie had said.

"A watered-down myth! The older legend is more gruesome. The Muses were supernatural beings that required human sacrifice to survive but would accept art as a substitute. For early civilizations, creating worthy art was a matter of life and death!" He'd laughed. "Remember that. You are dancing, acting, and singing for your lives. Make the story feel real enough for the Muses or they will feast upon you instead!"

Mr. Camoin put the *drama* in drama teacher.

Josie didn't think Mr. Camoin really believed in the Muses. It was just a tactic to get their best performances out of them. But sometimes, when she was alone and up way too late, she wondered, in a punchy, dizzy kind of way, if maybe they did exist. There had been times, after all, when she was performing and felt more than she could explain. The energy of the audience like an electric wind. The goose-bump-raising chill of ghosts rising up from the stage boards. And in the darkness beyond the light, around the shadows, a kind of hunger, something she must feed.

Just flights of fancy, but the spirit of it stuck with her. *Get immersive. Feel the music. Become the character. Make it real. Or else.*

She took a breath and took the karaoke stage. It was small, a hollow wooden stand just a couple of steps up, but a bright yellow light shone down. The prelude to "Stop in the Name of Love" began to play. She didn't think she needed the words, but she stared at the monitor anyway, desperate for its security. The microphone was damp in her hands.

"Oh, come on . . . ," muttered a man from a nearby table.

Josie only at this moment realized that this wasn't a good solo number, but it was too late to stop, even in the name of love. Seemingly on their own, her shoulders rolled in, her head bowed, her whole body wanting to make herself a little smaller on the stage. Some of the crowd looked away, talking to their friends and dates. Like indifferent casting directors behind folding tables, slowly unwrapping pieces of gum.

How long had Justin been wincing at the sound of her voice?

Josie sang a little quieter, not wanting to annoy the audience. Her hands were shaking and her voice followed, alternately whispering and squeaking. The best she could hope for was that the squeaking was somehow adorable, like a little piglet.

Nina, I am small, she thought, wishing to be even smaller. Invisible. Nonexistent.

The song seemed to last a Montana winter. Eventually the final words drizzled out of her mouth, and she stared down, her feet frozen to the spot. It occurred to her that profound awkwardness was basically a super-powered glue. If only she could store awkwardness in a bottle, she could make millions.

Nina sprang to her feet, her coral jumpsuit bright as a spotlight. She clapped.

"Yeah! That's what I'm talking about! You rock, Josie. YOU ROCK!"

Nina's completely unwarranted approval proved immensely useful. It increased Josie's mortification to such a profound level, her feet unfroze, and she was able to shuffle offstage.

CHAPTER 14

The next morning was strange and stiff and mostly silent. Nina had breakfast; Josie commented on the breakfast. Nina did her hair; Josie commented on her hair. By the time Nina had departed for the airport, the ache inside Josie had helped her make up her mind.

Josie walked Mia to preschool again, prepping her along the way that, since it wasn't one of her regular days, there would be different kids there. *New* friends.

The little girl didn't bounce and sing at the prospect of making new friends. She was solemn, gripping Josie's hand, staring straight ahead as they crossed the street.

"Mia," Josie began, but Mia shushed her.

"It's bad luck to talk on the crosswalk," Mia explained when they'd reached the other side. She began to hop on one foot, her ritual for undoing bad luck.

Josie blamed herself for Mia's obsession with luck. When she first started looking after Mia, she'd said, "Break a leg," before Mia was about to sing a song for her. Mia had wanted to know why she was so mean, so Josie had told her about theater superstitions and how it was bad luck to say *good luck*.

Josie supposed her insistence that talking on crosswalks was bad luck was as arbitrary as "Inside any theater, *Macbeth* must be referred to as the Scottish Play."

"Mia, if you'd rather not go today—" Josie started.

"I do want to rather go today," Mia said with a stoic face. "I am excited."

Josie tried not to laugh. "You are?"

Mia nodded slowly. "I don't want to scare it."

Josie supposed Mia thought of today as a precious, wild bird, and any sudden movements would startle it into flight. So Josie played along and was silent and careful too.

At the doors of Little Bookworm Preschool, Mia gave Josie's legs a businesslike hug.

"Thank you for making my dreams come true," she said. "I will make friends. And I will tell them about you."

And then, without a backward glance, Mia ran inside.

Josie lingered. Through the window, she could see Mia just standing there in the classroom. Mia didn't smile often, but what if this not-smile was Mia fear or Mia confusion or Mia-needs-her-nanny?

Mia is fine, she told herself. *You, on the other hand, are not. Clingy nanny freak.*

Josie had talked Victoria out of signing up Mia for

more preschool, saying that she was already being paid for full-time nannying and wanted to give Victoria her money's worth. But if she was honest with herself, she'd been afraid of having too much free time in this new place. Free time meant time to fill. And with what? The vast openness of her unpromising future felt as inviting as never-ending winter.

So Josie forced herself to march away from Mia and head for the library.

She'd realized that there was one way to know for sure that she had, in fact, experienced what she thought she had. Third time's a charm, as they said. Maybe they even said, *You just don't get it, do you? Third time's a charm!*

Either way, if Josie sat down on that bench and read a third book and entered a third fictional story for the third time, then there would be her proof. If that didn't happen, she'd try it again after having one of Bruce's teas. There was no way three hallucinogenic seizures could seize her in the exact same way and circumstance three times in a row.

It would be an experiment. Scientific method. Peer-reviewed study. Or something.

But at the same time, if she chose just the right book . . .

After the karaoke fiasco, she yearned to feel again as she had post-Zombloid triumph. But as she neared the library, she started to get those foreshadowy worries in her belly. To go into a dream sequence *on purpose* felt risky. Dangerous. There were moments in *Valentine* when Josie had almost forgotten she was in a book. The montaging had been a little scary, swooshing her through scenes against her will—almost a threat that maybe the story could keep her forever. Not to mention the time Hatchet had called her Melody and, for a split second, she'd thought that was her name. How could she be sure she wouldn't get stuck inside? And what would happen if she did?

Just one more time, Josie thought. *Maybe two.*

But before reaching the library, she veered left toward the bookstore instead. She figured she ought to stop by to tell Deo that she wouldn't be stopping by. If that was a thing that normal bookstore customers did.

The bell dinged. Deo looked up from the cashier's desk. And his face lit up.

"Wow," Josie said under her breath. It wasn't a thing a person could fake, being genuinely happy to see someone at first glance.

Deo turned a customer over to another bookseller and ran up to her.

"Hey," he said. "Josie Pie. Hey."

He took both her hands and then dropped them, momentarily embarrassed but unable not to grin.

Josie smiled back and meant it. When she realized that she meant it, her face went hot. "I just wanted to say thanks for your help with books and stuff. And I wanted you to know that I can't come back in to buy any more books for a while. Actually, I'm broke."

"Oh, that's fine, it's okay."

"But I wanted to stop by . . . to tell you . . . I just . . . I don't know what to say."

"I'm glad you came in. So . . ." He cleared his throat, looked at his shoes. "Are you still sorta involved with someone or could I take you out sometime?"

"Um . . ."

"Sorry, my sister tells me I'm too forward."

"No, it's okay. It's just . . . it's complicated. But I'm glad that you asked. I'm flattered, for real."

"Okay." He grinned wider, his gaze taking her in. He seemed to remember himself and looked down again. "Oh, hey, did you want another book?"

"I . . . uh . . . I'm broke. Utterly and completely."

"But a free one? We get loads of ARCs—advance reader copies, these cheaply bound books they send out before a book is published, for reviewers and booksellers and stuff. Do you want to take some with you?"

Bianca appeared suddenly from around a bookcase.

"Deo, I need you," she said.

"Just a sec," he said, taking Josie's arm.

Josie followed Deo into the back room. So different from the front of the store, the back room felt like a mini warehouse: Whatever organizational system it might have had was well hidden beneath the bare-bones chaos. Towers of cardboard boxes, steel shelving with stacks of hardcovers, a desk overflowing with mail pouches.

"Take as many as you want," Deo said, gesturing above the desk to shelves that were stuffed with softcover books.

"Wow, are you sure?" she asked.

He pointed to a handwritten sign: *ARCs for taking. Please take. PLEASE.*

Josie laughed. "Okay. Thanks. Thank you."

He smiled, pleased, and left.

As soon as she was alone, Josie slouched down in the seat, dropped her head against the desk, and surprised herself by breaking into sobs. The fight was out of her. She and Justin were over. She and Nina weren't the same. Nothing she'd hoped for had happened. She was not and would never be a star. That was a lot of nots, and it was too much to take in all at once.

The star got the applause. The big moment in the spotlight. Elphaba on the wires singing "Defying Gravity." Evita on the balcony singing "Don't Cry for Me, Argentina." Elsa on the mountain tearing off her gloves and belting "Let It Go." That was when people adored them. That was when they came into their own. When they were center stage, alone, singing their signature song, declaring what they wanted.

And they would get it by the end of the show.

Grizabella with her "Memory." Annie and "Tomorrow." Sally Bowles and "Maybe This Time." Josie had tried. She'd stepped out alone on the stage of her life and sung out her "I want" song with all the hope and pleading in her. And the universe hadn't listened.

At that second, all she wanted was to be Mia's age again, when she was too young to know that her dad was a mess and her parents were unhappy, when she believed she was still their baby and always would be. When she was sad and could lay her head on her mother's lap, and her mom would pet her hair and sing. Sing something soft. A song that promised everything would be okay.

"Ouch," Josie said, because becoming an adult hurt.

She glared at the shelves of books, daring them to fix her. If only she could manage to get lost in another character, she wouldn't have to feel all these big feelings anymore. The shelves of ARCs were divided into categories, and the one right at eye level was YOUNG ADULT. She hadn't read much young-adult fiction in high school, too busy and caught up in school and theater to read for fun.

She pulled down a small stack and examined the first book. The cover was a close-up of a girl's mouth and cheek, off-center, her head backlit by car headlights.

FEMURS IN THE ATTIC
An Emma Knickerbocker book
by Phillip R. Underwood

Josie's first thought was *Why are those rodents from Madagascar in somebody's attic?*—before she realized it said *Femurs*, not *Lemurs*. She opened it to a random page. The words looked a little small, so she put on the glasses and started to scan the page, to see if it was a story worth taking back to the bench.

Emma scowled at the wall. The crisscrosses of yarn were like a spider's web, and she couldn't help but wish that Charlotte the spider had spun this particular web and spelled out some helpful hints. Just a word or two. A clue here and there. Strike that—Emma already had plenty of clues. What she needed was a connection between them. If only—

Oh! It was happening. The swooshing, tumbling sensation, the world of colors draining and then hardening. A breath-stealing jolt.

And Josie was somewhere else. Alone, standing in a small, unfamiliar bedroom. How? How had this happened again? She hadn't drunk any tea or been on the park—

"The glasses." She breathed out the word. "Not the bench. Not the tea. *The glasses.*"

She must not have been wearing them those other times when she'd read but stayed firmly in the real world. And now she was—where was she? She hadn't even noticed what genre of book she'd entered, but she was *so* ready to be somebody else, her legs trembled in anticipation.

She looked down at herself: too-big T-shirt that went to her knees and mismatched socks. The twin bed was unmade, ruffled pink comforter shoved in a corner. Clothes lay around in piles, like pots of potpourri giving off the scent of Teenager. Josie turned and—"WHOA."

One entire wall resembled a set from a show about an obsessed detective.

At the center was a photo of Bianca. In black-and-white, she was smiling at the camera as if in a class photo but blown up large. Other photos were stuck to the wall with thumbtacks: Justin, Deo, Blonder Trophy Wife, Cowboy, Bruce, Misty. Strings connected the photos to one another and all of them to Bianca in the center. Also stuck into this web were:

- a receipt for a ladder, a bucket, and two pounds of lard
- a ticket stub for a movie called *Yosemite Pam*
- a computer printout of an attendance record for Tiffany Schloop at Flavor Flav High School
- Post-it notes full of questions:
    Where was Johnny at 3:10 p.m.?
    Groundhog Day = bank holiday?

Could Tiffany whistle?

Hairdresser allergic to hamsters?

There were more Post-it notes, but before Josie could read past *Is skim milk a beverage?* Nina burst through the bedroom door. Her hair was braided back, her hoop earrings touching the tops of her shoulders.

"Hey—" Her smile faded as she looked at the wall. "No. No no no no."

Josie tried to smile sanely. What would a character say in this scenario? "This . . . isn't what it looks like?"

Nina took Josie by the shoulders and shook her, eyes desperate as she yelled, "Tiffany is dead! You have to let it go!"

"I'll never let it go until"—Josie made a guess— "I find the murderer?"

"Not this time." Nina backed away, waving both her hands. "I won't be pulled into your schemes. If you want to go murderer hunting again, you'll need a new best friend."

This book must be a sequel, Josie realized.

"You know what? I should go," said Josie. She wasn't here to solve a murder. She just wanted to be in a story where she had a little more control than in real life. And to get to sing. And to feel likable, maybe. And to practice exits so she could feel confident that she wouldn't get trapped.

How had she done it before?

The last times she'd exited a story, she'd been kissing Not-Justin. Was that the key?

"Um . . . do you want to . . . kiss or something?" said Josie.

Not-Nina looked at her with shock and then slapped her face. "Snap out of it!"

Josie blinked her eyes hard, trying to dispel the stinging. So, kissing wasn't a reasonable option. She closed her eyes and tried to pull back—less like leaning back and more like sinking deeper into her own chest. She felt sticky, a part of her resisting, unwilling, but she stretched and stretched till—*jolt!*

Josie was sitting at the desk in the bookstore back room.

"Ha-ha!" she crowed. She'd done it! Gone in and out quickly, no danger, easy as singing scales.

Josie took off the glasses and examined them. They seemed perfectly harmless, just a pair of old-lady reading glasses. She held them up to the window light and snorted. She'd never noticed before, but the lenses were slightly pink. Rose-colored glasses. How perfect.

Well, now I know, she thought. *Or at least I know the glasses are involved in whatever the holy crap is happening to me.*

She checked her phone. She still had a couple of hours before she needed to pick up Mia. Besides, very little time seemed to pass when she was inside a book. How much exactly? Wanting to time herself was an excellent excuse for going into another story.

She leaned back in the chair, put her feet on the desk, and picked up the next book on the stack.

THE TREMBLING
by Scott Goth

Black cover with a rectangle of an open door, smoky light coming through, outlining the silhouette of a child. She wasn't sure she was interested in whatever story this book offered, so she just peeked at the first couple of sentences:

———————— 📖 ————————

It was spring outside, but overcast and gloomy. What little light filtered through the blinds had a sallow, sickly tone. Cassandra leaned against the cool marble of the counter—

Jolt.
So fast this time! Josie felt herself vibrating from the transition. She gripped the marble countertop before her till she stabilized. She was in a mostly white kitchen, a peanut butter sandwich on a plate in front of her. From behind a closed door, a sound was echoing as if it came from a deep cellar: *BOOM. BOOM. BOOM.*

"Quiet!" Her mom, Lorna, sat in a single lounge chair in the adjoining room, facing a television. Josie couldn't see her face. "Quiet!" she said.

"Mom, what are you—" Josie started to say, but the closed cellar door creaked, as if something was pushing against it. Through the thin gap beneath the door came a creepy little-kid voice: "*Mommy? Mommy, can I come in? Please, Mommy, please . . .*"

"Nope, nope, nope," said Josie, backing away.

It was called *The Trembling*! What did she think it'd be, some feel-good rom-com? Josie avoided horror stories in real life because after, when the book or movie was over, she couldn't turn off her imagination. Insomnia for days.

Her first instinct now was to flee. But she stopped. This would be an excellent opportunity to hone her imagination after all, with the stakes so high. Lethally high, even. Just how much could she control in these fantasies?

She stared at the door, feeling certain she needed to imagine something harmless first, before some creepy monster kid showed itself. Once the story declared something to be fact, it might be harder to change it.

"Door, open and show me John Cena!" she commanded.

The door didn't open. There was a scratching sound like fingernails against wood. Josie shivered. She scurried into the other room.

"Hey, Mom? What's behind the cellar door?"

Lorna turned slowly to look at Josie with blank eyes. "Just your sister," she said.

"Welp, at least *you* are your same old self, Mom," said Josie.

The woman with Lorna's face didn't blink.

"Ha-ha, that was a joke, let's laugh and relieve the horror tension, hee-hee, ho-ho, never mind."

Josie walked slowly back into the kitchen and stared at the door again. *Be Lila. Be my sister, but be nice. Be a nice Lila.*

She not only thought it but wished it, felt the desire so deeply that she realized she wasn't faking it. How much would she love to have a nice older sister? Someone who was around, who loved her, who knew her and supported her?

The scratching stopped. "Lila? You can come in." Josie steeled herself and turned the knob.

There stood Lila with her familiar dark eye shadow and pierced lip, but with a shockingly big smile. She was holding a jar of peaches.

"Hey, little sis!" said Lila. "Just went to the cellar to grab some peaches and got locked out. Thanks for opening the door!"

"Uh, sure, anytime," said Josie. "Should we all have a, you know, family dinner? Together?" *Like the kind we never ever had but I really wished we would?*

"Let's do it!" said smiling Lila.

Lorna walked in, staring blankly. And then Josie's dad entered the kitchen.

Josie startled, took a step back, and without thinking twice leaned away from the story, pulling and pulling till—

She stared at the book in her hands and dropped it on the desk.

Trying to change the narrative was hard enough without battling all the emotions her family sparked in her.

She shoved *The Trembling* back on the shelf and took a few deep breaths. Though she was still buzzing with nerves, she already knew she was going to try at least one more book hop. She just needed a story that would leave her on a high, like the kind she'd felt after defeating a Zombloid army.

Glasses off, she sorted through her stack.

HEIR OF RUST AND HORNETS
The Magicurium, Book Two
by J. L. A. Montmorency

Jewel-blue cover, embossed gold lettering, image of a wicked-sharp dagger. "Sequel to *Child of Fungus and Teeth*." Ooh, it looked like high fantasy. Glasses off, she opened the book and held it as far back as she could and squinted at the letters. It was no use: The font was too small. She couldn't read without them. It was a risk to keep going in without any story prep, but she put the glasses back on and remembered to set her phone timer before opening the first page.

─────────────── 📖 ───────────────

Belisandre's skirts whispered around her ankles as she strode into the chamber. She grounded herself in that sound and the others surrounding her: the soft murmurings of courtiers, the creak of leather as a guard shifted his position, the crackling of the Eternal Dragonfire in its brass brazier. No one even looked at her, not one set of eyes to mark her entrance. She smiled to herself, content with her own anonymity. If only they knew, if only they could guess what she—

Even though she was expecting it, Josie still felt as if someone had played a prank and pulled the chair out from under her, but instead of hitting the floor, she just kept falling, the world in slow motion, so slow it blurred, too slow to hold its own shape and color. Then, instead of falling, she was floating.

And then she was there.

She'd read enough fantasy in middle school to recognize the throne room of a generic Renaissance Europe setting: There was Misty looking haughty on the big gold chair on a dais and all the usual suspects milling about on the marble floors between marble pillars under the domed marble ceiling.

Everyone was dressed in head-to-toe brocade, like ambulatory sofas. Except the guy in ninja black lurking in a corridor off the palatial room. He turned, and Josie inhaled sharply. He had Justin's face. Seeing him after deciding to let him go felt like a gut punch.

Ninja Justin noticed her and quirked an eyebrow— a question.

"Where are our henchmen?" Misty was shouting. "We will not tolerate late henchmen!"

Josie told herself not to follow him, but she did anyway. His was the face she trusted, his company always meant safe harbor, and Misty-the-queen's shouting unnerved her. Josie moved past Cowboy and Blond Dreadlocks toward Ninja Justin. Her hips were huge and padded, and her shoes had high heels, so when she walked, she couldn't help listing from side to side like a ship in rough seas. She pulled into port between him and a potted tree.

"How did you escape being dressed like a couch?" she asked.

He raised an arched eyebrow. *Pardon me?*

She indicated the upholstery fabric of her dress.

"Ah. Well, as Her Majesty your sister's royal assassin, I must dress in loose, flexible fabric, in case I need to . . ." He did a sudden armless cartwheel. When he landed on his feet, his previously empty hands now held two daggers. He released them while dropping to the floor and was halfway through a full somersault when the daggers hit their targets—the eye holes of a wooden statue.

"Huh," she said.

His eyebrows wagged up and down. He seemed to be relying a lot on his eyebrows for communication.

"It serves the ruse well, milady," he said. "Dressed as a proper princess of the court, no one suspects that you are secretly the most deadly of us all."

Secretly the most deadly? Josie had never been deadly before. Unless you were a Zombloid.

"Have I slain anyone recently?" she asked out of curiosity.

"Only my heart." And with ninja stealth, he was suddenly behind her, bending to kiss her bare shoulder. Goose bumps ran down her arm.

No, no, this was all wrong! She couldn't be flirting with Justin-faced characters anymore. It was creepy. And pathetic. And desperate. And pathetic. She took a step away and looked around for Deo. Maybe a little harmless flirting with the bookseller would help cure her of this tragic codependency.

All she spotted was Blond Dreadlocks striding toward them. A knife was in his hand.

"Look out!" said Josie. She raised her hands, and

sparkly magenta streams of energy came burning out of her fingertips. The energy slammed into Blond Dread-locks, knocking him onto his back.

"Cool," she said.

She didn't know how she did it. It felt as natural as throwing a ball or catching a grape in her mouth—something that she used to practice during long rehearsals.

Two bookstore clerks came running at them with swords.

"I've got this," she said, and hit them with her magenta energy. They flew backward with the force of her awesome magic finger lightning.

She was super impressed with herself. She hadn't even been singing, which she'd thought had given her more control in past stories. Maybe she could always do whatever her character in the story could do, but if she wanted to change the story, assert her control, that was when she needed to focus more. And singing helped her to focus.

Even in real life, when she sang, she imagined what she wanted the audience to feel. But in the horror story, it hadn't even occurred to her to sing; she'd just willed the character into her sister. By wishing. Imagining. Hoping for it.

Yearning was a power.

"Thank you—" Justin-the-assassin started to say, but just then a chunk of ceiling came loose, cut by her blast of magic. At once Josie threw up a sparkly shield, while Not-Justin grabbed Josie and shoved them both out of the way of falling rubble. They hit a wall, Justin pressed against Josie. His face was close to hers, his gaze full of adoration, and her heart started pounding.

Desperate, pathetic, desperate, pathetic . . .

"Princess," he said, his lips an inch from hers, "you are indeed the chosen one, of whom it is written, '*She, who wears the burden of power; she, who cuts through the world like a blade; she, who will destroy before naught can mend; she, who is all and yet must walk alone—*'"

"No, no, no . . . ," said Josie.

This nearness to Justin was almost physically painful, a blade to her heart. Time to go.

She closed her eyes, wrestled with her sticky self . . .

And she was out.

"Whew!" she said, standing up, that expanding feeling inside her again. She felt so powerful, as if she could suddenly do backflips.

Wait, could she?

Josie tensed up her muscles, crouched, and made an exploratory leap. A tragically tiny leap with zero flippage in it.

But having magical powers in a dream sequence still made everything feel more possible. She picked up her phone and paused the timer—only a few seconds had passed while she was in the book. She shoved some other books into her bag, and the weight of them felt a little bit like hope. Real life was pointless. But inside the dream sequence, it was all more real anyway.

On her way out of the bookstore she looked for Deo. Yearned for him? Well, she wouldn't go that far . . . yet. But no sign.

"Can I help you?" Bianca was watching her curiously from behind those glasses.

"Hey! I just wanted to tell your brother thanks for the books before I left." She paused, leaned in. "Um, quick question. He gave me some reading glasses, said they were a free sample. I was just wondering, do you know where they came from?"

Josie showed her the glasses.

"Oh yeah," said Bianca, turning them over. "There was some guy in here a few weeks ago, wanting to be our supplier. He left these for us. But we already have an account with another supplier, so we never called him. Can't remember his name." She handed Josie the glasses. "Anyway, I'll let Deo know what you said. If you're sure you want me to?" She blinked innocently.

"Yes, I think so . . ." Josie felt sure of very little when addressing this blond beauty, except that she wanted to get out of her gaze as quickly as possible, so she made an excuse about needing to fetch Mia again and left.

CHAPTER 15

All Josie wanted to do was go back into a book.

But she was going to be a grown-up about all this. She cleaned the condo. She played games with Mia. She was caller fifty-seven to talk to a bank representative and waited two whole hours before giving up on that. She even made a hot dinner. Spaghetti. It wasn't tasty. But it was made.

The next morning, she woke up with a familiar but long-absent feeling stretching inside her. The yearning, like a yawn, was infectious. It was time to open herself up to the possibilities of the future. She even managed to think the words without grimacing: *community theater*.

Josie showered and got fully dressed before realizing she was channeling a bit of Crossbow Melody in jeans and a close-fitting black shirt, with her hair still pseudo-eighteenth-century wench. She managed not to doubt herself all the way to Mia's preschool. But after the girl was checked in, Josie hesitated on the sidewalk.

Community theater? Really?

She almost turned back toward the condo when her phone buzzed. She checked. Not Justin.

Hey Josie, did you ever get my email? If you can't get the drama club comp tix it's ok, but we still want to see your show when we're in nyc!

Josie muted the number, squared her shoulders, and walked instead toward downtown. Determined. So determined it was an adverb. She walked forward determinedly.

The Missoula Repertory Theatre Company was a fifteen-minute stroll from the preschool, but it was another annoyingly pleasant Montana spring day. In a green space, college students were out in force, tossing those Frisbees and hacking those Hacky Sacks and drumming those drums in one big drumming circle like a drummer hive mind.

Josie passed Cowboy crossing the street and exclaimed in surprise, and then tried to hide it by bending down and feeling her ankle.

"You okay?" he asked.

She said yes and hurried on.

Josie had been expecting to find the community theater in someone's basement, but it was housed in a pretty nice revamped elementary school complete with abstract art out front, of the tall-pole-with-dangling-things variety. Josie had never understood abstract art and so always felt impressed by it. Clearly this was art so smart it was beyond the powers of her reasoning.

The lobby of the theater sported three-star-hotel carpet and wallpapered walls lined with framed photos of past productions:

Violinist on the Porch
Ginger Orphan
Lease
Boatshow!

At first she thought this theater must specialize in parody, but there was an unaware, earnest quality to the photographs. Apparently the theater's earnings had not allowed for paying royalties on actual musicals.

I'm here to perform my best for you, theater Muses, she thought as earnestly as the production photos looked. *I know it's only community theater, but please don't eat my soul.*

On the counter of the empty concession stand, Josie found the audition forms. Those old audition nerves perked up, chewing her up from the inside. But it was kind of a good feeling, the butterflies in her belly humming a familiar tune, dancing around in there to some Spice Girls song, probably. This confidence felt amazing—just like high school!

Name: *Josie Pie*
Past experience: **see attached**

No need to list all her theater credits when she had a professional résumé in hand.

What role are you seeking? ____

The upcoming show was something called *Nebraska!* and since Josie had no idea what that was, she wrote in: **the lead.**

If you are not cast, would you be interested in participating in a backstage capacity?
Y __ N __

Josie scoffed. *Community theater* . . .

Y __ N **x**

She pinned on her number, lucky number eighteen, went into the auditorium, and slipped into a seat near the back. A college-age girl was belting out "Somewhere Out There," her bottom lip quivering with the effort. A man (the director?) was sitting in the center of the house seats, holding a clipboard with attached reading light. A couple dozen auditioners sat scattered in the theater, those in pairs quietly whispering to each other.

Number fourteen, number fifteen, number sixteen . . .

Josie bounced on the edge of her bouncy seat. A woman (they were mostly women) did pretty well by "Send in the Clowns." Josie added hoots to her applause and congratulated herself for being such a good audience member. Maybe she and the woman would be in the cast together. Aside from Justin's and Nina's unconditional acceptance, being a cast member felt the closest to having a true family that Josie had ever experienced.

Her hands were trembling, not because she was nervous but because she could not wait. In high school, all she'd had to do was step onto the stage and feel. Sometimes, as she was singing, emotions she didn't know she possessed rode the music out of her body and into the audience, infecting them with the same sorrow, the same joy, the same understanding. It was a wild magic. She was more than the sum of her parts because her power was untamed and unpredictable.

The elderly pianist rose painfully from the piano bench, picked up a megaphone, and called out, "Number eighteen!" She was also the stage manager, because she shambled across the stage and down the front steps toward Josie to collect her audition form.

The woman had ghost-white hair, a face wrinkled like a fingertip after a long, non-Mia bath, and was wearing a blue terrycloth zippered pantsuit.

Josie handed over her papers, including her music notation that she'd photocopied from a book at the library.

"The résumé is attached," Josie explained. "And there's an eight-by-ten glossy there too."

The stage manager took it without comment, not even an *I'm impressed* eyebrow raise. Josie followed her as she doddered up the aisle to where she could hand the papers to the director.

"Thanks, Mom," he said.

Josie did a double-take. She was his mom? The director wasn't wearing black or even so much as a hemp-fiber necklace. In a cheap plaid shirt stretched over his gut till the fabric strained, he looked less director and more neighborhood dad, which, she realized, he probably was.

Community theater.

Josie sprinted up the stage, tripped on the last step, and fell flat on her face. She popped back up and waved, to show that she had a great sense of humor. *Trips happen! I'm down with that! No prob!*

She took her place downstage center, her hands behind her back. Confidence. That's what she'd been lacking at the karaoke bar. She was Josie Pie. She could do this. She could do anything.

Her feet flexed inside her shoes, just so happy to be on a stage again.

Nearby stood the ghost light. It was both tradition and superstition in a theater to keep a ghost light onstage—usually a plain metal stand with a single bare bulb. Some said the light was an offering for the theater's inevitable ghosts, illuminating the stage for their midnight productions so the ghosts wouldn't mess with the actual performances. Others claimed the light was there to scare the ghosts away and keep bad luck out of the theater. Its presence was charmingly familiar, and Josie felt like she was sharing the stage with an old friend.

"Josie Pie," said the director. He flipped through the pages of her résumé. "This is it?"

"Yep," she said brightly.

"Mostly high school productions?"

"Yep," she said not quite as brightly.

A tiny twitch in her cheek muscle was the only sign that she had stopped herself from clarifying just how big a deal she'd been.

The director was quiet again, reading. Josie felt that hot, delicious confidence start to cool. She quickly struck a pose: the noble loner, one she'd picked up from Hatchet. But there was no rock here to prop up her foot, so with hands on hips, she just kind of stuck her leg out, crooked and maybe attractive? A little?

No, she decided. *Not good.* But she'd already gone for the pose. Pulling back now would show a lack of confidence. And Mr. Camoin had said that in auditions, confidence was second only to talent.

Maybe they wouldn't even bother to make her come to callbacks. Maybe they'd just offer her a place in the cast right then and there. She would do her best to be properly flattered—surprised, yet gracious.

"I moved here from New York," she offered. "New York City," she clarified, lest he assume Albany or Buffalo or something. "I was invited to an Equity audition. And I participated in workshops with some of the best experimental theaters in Queens. You might not recognize the names because they're not famous yet. Emerging playwrights and composers. But the workshops were definitely in the geographic boundaries of New York City. In one of the five boroughs."

She was monologuing. She pressed her lips together.

"Oh, and I won a Jimmy Award!" she said.

"All righty, then," said the director.

He signaled to his mother, who had just made it back to the piano bench. She lifted fingers visibly crooked from arthritis and began to pound out the introduction to "Defying Gravity." Josie spied the audience, anticipating gasps of the *you'd have to be insane to attempt this song, and at an audition no less!* variety. *That's right, Missoula, Montana. Josie Pie is that good. She's "Defying Gravity" good, so prepare yourselves.*

She hit the first note, singing out strong and gesturing wide. So wide she knocked over the ghost light. The metal post tipped over and clunked down on the stage. She ignored it, because that's what she was trained to do. The show must go on!

But so must the ghost light, because it began to roll

down the slightly sloped stage. Slowly at first, and then a little faster—*clunk-clunk, clunk-clunk*. Josie sang on but nervously watched it get closer to the empty orchestra pit. Finally she sprang forward but just missed it as it thudded off the edge of the stage.

"Sorry," she said, but then kept singing. Because the show. It must go on.

But she made the amateur mistake of looking at the audience. They were not joining her song, improvising drums on the floor and backs of chairs. And they were not falling before her feet, slain and dissolving into Zombloid goo. They were staring at their own fingernails, reading over their own résumés, whispering to one another.

Josie panicked.

Confidence.

She went bigger still. But there wasn't much room for her to go any bigger than the bigger she already was going. She upped the volume. Josie Pie could belt it out, baby! She struck her fist-in-the-air triumph pose, and her voice cracked.

"Okay, okay . . . ," the director said.

The stage manager stopped playing.

"Thank you," he said.

"Thank you?" she said.

"I've got what I need," he said.

Josie stood there, her arm still lifted in the air, though slowly falling as the non-defied gravity kicked in.

"Do you want me to sing something from your musical? The lead's role?" she said. "I can read music."

"Um . . . we're looking for someone with a little more experience."

More experience? But . . . but . . . *community theater?*

"Number nineteen!" the stage manager was shouting into the megaphone. "Number nineteen!"

Confidence, Josie thought.

"I can do anything!" Josie blurted.

She could hear the quiet room go quieter. From the dark of the audience came the squeak of a chair, a held breath, an amused snort.

"Thank you, that's all we need today," the director said.

Josie shuffled off the stage. She hopped down into the orchestra pit and set the ghost light back on its base, giving it a pat before trudging out.

When she hit the street, she pulled out her cell to call Justin. The realization that he was on a trip at some possibly female friend's house hit her with such surprise and pain it took her breath.

She texted Nina.

JOSIE
Botched my audition

NINA
Liar

JOSIE

Tripped onto stage. Sang so aggressively I lost the tune. Knocked over the ghost light. Is that bad luck?

NINA

Maybe

JOSIE

Told director "I can do anything"

NINA

I hope you're kidding. Please say you're kidding

JOSIE

I'm kidding. Call you later

She was early to pick up Mia. So she sat on the weedy parking strip outside the preschool and waited.

I can do anything.

CHAPTER 16

She could do anything. In the books, at least.

"How was preschool?" Josie asked.

Mia sighed, and Josie easily interpreted the sound of this particular Mia sigh to mean, *Duh, it was perfection—why do you even ask me these questions?*

"Are you hungry?" Josie asked. Because she was. Starving. But not for food.

She couldn't stand this post-audition funk, this petty emptiness, this catastrophic disappointment. She could only think of one thing that would distract her from it.

Instead of heading back to the condo, Josie dug a granola bar out of her purse for Mia and led them to the library.

Last night (without the glasses—her eyes hadn't even needed them) Josie had looked over the books she'd brought home, and none of them had seemed right. So much drama in young-adult literature! She knew that the twists and triangles and jeopardies and apocalypses made for exciting stories, but she really didn't want to live inside another life-threatening scenario at the moment. Where were the stories about a nice guy and a girl just, like, having great conversations and eating good food and being cozy in sweaters?

Her eyes were fine again today without glasses, so she read Mia a stack of books in the kids' section until the little girl was ready to explore some picture books on her own. Josie, guided by a giddy impulsivity, browsed for her next dream sequence.

The first book to catch her eye was propped up in the nonfiction stacks, simply titled *Greek Mythology*. When Josie had been very little, before her dad left and his family began to ignore her and Lila, Josie used to hear all about Zeus and Hera from her Greek grandmother's stories. There was a time when she thought that as a good little Greek girl, she should still believe in the myths. They had been sacred religion to her heart, and, at the very least, she still considered them her inheritance.

She flipped through the book, and a section on the Muses caught her eye. Curious what this nonfiction book might look like from the inside, she put on the glasses and read:

———————— 📖 ————————

In some myths, the Muses were the daughters of Zeus and Mnemosyne, the goddess of memory. They became women of great beauty and artistic talent—

Jolt. And Josie found herself sitting in a lecture hall, as if on a college campus. She was the only person in the seats. On the stage at a podium stood Mr. Camoin—or, likely, the narrator of this book sporting Mr. Camoin's face. He wore a shirt and tie with an ill-fitting tweed jacket and spectacles on the tip of his nose. He was droning on and on in a monotone voice.

"In the more modern myths, the Muses were benevolent creatures who inspired people to create art, poetry, music, dance, and theater. But digging into the oldest of the stories reveals a much darker origin, wherein the Muses were creatures born from the consciousness of the earliest humans. Not humans themselves, they were embodied thoughts that fed on human memory—"

"Say something more interesting," said Josie.

The Mr. Camoin lecturer didn't pause at her command, droning on. "—symbiotes that needed human thought to survive, the precursors to the myth of psychic vampires. Some stories suggest that early humans performed human sacrifices to the Muses to keep them at bay. The early Greeks discovered that the Muses could feed on fictional stories nearly as easily as on real lives, and so art was a sly substitute for a human life, a way to appease their terrible hunger. Without a sacrifice of music, poetry, dance, or theater, the starving Muses would instead turn back to human sacrifice, breaking open human bodies to suck out their souls.

"The more passionate the art, the longer the Muses stayed fed. And, in turn, the Muses could grant humans their sincerest desires . . ."

Josie closed her eyes and concentrated on an idea, yearning that he would—

"Bunnies, too, are a fascinating study," Mr. Camoin continued in the same voice. "I will now demonstrate the mechanics of a bunny's hop. Watch as I drop to all fours and hop around this stage."

He was still hopping when Josie pulled out of the book.

She stumbled a few steps forward before gaining her feet again in the real-world library. Feeling already a hundred times more awesome, Josie hunted for another book to soothe her troubled soul.

She smiled at a displayed novel titled *Old Men in Rural Pain*.

"Not in a million years," she whispered. It did sound like something Misty might enjoy, though.

A comic book on display drew an unexpected laugh out of her throat. What would it feel like to go into that story?

Josie opened the comic. The first page showed a tropical island and a grand fortress—*Jolt!*

". . . OUT!"

Josie was standing in the library, the comic book in her hand.

"Psst." A kid tugged on her sweater. "You're not supposed to yell in a library."

"Sorry," Josie whispered.

She took a deep breath and remembered that she had been able to breathe all along, of course. There was no atmosphere in a comic book. Her real body had been just fine. But it had felt so real.

All of it. Josie shivered. She had been flying! And saving people! And kicking mechasaur heinie! She hadn't even meant to leave. Being a hero was such an amazing high, she was tempted to try to get back into that comic immediately.

Instinct buzzed a warning in her belly: *too dangerous.* But why? Because of the claustrophobic shrinking trap? Or the risk of staying forever?

She dismissed the feeling and, glasses off, flicked through the comic book, hoping to find a panel where Lady Justice and Dr. Dominion kiss. Nothing. That moment had been entirely her will. She shook her head at her own desperation.

She'd just set the comic book back when she spotted an old book friend, gasped, and seized it from a shelf.

Anne of Green Gables by L. M. Montgomery. The cover featured a beautiful watercolor pastoral scene, a girl with red hair in braids picking wildflowers beside her raven-haired best friend.

Now, this was a book with very little drama or danger, a place to lie back and watch the clouds, and, most importantly, it centered on the perfect friendship. Anne and Diana: kindred spirits. Just as Josie and Nina had been in high school, before Josie lost her starry shininess and everything flopped.

Josie made herself comfortable in a reading chair and, without the glasses, flipped through chapters, squinting as she scanned for one that had both Anne's and Diana's names right off. Aha—chapter 29 looked ideal. So she put back on the glasses and read:

———————————— 📖 ————————————

Anne was bringing the cows home from the back pasture by way of Lover's Lane. It was a September evening and all the gaps and clearings in the woods were brimmed up with ruby sunset light.

And then Josie was there.

She wore a pale blue dress and a white apron trimmed with lace. The grass was so high, it rubbed against her long skirt with a sound and feeling like wading through high water. Prince Edward Island. This place was a landscape of her imagination as magical as Narnia or Hogwarts. The breeze brought the warm smells of turned soil and crushed grass, and promises of perfect friendship and endless afternoons with nothing to do but drink raspberry cordial and imagine. Josie sighed, feeling utterly and perfectly Anne-ish.

Anne met up with Diana on the first page of this chapter, so Josie scanned ahead for her best friend, expecting to see her at any moment. Maybe she'd linger in this book for a while and find Gilbert Blythe, too, that darling, intelligent Canadian boy who had such a crush on Anne for so many years. Would he have Justin's face or Deo's?

Ahead was a sturdy fence with a gate too narrow for cattle. Josie sidled through it and spotted Nina coming down the lane. She was wearing a brown dress that hit her mid-calf, with black boots, and she was carrying a straw hat in her hands, two braids hanging down her back. Dreamily, she walked behind a few slow, contented cows, reciting poetry with great passion as she went:

> *The stubborn spearsmen still made good*
> *Their dark impenetrable wood . . .*

Josie was just about to call out, "Good evening, Diana!" but Nina spoke first.

"Isn't this evening just like a purple dream, Diana?" said Nina.

Nina wasn't speaking to her. She'd called out

to someone else who was coming down the lane—dark-haired Frisbee Girl. She had an air of wisdom and self-confidence, like the kind of girl Josie imagined Nina had befriended in Chicago.

It was then that Josie realized Nina had red hair. She'd thought the fiery tint was from the sunset light, but nope. Nina was Anne, not Josie.

And worse, Josie wasn't even Anne's best friend, Diana.

"It makes me so glad to be alive," Nina was saying in a flawless Anne-like way. "In the mornings I always think the mornings are best, but when evening comes I think it's lovelier still."

"It's a very fine evening," said Frisbee Girl, who was obviously Diana. "Oh, hello, Josie."

The girls had spotted her. Nina folded her arms and stared her down.

"Josie Pie," Nina said without enthusiasm.

She knows me! Josie thought for a split second before realizing that Nina-Anne was probably spelling the last name *P-Y-E*. Great. Here she was, in one of the most amazing friendship stories ever, playing the part of Nina-Anne's nemesis.

This was terrible. Josie very much wanted to order the story to change—make herself Anne, change Nina into her best friend. But not only did she doubt she had the power to actually switch places with a character, it felt wrong to even try. Not with Nina—or a character who looked like Nina, at any rate. Frustrated at the ruination of such a gorgeous story, Josie wrinkled her nose.

Nina-Anne seemed to notice Josie's stink face and, perhaps thinking it was directed at her, promptly turned her back. "Marilla is making me a new dress, and it is very pretty, Diana," said Nina, effusing to her story friend. "Navy blue and made so fashionably. It is ever so much easier to be good if your clothes are fashionable."

Maybe, Josie considered, this story defaulted to Nina as the protagonist because she had been in charge of her own story for a long time.

In high school, Josie had seen herself as the one with the story, the friend driving their joint plot. But Josie hadn't noticed that all along, Nina had been writing her own story. Now Josie was a supporting character. It had taken her too long to realize it.

Worse, she wasn't even Nina's supporting character. Here, she was an antagonist.

Josie took a lingering look around Prince Edward Island, breathed in deeply, and waved goodbye to the breeze that was nudging the brim of her hat and nestling in her apron. It was beautiful. And it wasn't hers.

Josie sighed as she thumped back to the library chair. She shut *Anne of Green Gables* gently and put it back on the shelf.

Her phone buzzed in her back pocket.

Justin!

Stop doing that, Josie! she scolded herself. You're being pathetic. It's not going to be Justin!

And it wasn't. The number had a Montana area code. She quickly stepped outside the library's front doors and answered.

"Hi, can I speak to Josie . . . Pie?"

"This is Josie."

"Hi, this is Shelley from Missoula Repertory Theatre?" she said, as though it were a question that Josie could confirm. "I'm the assistant stage manager for *Nebraska!* and I wanted to let you know that the director would like you to come in for callbacks."

"Oh! They want me back? I just didn't expect . . . I mean, my audition was pretty bad."

"Well, you're on my list to audition for a spot in the chorus? But on your paper you wrote you wanted the lead, and the leads are already cast? From our repertory actors? So I just wanted to make sure you were okay with trying for a chorus spot before you came in?"

"Oh, I'm not sure yet if I . . . can. Is it okay if I call you back later?" said Josie politely while thinking no way in Hades would she stoop to being in the chorus of a community-theater production.

"Great. Hey, do you mind me asking, did you really tell the director that you can do anything?"

"Um . . . yeah, I did."

"That's so awesome. Everyone's been talking about it. You're such a riot!"

"Thanks?"

"No, seriously! I love it! I hope you get in the show. After rehearsals we all go for cheese fries at the Iron Horse."

"Okay, well, thanks for the call."

Josie hung up and didn't take a moment to process, didn't spend a second mourning whatever this was that she'd become. She knew exactly what she wanted, though she'd been lying to herself about it. Not anymore. Who knew how much longer she had to live out her fantasies? What exactly was the half-life of a pair of magical glasses? Embarrassing or not, if she had this power, she was going to make it count! So she marched straight back into the library and, after checking on Mia, looked through the young-adult fiction recommended titles and made her choice.

This, she hoped, was the one.

CHAPTER 17

Josie's hands were shaking with eagerness, her heart pumping at the idea of escaping now, immediately, from this reality.

LAVENDER GARCÍA AND THE
UNEXPECTED CANADIAN SEMESTER
by Mary Tenacious White

The cover showed a long-haired girl in a breezy summer dress, the top of her head cut off. Not actually sawed off or anything horrific—just, the top of the picture ended.

After *Valentine*, Josie was suspicious of misleading titles, but the cover was pretty clearly promising a teen rom-com, and she remembered several friends gushing about this exact book in high school. She read the back cover: *Lavender García is new at Buttercup High . . .*

Josie inhaled hard. Yes. This was it. She could actually

go back to high school! And maybe just stay there for as long as she wanted! It was her deepest, most secret, most shameful desire. She'd never confessed it even to Nina; she'd barely even confessed it to herself. She gripped the book as if it were a magic lamp, and with just a rub her wishes could come true. And no one needed to ever know that high-school dropout Josie Pie wished she could return and this time stay forever.

This is dangerous, she thought, then laughed at herself. She was getting so much better at control, and since *Valentine*, she'd had no trouble getting out of a story.

She ran to use the bathroom, as if she were about to go on a long trip, and then she checked Mia again. Josie felt extra anxious this time, but she dismissed her fears. The longest she'd been away had been in *Valentine* for about five minutes, even though she'd passed days in the story. If she just made sure she was in and out in less than a couple of story days—a week tops—then nothing could go wrong.

She settled into a chair near Mia, put on the glasses, and opened herself up to her sincerest fantasy.

There was no time for breakfast. Lavender slept through her alarm, and she couldn't risk being late for her first day at a new school. She hopped down the stairs and ran into the kitchen, poured a cup of her mom's amazing hazelnut coffee into an environmentally friendly reusable cup with plant-based biodegradable lid—

Jolt.

Josie was standing in her kitchen at home in Arizona. Morning sun shot in through the window above the sink, painting the wood cupboards a buttery yellow. She held a warm cup in her hand; a backpack hung on her shoulder. She smelled bacon and pancakes, which must have been a detail in the novel, because real home smelled like microwave pizza and neglect.

Lorna walked in the room. "Look at you!" she said.

Josie flinched, looked down at herself. Had she spilled coffee all over her clothes? "What? What's wrong?"

Lorna smiled. "Nothing's wrong. You look beautiful. I can't believe my baby girl is so grown-up."

Josie laughed without meaning to. *Baby girl?*

And then her dad walked in. His hair was combed; he was wearing a tie—*a tie!*—and a disconcerting smile.

"You're going to do great, sweetie," he said.

"Thanks," she said. She met his smile and knew she should be glowing with contentment, but instead she felt kinda disgusted. By them? By herself?

And then, the cherry on top, her sister, Lila, popped in the kitchen, completing the whole stock-photo "happy family" look.

Lila was dressed in pastel colors. This particular detail had to be in the book, because it was beyond Josie's powers of imagination.

"Go out there and be your awesome self!" said Lila. "I'm so proud of you, little sis."

"Thanks," said Josie, hurrying toward the front door.

"Have a good day, dear!" her mom shouted after her.

Josie shut the door and shuddered. Of course, that was the family she'd wished she'd had, but seeing her subconscious yearning played out before her, so raw and naked, felt grotesque.

If this were a musical, she would sing "Let It Go." *Let it go, Josie. This family was never in the cards for you.*

Well, never mind about her home life. School itself would be amazing. Josie walked the route she knew so well, focusing on imagining it all as perfect as it had really been so she wouldn't have to fight the story if it started off wrong.

Time skipped forward a bit faster than normal, as if the sidewalks were mechanical airport walkways, and suddenly she was in the hallway of her old school: Millennial High in Yasmine, Arizona (no sign of the Canadian location promised in the title—sorry, Canada!). It smelled exactly like she remembered—spoiled milk, copy paper, feet, and fear. Josie breathed in through her nose and tingled with joy. She'd missed the place, but she'd especially missed who she'd been here, once upon a time. She'd left too early, given up her precious senior year. Now she could reclaim it—or at least a week of it. A month, tops.

Ahead of her, Frisbee Guy was greeting Marcus with an energetic high five. When Blond Dreadlocks bumped into him, Frisbee Guy said, "Watch it, chump!"

"You watch it, jackwad," said Dreadlocks.

Hmm, Josie seemed to remember a lot more actual swearing in the halls of her actual school.

From behind, she recognized Deo carrying a backpack over one shoulder like a cool kid, not over both shoulders like kids who are smart enough to avoid chronic back pain but still somehow not as cool. Would he be the love interest in this story? She wasn't opposed to the idea. Maybe dating him here, where nothing counted, would help her feel capable of really dating him. Or anyone other than Justin.

Josie pushed her hair over her shoulder and tried her best to embody the kind of girl who tended to be in these stories: i.e., a beautiful girl who didn't know that she was a beautiful girl. Which in practice was way harder than she'd thought. She kinda pursed her lips like she was thinking hard about something, tilted her head, let her eyes look up thoughtfully. Belatedly she realized that beautiful-girls-who-don't-know-they're-beautiful-girls probably had naturally excellent posture, so she pulled back her shoulders, but too quickly, too obviously. She glanced around to see if anyone had noticed. Unconsciously pretty girls did not engage in self-aware posture correction. (Not to be confused with *unconscious* pretty girls, of the Snow White and Sleeping Beauty variety, who always maintained excellent posture by sleeping board-straight on their backs.)

"Hey—" she started to call out to Deo, when someone bumped into her. She stumbled forward, dropping her book bag, the contents spilling over the painted cement floor.

"Here, let me," said Justin.

Yep, there was Justin, picking up her books. He looked so much like his real self, except perhaps a little taller and a little more high-school-movie-ish, complete with swoopy hair and a letterman jacket. He smiled shyly, said, "Hey, I'm—"

"Justin," she said.

"Right, Justin. I'm new; I didn't think anyone knew my name."

He stood there, still smiling, waiting for her to tell him her name, and part of her reallyreallyreally wanted to replay the beginning of their relationship, before it got stretched out and misshapen.

"I . . . ," she started. No, she was not going to do this again. "Thanks."

And she took her stuff from his arms and scurried off.

I guess that was the meet-cute, she thought. Situation averted. Now to find Deo, who had disappeared.

As she walked down the hall, she spotted a cell phone on the floor, getting knocked this way and that by the foot traffic. She rescued it from beneath the boot of Blond Dreadlocks and looked up to see she was directly in front of the office. As the story seemed to be leading her, she went inside and said to the school secretary, "Can you put this in your lost and found?"

Maybe it was Deo's. Maybe he would come in to claim it, and that would be their meet-cute.

Josie turned to look at the office doors, and just then, they did open.

Justin walked in.

"Hey, I dropped my phone—oh! That's the one!" he said, pointing to his phone on the counter.

The school secretary, played by Blond Trophy Wife, tilted her head toward Josie. "She just brought it in."

"It's you again!"

"Yep," said Josie, as she was walking out the door. She was not falling for this.

Nina was waiting for her in the hall. "Hurry up, we'll be late for chem!"

As they ran down the hallway, skirts swishing around their thighs, Josie couldn't help but laugh out loud.

"What?" said Nina.

"High school!" said Josie. "It's just ridiculous, isn't it?"

Nina quirked a smile. "Yep."

"But also . . ." Josie took her best friend's hand. "Also good?"

Nina laughed, and they held hands as they ran.

Wait, Josie realized—wasn't Lavender's character supposed to be new and know nobody? Oh well, too late. She was claiming Nina as her already-best friend, the way it should be.

The classroom was organized in rows of two-seater tables. There were no two seats together left, so Nina took the one in back. Just as the bell rang, Josie grabbed the other empty seat.

"Oh, hey! It's you!" said her tablemate, who had Justin's face.

Josie sighed. "Always."

Bruce stood in front of the room, arrayed in plaid and glasses, and declared, "Your tablemate will be your lab partner for the entire year."

Josie sighed again. *Of course he will.* The story had decided: Justin was the love interest.

The story didn't seem to care that it was physically painful for her to sit so close to him and pretend indifference, to just have to wait for it all to be over.

She'd really thought that she'd been yearning toward Deo and that the story would have arranged that. But clearly the story was reading deeper, where she couldn't fool herself. Maybe she could pop out of the book, adjust her deepest desires real quick, and then pop back in? But that sounded more like a job for copious amounts of therapy, and she didn't have the patience for that right now. Not to mention that she'd never managed to get into the same book twice, wasn't even sure it was possible. The reading glasses hadn't exactly come with a manual.

Justin smiled at her. "We just keep meeting. It's like . . . fate."

"It really is," she said.

As soon as the bell rang, Josie jumped to her feet and strode into the hallway.

And she started to sing the Spice Girls' "Wannabe."

"Um, are you singing to me?" Justin asked, following beside her.

"No," said Josie. "I'm singing to the announcement board."

Her longing was so powerful, she didn't think she needed the song to focus, but she kept singing and imagining, singing and imagining, till when she was close enough to see, sure enough, there was a flyer that read TALENT SHOW TRYOUTS—IN THE AUDITORIUM RIGHT NOW!!!

Josie laughed out loud.

"Ooh, a talent show," said Justin. "Are you trying out?"

"Indeed I am." With a toss of her hair, she said, "Later, lover boy," just because she'd always wanted to. He followed her into the auditorium, where Meaghan was finishing her audition, a robust flag routine set to Madonna's "Material Girl."

Mr. Camoin clapped for Meaghan as he walked onto the stage. "Wonderful. Very . . . enthusiastic. Anyone else?"

Josie smiled and thought, *Prepare to have your world changed, Mr. Camoin. Prepare to regret your decision to cut me out of your life.*

She jumped up onto the stage, about to sing "Wannabe," before remembering again that it was an ensemble piece. What was her deal with trying to go solo in group numbers? No, this was the moment for a power ballad. Some quintessential Broadway "I want" song. And not the one from *Oliver!* that had won her a Jimmy Award. She wasn't a one-hit wonder.

She knew just the song. She looked at the old-lady stage manager at the piano and said, "Hit it." And her yearning was so clear and immediate that without hesitation the woman began to play "Maybe This Time," the big "I want" song from the musical *Cabaret*.

The song itself was already so ripe with longing that Josie's own longing filled it out perfectly. She hit every note, every inflection, every emotion, all the while imagining that her song had real power, that she was magically gifted, that all the auditioners out there in the dark auditorium thought she was the greatest thing since sliced bagels. Students came in from the hallways, murmuring about the amazing singer onstage. *Who is she? She's miraculous!*

Josie finished the final note, and the auditorium flooded with students on their feet, clapping and cheering. Mr. Camoin was folded over, sobbing.

"You're in!" he said. "Any slot you want! Just take all of them!"

Justin was standing in the aisle, applauding, looking up at her with shining eyes.

Josie lifted her arms out to them all like Evita on her balcony, glowing and smiling and loving, and . . . it wasn't satisfying.

Why wasn't it? She'd nailed that song!

But in the tragic musical *Cabaret*, Sally Bowles never got what she wanted. She sang "Maybe This Time" with all the hope and pleading in her—that her life would change, that this time she'd have a real shot at love and meaning. And then the musical ended with Sally back where she began, though the future was even bleaker and more hopeless than before.

Josie descended the stage steps into the aisle, where students were gathered en masse to thank her, as if she were a superhero who had just saved them from a collapsing building or a sentient cafeteria meat loaf or something.

"You were amazing!"

"You're a star, Josie Pie. A star!"

"Hey, you were great. Really, really great." Justin looked at her as if she were the whole world.

Was this what she wanted? All this fawning, this love she hadn't earned. It wasn't real, and it felt as shallow as a dinner plate.

Tears streamed down Mr. Camoin's face.

"You are a revelation," he said.

"Thanks . . ."

"I mean it. You are gifted. You don't belong in high school. You should go straight to the top—pack your bags for Broadway!"

"Whoa, let's pump the brakes," said Josie, but all the students were nodding in agreement.

"You belong on Broadway! You should go there now!"

"But . . . high school?" she said.

The crowd began to chant: "Broad-way! Broad-way!"

Josie wrestled free of them, ran backstage, and took a breath in the cool, dark emptiness. Nothing felt right, and yet she'd imagined it all in the way she remembered. *Thought* she remembered. Well, in actual high school there'd definitely been 100 percent less chanting. In fact, she couldn't remember anybody being enthusiastic about her decision to audition in New York. Except Mr. Camoin.

At that moment, as if called by her thought, he stepped backstage. He was clutching his hands, his posture unsure. Josie faced him. Mr. Camoin. Every cell in her wished him real, to be the Mr. Camoin she knew, who knew her, too.

242

"How could you leave me?" she said. "How could you promise me so much and then abandon me? You were the adult who was supposed to never abandon me. You were the one who got me. Who believed in me."

"I'm so sorry."

He looked a little scared, and he turned, exiting the backstage into an empty hallway. She followed, calling after him.

"I depended on you. I believed in you. I believed in you believing in me."

"I made a mistake," he said, still trying to walk away.

Josie hurried around and stood in front of him, forcing him to stop. "No, you were the adult. You'd lived the Broadway life. You should have known better than to lead me to these impossible dreams and then dump me when it got hard. I wanted . . . I wanted you to be my dad!"

And then he said what she'd already come to guess: "Adults can be messed up too, Josie."

She let him walk around her then. She let him leave. And she thought she'd like it to be the last time she ever saw him.

The bell rang and the hallways filled up with students. They greeted Josie as they passed.

"Hey, Josie!"

"You were amazing, Josie."

"I can't wait to hear you sing again, Josie!"

Josie turned, hoping to see Nina, and there she was, smiling wryly at the commotion.

"High school isn't really like this," said Josie. "It can't ever have been really like this."

"Instant popularity? Universal adoration?" said Nina. "But you deserve it. You're so talented and kind—"

"No, not you, too, Nina. I mean, you were always supportive of me, but I can't stand it if my deepest desire is for your constant, unconditional approval. Is it? Am I that needy? That shallow?"

This Nina tilted her head, as if not understanding Josie.

"None of this feels real," Josie muttered to herself. "All the good parts, shined up, waxed, and set out on display. None of the bad parts."

"JOSIEyouaresoAMAZING!!!" a freshman boy screamed from down the hall.

"It'd be boring, ultimately, if every day were like this. And high school isn't boring. Is it, Nina?"

"Sometimes," said Nina. "Frequently."

"Yeah." In her memory, Josie tended to montage past the boring parts: the homework, the lack of completed homework, the dread of going to school without having finished her homework. The days when she was too tired after rehearsal to shower and went to school the next day with greasy hair, wincing away from people, afraid that someone would smell her and her star status would slip. Or that she'd do something embarrassing—answer a question wrong, say something stupid, walk out of the bathroom with toilet paper hanging out of her pants—and the image she'd so meticulously crafted would crumble. That everyone would see that she was a fraud after all. Josie the Star didn't exist. She was just a kid trying to be special so people would love her.

Josie and Nina walked together to the cafeteria, filled their trays with unrealistically delicious cafeteria food—sushi and slaw and slushies—and by the time they sat at a table, Josie was silently crying.

"There, there," said Nina, giving her shoulder a little pat. One or two. In real life, Nina never had much patience for consoling either. Distraction was her tactic. This Nina gave Josie a minute of quiet blubbering before saying, "This moment isn't everything, you know."

"It's not?" Josie said miserably.

"It feels like it's everything, but we are both of us so much more than what we are in this second. We are who we used to be, who we are now, and who we will become. Even if we can't see it, we are never-ending, eternal, with limitless potential, the magnificent way that God sees us."

Did Nina believe in God? Josie felt a chill of regret as she realized that she wasn't sure what her best friend believed. Real-life Nina had grown up in a churchgoing family but had felt unwelcome in that congregation once she came out as transgender. Josie hadn't thought to ask how Nina felt now. She'd been too busy feeling her own vastly important feelings, she supposed.

Josie blew her nose in a rough little napkin. "I'm

sorry," she offered, meaning it for more than awkward tableside snot issues.

"We tend to think of life as all linear," Nina went on, "as if each moment, each year, has to be better than the last, and if it's not, we failed. But we're all of it at the same time. And then some. So be patient with yourself, Josie. Don't judge yourself by any one moment. Allow yourself room to change."

Josie stared at Nina in amazement. Did the character Nina was playing in the book believe this? Or had Nina said such things before, and they were buried in Josie's psyche?

"That's a beautiful thought. And have you? Given yourself room to grow?"

"I'm already so huge I fill up the room!" Nina said, extending her arms as wide as her smile.

"That's true." It had always been true.

"And know what I discover again and again? When I hit the ceiling, the room just gets bigger. There's no end to me."

"Or me?" Josie tried to sound hopeful, but her intended exclamation point twisted into a question mark.

My yearning and regret made me small, she thought.

No, she thought again, *I worked to make myself smaller than my yearning and regret. I tried to get out of their way, curled up beyond their touch.*

"Of course you are limitless," said Nina. "You are

Josie Pie, and I will always have your back, no matter what."

Josie took a breath. This Nina-faced character was offering her the exact platitude she'd thought she needed, but it fell down on her with a hollow thunk, empty because it wasn't real.

"Nina," Josie whispered, "if you *can* be yourself, will you now? Please."

Nina stared at her. Josie cringed.

"Okay," Nina said, leaning her elbow on the table and shoving away the food tray. "Okay, Josie Pie à la Mode."

Josie's jaw dropped. "Wait . . . it's really you?"

"Yeah . . ." Nina took a sip of her chocolate milk and glanced around. "It's not *quite* Millennial High, you know what I mean? It looks convincing, but something's off."

Josie blurted, "What's the name of your roommate in Chicago who brought her entire Precious Moments statue collection to college?"

"Lezleigh," said Nina.

"What role did you used to say you played in our high school shows?"

"Ensemblé," said Nina, with an accent on the last syllable as if it were the name of a French character instead of an unnamed background player.

"What word am I thinking right now?" *Pumpkin, pumpkin, pumpkin . . .*

"I have no idea. I'm not telepathic."

"Are you actually Nina and you got pulled into the fantasy with me? No, that's impossible, I must just be imagining fantasy Nina to have the same knowledge and character as real Nina, or at least the way I see real Nina."

Nina shrugged, looking exactly like real Nina shrugging. For some reason that made Josie cry again.

"Nina, I'm such a mess. It's my fantasy, I have the power to make it *perfect*, and I'm *still* failing at it."

Nina groaned in exasperation. "Can you get over yourself for five minutes?"

Josie pulled back, wounded.

Nina put on a more patient face. "What was it that I told you when you dropped out of school?"

"That high school is a blip and doesn't define me." Josie paused. "I thought you were telling me I was going to make it big! But you were warning me, weren't you? That it was a mistake to push myself into the world too soon. That I still had growing to do."

"Yeah, you didn't used to be very good at listening."

"Didn't used to be?" said Josie, and they both laughed.

Nina smiled at her. "There's something you've been trying to ignore, something that you can't pretend not to see anymore."

"Yeah . . . ," said Josie, though she was still afraid to speak it aloud. But Nina just sat there, patient, waiting.

"I'm losing your friendship. Back home in the real world, I'm losing you."

"I know this is hard for you."

"I feel like I've lost Justin already, and the theater. And Mr. Camoin, and high school, and really everything I used to be. What will I have left? Who am I without my people?"

Nina tilted her head, one eyebrow lifted.

"Oh! I get it. You found *your* people." Josie straightened up as truth rushed through her, cold as ice water. "You found your people in Chicago, and I'm not one of them."

"People grow up," said Nina. "People change. That's okay. We don't have to peak in high school and spend the rest of our lives sliding downhill."

But . . . but . . . but, Josie wanted to say. *But we're kindred spirits. But we're best friends. But we're practically soul mates! Or, I thought we were. I wanted us to be. I fooled myself into believing—*

"I'm so mortified," said Josie. "It must seem like I've been expecting you to be my, like, sidekick for the rest of our lives. You'd need me, I'd protect you, and that would somehow be perfect for me. But you're a real person with a real life and all that unlimited potential you were talking about—that is, real Nina is real. This is all giving me a headache." She took a breath. "Nina, what do you want?"

"I don't know," said this Nina, because she was only

who Josie could imagine her to be, which meant Josie didn't really know what Nina wanted.

"I love you, Josie," said Nina, because Josie at least knew this was true. "I always will. You were there when no one else was. Literally no one. You know I think you saved my life."

"I know. But . . . despite our current environment"—Josie glanced around the cafeteria—"we're not in high school anymore."

"Remember when Mr. Camoin put on *Wicked*, and you wanted to play Elphaba because it was the better role? I said, 'In our friendship, I'm the one who is Elphaba. You're more Glinda—the popular girl, the girl everybody loves.'"

"I remember."

"What I was trying to say is, you were the girl who tried to be perfect, who thought she got it, but she didn't. You wanted to, but you didn't really get what your best friend was going through."

"I'm sorry, Nina."

Nina waved her hand in the air, already over it. "Chicago was a revelation to me. For the first time, I was in control of how I would focus my mind, explore my passion, start to carve my life out of rough stone. And I found this funky, open-armed church and all kinds of people who got me because they were like me, and I got them. We didn't have to create a context for everything we said to each other. We were the context, you know?

It felt so good and right that it got to be exhausting to be around anyone else."

How did fantasy Nina know all this about real Nina? Josie's stomach dropped as she realized: Nina must have told her in real life, but Josie had probably barely acknowledged it before returning to her own problems.

"And then you were always calling me," said Nina, "begging me to move to New York . . ."

"I worried that as soon as I started to struggle, Justin would leave me, but I always assumed that you'd be my constant no matter what. I leaned on you more than was fair."

"You needed me. And I really thought about moving to be with you. I owed you so much. I looked into transferring to a college in New York."

"You were willing to give up your life in Chicago for me. I didn't know. Or I didn't think about it. Nina—"

"I'm a saint, what can I say? But I couldn't do it. Then when you moved to Montana, you wanted me to move to Montana too, like it was my job to follow you around and prop you up—"

"And now it's time to let go," said Josie. She sighed. "That's why you flew to Missoula to see me. But I was such a mess you didn't burden me with a best-friend breakup."

"You want to keep living as who you were in high school—"

"And you want to move past those years." Josie held her face with her hands. "I'm sorry. I know. I'm sorry."

"It was your highest high. And my lowest low. I can't stay there with you anymore. You'll always be precious to me. But I can't be your link to your high school self. And I can't be your Justin replacement. Just, I can't be your *everything*."

"I've known for a while; I just didn't want to know." Josie sniffled. "It's fair, and I understand, but it hurts still."

"Which is why I've put off telling you for so long."

"You in the real world."

"I guess," said Nina. "I don't really get what's happening here."

Josie nodded. Who did?

"I mean, you always were an odd duck," said Nina, "but this, whatever this is you're doing with the books and the fantasies and everything, this takes the cake."

"The duck cake."

"The odd-duck cake." Nina frowned. "Let's clarify that this metaphorical cake is a duck-shaped cake and not a duck-filled cake. I'm vegetarian."

"Are you really? In real life?"

Nina shrugged. "I don't know."

"Excuse me," said Blonder Trophy Wife, wearing an apron. "We made too much dessert today. Would you like some?" She handed them pieces of cake on paper plates— one the shape of a duck head, and the other a duck butt.

Josie and Nina started to laugh so hard, they put their arms around each other, laughing and weeping. And eventually eating the cake—which was vegetarian and entirely duck-free.

"Josie, you are far more than the talented girl who thought she could live her high school high forever and instead gave it up before she was ready. With or without me, you aren't less. You are *more*. Got it?"

Josie was still laughing. "Thank you, figment of my imagination in the shape of Nina telling me deep truths. I am such a weirdo!"

"Sure, but what a ride you've had." Nina toasted her with her chocolate-milk carton. "What a ride."

Josie raised hers and they clinked cartons. She sighed.

"Now that I know I'll have to give you up when I leave, staying here forever is starting to feel like an excellent choice."

"No, you should . . ." Nina looked around the cafeteria as if for eavesdroppers. Then she leaned in closer and whispered, "You should probably get out of here. I get the feeling leaving will be harder the longer you stay."

"Stay . . . in the school? Why, is it going to rain?"

Nina opened her mouth as if to speak again, but just then a group joined their table, chatting loudly, trays clattering down. One was a tall skinny blonde Josie recognized, though it took her a moment to place her as Bianca the bookseller, her glasses still making her look like the pretty girl in a Hollywood movie poorly disguised as the plain girl.

"Hey, Josie," said Bianca. "I heard you killed it at talent-show tryouts. I'm having a party at my dad's this weekend and you should definitely come."

Josie shuddered. Nope. Staying and pretending would be more painful than leaving.

She stood up, taking one last look around.

"Josie?" said Bianca.

Nina raised her milk carton. "Josie."

There were parts of high school she would miss. Maybe forever. Those things did not include the smell.

She closed her eyes and pulled back.

Mia was sitting by her feet, staring up at her. Josie startled.

"Hey, Mia! Um, how long have you been there?"

Mia shrugged.

"Was I reading a long time?" asked Josie.

Mia shrugged again. "Do you like your book?"

"It was okay," she said. "I used to like it better, but I think I've outgrown it."

Mia nodded. "Like my baby books with the animal sounds."

"Exactly like that."

"I'm hungry." Mia stood and stretched.

"Do you know what you want?" Josie asked.

"Grill cheese," said Mia. "But you can get another book first if you want it. A grown-up book like you."

It was an unexpectedly generous thought from the five-year-old, and real Josie felt a touch misty-eyed. And maybe a bit too seen.

Josie pulled out her phone and stared at it bravely for a few seconds before putting it away again. She owed Nina a breakup call. But she couldn't do it, not right now, not while feeling so low.

She'd intended the high school book to be her grand finale, but the way that it had ended felt too tragic. And the idea of returning fully to the mundane, with no hope of future escapes, was fully depressing. Go back to the condo, make Mia a sandwich, try to let go of high school, and . . . what? Face the Great Unknown Future of a high school dropout?

I know what I want, she thought.

Though she felt no triumph from having made her goodbyes to high school, there was a lingering sense of pride. Maturity. Maybe even hope. Perhaps there was a way for her to experience her one true fantasy, know what it'd really be like, and then say goodbye to that, too. Like a grown-up. Broadway couldn't actually be as wonderful as she'd imagined. If she lived it out, she could let it go, too.

She spent a few minutes searching in the library's online catalog and found something perfect.

Title: *Love in the Spotlight*

Summary: A chorus girl is ready for her big break on Broadway to steal the spotlight, but is she also ready to steal the star's big heart?

Josie read the synopsis to make sure there wouldn't be any undead hordes, exploding tree houses, showerless uncivilized wastelands, horror sisters hiding in cellars, et cetera. It seemed to be a chorus-girl-makes-good wish-fulfillment tale. Josie wasn't looking for high literature. She just needed a book to provide the right setting, and then she could take care of the rest. A place to perform. Test herself. Live big before it was time to give up and grow up for good.

CHAPTER 18

Even worse than peaking in high school was to never peak at all. To treat life like a big waiting room, idly reading whatever magazines were available, playing a game on your phone, killing time till your name was finally called.

It wasn't in Josie Pie's nature to wait. Broadway was never going to call her name. Community theater was barely even bothering. Time she got out there herself and started re-peaking. And she couldn't do that until she let it go.

In the morning, after a hearty breakfast of Frosted Corn Shreds (teenage nannies FTW), Josie and Mia put on their jackets and headed outdoors. The morning, scrubbed clean by overnight rain, was springy and sunny, the birds singing in a frankly over-the-top optimistic way. Mia had wanted to find friends at the park outside, and Josie, clutching her library book, liked the idea of taking this big fantasy plunge back on the bench where it had all begun.

It won't be as good as I imagine, Josie thought. *My high school dream wasn't. This is therapy on a budget. Live out my Broadway dream and see that it's lacking so I can finally say goodbye.*

When the bookstore was a block away, Josie's stomach switched from doing a few flip-flops into a full gymnastics routine.

She gripped her phone in her pocket. It was ridiculous that she wanted to call Justin and ask his advice about going on a date with Deo. Ridiculous! She gripped her phone tighter. She hadn't been able to get ahold of him last night, and she didn't want to break up over text. She also had the nagging feeling that breaking up with him was moot at this point. Maybe his reaction would be, *Wait . . . did you think we were still together?*

If there was one thing Josie's family knew how to do, it was fight. It had been disconcerting when Justin wouldn't fight with her. In the past, she'd taken that as a sign of their infinite compatibility. But maybe he'd just been burying his discontentment, avoiding confrontation until it was too much and he just gave up?

The bookstore was around the next corner. She checked her hair in the reflection of a yoga-studio window, panicked, and crossed the street.

"Where are we going?" said Mia.

"The park still," said Josie. "This is the longer way, but it's . . . good exercise! Yay, exercise!"

Josie's heart was still raw from her virtual Nina conversation, and she didn't think she could bear relationship stuff at the moment, current or potential. She was also avoiding the coffee shop. Those free teas were piling up in her unpaid-debt column. At some point, wouldn't Bruce expect payment? The worry about money was like a constant ticking noise in the back of her head. Sometimes ticking noises were just overemphatic clocks. Sometimes they were bombs.

"Don't!" Mia screamed, tugging Josie away from a shallow puddle on the sidewalk. Apparently puddles were now one of Mia's bad luck items. Josie added it to a mental list of things she wanted to tell Victoria about.

After preschool yesterday, Mia's teacher had talked to Josie about some unusual behavior. Insistence that things be just so, excessive concern about germs, a terror of bugs. At what age was Mia supposed to grow out of the little-kid quirks? The rituals and obsessions? At what point was this not normal but a sign of something more troubling?

Josie had started composing an email to Victoria in her head: *I don't know what I'm talking about, but it seems like maybe Mia worries too much about stuff? But maybe it's not a big deal* . . . No. It wasn't her place to analyze Mia. She was just here to keep her safe and fed.

As soon as the park was in sight, Mia let go of Josie's hand and ran ahead. The trio was out in the achingly clear post-rain weather, dressed in light blues, white, and yellows, their hair prepped as if for a close-up.

The whole world looked ready for a close-up. The hills were a bright, just-woke-up green. The river was clear where it wasn't poetically bubbly. The air was so clean the breeze nearly squeaked. Josie felt a little annoyed by how beautiful Missoula was, as if it were calling her a fool to think she could find any place better.

She sneaked behind the book-club bench, where Meaghan and Misty were reading something called *The Nauseous Life*. She passed by the swings, where Marcus was crouched down to tie Atticus's shoe.

"Oh! Hey there, Marcus."

"Josie Pie," he said. He glanced over his shoulder at the reading bench and then asked, "I wanted to ask you—what did you think of that book you had the other day? The one with the sexy-wench cover?"

"*The Highwayman Came Riding?*" said Josie. "If you don't mind egregious overuse of the word *manly*, it's a lot of fun."

Josie winced, unsure if she'd used *egregious* correctly, but he didn't make fun of her.

Mia bum-rushed Ahab, tackling him to the sandy ground, while explaining the complicated rules of a game she had invented called "sewer pants." Happily,

Misty was too busy reading to notice Josie's kid clobbering hers.

Josie watched till she was sure neither child was injured, then settled onto the supremely uncomfortable but probably not mystically powered bench and reached into her bag.

Love in the Spotlight looked, and smelled, a great deal like the library books she remembered from school: old and inky and dusty. She inhaled deeply, told herself to break a leg, and, to get a sense of the story before her deep dive, she decided to be responsible and read a few chapters first without the glasses. She held the book at arm's length, expecting to have to struggle, but though it was morning, she had no trouble making out the text. The eyesight problem seemed to come and go randomly.

📖

CHAPTER 1

"Thirty minutes to curtain! Thirty minutes!" the stage manager called over the speaker.

The dressing room erupted in a chorus of moans and exasperated sighs. A dozen girls patted powder on their faces at the same time, making the air as thick as foggy old London.

Loretta Sweet dabbed an extra puff of powder on

her button nose and considered her face in the light bulb–framed mirror.

She was too short for sure. Gloria, the show's star, had legs so long they could qualify for their own bus stop.

Plus Loretta didn't have enough curves by half. Every time Gloria went swimming, cartographers named new islands.

Well, maybe Loretta didn't have the bazoombas or battleship hips of Gloria, but she had a neat little figure. Strong legs, trim waist, and enough of a curve in between to shake out a rhythm. Her heart-shaped face was pale, but a natural pink shone in those round cheeks and on those doll-like lips. Her black hair was as straight as the county judge and would never hold a curl, but it shone like the top of the Chrysler Building.

Nope, nothing flashy about Loretta Sweet of Middletown, Ohio. If she looked close enough, she could still see a big floppy hat on her head and a milkmaid apron hanging from her neck, her face and hands smudged with mud and who-knew-what-else. You can take a girl out of the farm, as they said.

There was a secret written right into her features, a secret no one in New York City had yet guessed. Makeup wouldn't cover it up. So far stage lights hadn't called it out. But surely soon, someone would notice. Someone would know.

A tall blonde elbowed Loretta, waking her from her reverie.

"Move over, sweetie," ordered the blonde. "There's not enough mirror space around here, so quit hogging one all to yourself."

She pursed her generous lips and applied cherry red paint.

"Tell me the truth, Hildy," Loretta pleaded. "Do you ever get tired of tap-dancing at the back of the line, keeping time, with the same stupid smile on your face?"

"Don't tell me you're calling it quits already, baby doll," Hildy joked. "You've only been in this one-horse show a few days."

"One-horse show?" Loretta exclaimed. "This is Broadway!"

Hildy smiled. "I'm just pulling your leg. But what gives?"

Loretta smiled too.

"My whole body yearns for the spotlight like parched earth craves rain. You think I got a shot?"

Hildy rolled her eyes.

"Rub that moonlight out of your eyes, kid. This

here's a classy joint. The stars? They're all gradu-
ates of the most expensive, fanciest, most elitist of
theater schools in New York City. And the chorus
line? They pull us from Little Town, USA. Ain't no
upward mobility on Broadway, baby doll. You're
born in the chorus and you die in the chorus."

Josie was already imagining herself as Loretta Sweet,
and in her mind Hildy looked like Nina. Even though
the text went on to describe the stage manager as "a
burly Irishman with a rosy nose and forearms thick as
hams," she still pictured the elderly woman from her
own recent botched audition. And she assigned the
community-theater director's round, fatherly face to the
book's director, even though the narrator called him "a
thin, harrow-faced man who looked to have gotten into
a fight with a bottle of whiskey and lost."

The slang was pretty thick. She wasn't sure what
year the story took place. The 1950s? Maybe it would
become clear if she read on.

The dressing-room door slammed open, and a gust
of cold air rippled Loretta's hair and sent papers flying. Gloria Astor stood on the threshold, trembling
in all her honey-blond glory. She wore a Japanese
silk robe, her hair still in curlers. Her perfect lips

were glossy red; her enviable high cheekbones were blushed. Her enchanting blue eyes were on fire with anger.

"You!" she shouted, pointing a manicured finger at Loretta.

"Me?" Loretta whispered.

Gloria squinted. At first, Loretta assumed the starlet was squinting with contempt, but her eyes darted around, taking in all the faces, as if trying to decide.

I bet when no one's looking, she wears cheaters, Loretta thought.

Cheaters? What were cheaters? Oh yeah, an old-fashioned term for glasses.

Maybe it was a sign: time to put on the glasses! She'd intended to read more . . . but she was too antsy anyway.

From atop the play set, Mia caught sight of her and waved. Josie waved back. She stood and took a step forward in case Mia wanted her for something. But no, she was busy again, playing with "Memmon" on the jungle gym.

The sunlight struck through the trees, filtering out the harsher colors and pouring a golden yellow onto the playground. Mia's profile and hair lit up around the edges, so brilliantly the beauty cut Josie like a knife. It seemed too perfect somehow, as if the moment were more an heirloom than a span of time. A picture she could hold in her hand. Something to cling to when the moment had passed.

A coldness seized Josie's ankles and crept up her legs, as if the river were flooding its banks. The chill climbed all the way into her heart. She pressed her palm there, took a breath, and considered returning the book unread.

Josie shuddered to shake off the chill. She waved at Mia again, who didn't wave back because she was playing and having a perfectly splendid time and nothing was wrong and foreshadowing didn't happen in real life, silly. Josie had never been gone in real time for more than a few minutes. But the worry, like a stone in her belly, wouldn't budge. So she promised herself: *I'll only stay one day. One story day. Then I'm out, no matter what. And Mia will be fine.*

Josie sat down and slid the glasses onto her nose. She noticed now how her eyes were fighting against the prescription, straining to make out the words that looked small and distant. As far away as Mia, as tiny as ants, getting smaller and smaller until she could read . . .

Loretta took a step—

That was as far as she got before the story snatched her. Slurped her in, hungrily, eagerly. A few moments of disorientation, tumbling through the digestive tract of whatever power pulled her into stories . . .

And then she was standing. In black shoes—character shoes, they were called, with a two-inch sturdy heel and a strap around the ankle, good for dancing. The rest of her outfit was like something out of a fever dream: seventeenth-century Puritan meets New York City dance club, with some Broadway sequins thrown in for good measure.

She looked up. Misty, in a Japanese silk robe and hair curlers, was pointing a manicured finger at Josie and saying, "You."

CHAPTER 19

The dressing room was breathlessly quiet. Misty was still pointing at Josie, her nostrils flexing and relaxing, flexing and relaxing.

A thousand angry butterflies raged in Josie's belly. It was another actor's-nightmare moment—trapped in opening night with no memory of rehearsal. Why hadn't she made herself read the whole book first?

The characters bore other familiar faces: Nina (with a platinum-blond bob), the Trophy Wives, Meaghan, Frisbee Girl, and the female book clerks, all wearing bedazzled, too-short Puritan costumes. What show were they putting on?

"Me?" Josie finally squeaked.

"Yes, you, whoever you are. Yesterday during the baby-tossing number, you walked in front of me instead of behind." Misty narrowed her eyes. "My dresser says you were *dared* to cut me off. Who dared you?"

"No one, I swear! It was just a mistake." She could feel a light sweat mist her forehead and upper lip. "It won't happen again."

"No it won't," said Misty, "or I will have your head. And by head I mean job. And by that I mean you will be out of a job, not that I'll take yours. Because your job is beneath me. I am the star."

Misty turned so fast, her robe made a cracking sound like a whip, and she stormed out of the dressing room. The door slammed. Josie heard several exhales.

"Hey, thanks for taking the fall for me," said Blonder Trophy Wife, "I owe you one. That was some acting job you did. I almost believed you myself."

"Yeah, this one ain't just a pair of legs and a set of lungs," said Nina. "She could be a spotlighter."

A spotlighter? The transition was disorienting enough without having to parse all the slang.

"Don't give her ideas," said Meaghan. "You know how this biz works."

"Born in the chorus, die in the chorus," several said in unison, followed by giggles.

Josie smiled at Nina. Under her white Puritan-style apron, her black dress shimmered with sequins and sported a thigh-high split. In real life, Nina was self-conscious about her legs. Josie wished she could tell her not to be. They looked fantastic.

"What are you gapin' at?" said Nina.

"Your legs," said Josie. "They look fantastic."

"She's got sense, this one," said Nina. She patted Josie's head. "Her machine's full of gumballs."

The elderly stage manager opened the dressing-room door. Everyone covered their ears in anticipation just as she lifted a megaphone to her lips and shouted, "Ten minutes to curtain!"

With ringing ears, Josie followed the troupe up the stairs. Ten minutes till Josie would find herself onstage before a live Broadway audience, expected to sing and dance. A chorus girl who didn't know what she was doing would stand out like a flamingo in a snowfield.

The carnivorous butterflies in her belly buzzed hungrily. She'd exerted some control over a half-dozen stories before this, but for the first time, she was experiencing literal stage fright. She just needed a few minutes to herself to try to imagine—

Two people were climbing the stairs beside her, squishing her between them: Meaghan on one side, Marcus on the other. He was wearing a brown sequined jacket over a white shirt, and his breeches were more Modern Mr. Darcy than Historical Puritan—fashionably cut and tight as a drum.

"Oh. Hi," said Josie.

"I heard you dissed Gloria," said Marcus.

"In front of everyone," said Meaghan. "Lied and everything."

"I found this stuck under Gloria's dressing-room

door, as if someone was trying to trick Gloria into read-ing it," said Marcus. He swatted Josie on the nose with a folded newspaper. "It was you, wasn't it?"

They'd reached the top of the stairs, but Meaghan and Marcus stepped in front of her, blocking her path.

"Excuse me," said Josie, but they didn't budge.

"You just don't get it, do you?" said Meaghan.

Josie rolled her eyes without meaning to. Marcus and Meaghan took one step closer.

"You're mocking me?" Meaghan said.

"No, no, it's not that," Josie said. "It's just that line, you know? 'You just don't get it, do you—'"

"You think *I* don't get it?" said Meaghan.

"No, I mean, I'm sure you do, I was just quoting that line—"

"Cut the gas, girlie-girl. I've fought to get here. Liter-ally," said Meaghan.

Without breaking eye contact with Josie, Marcus pointed his thumb at Meaghan. "She won the Chorus Girl Smackdown three years ago."

Meaghan pulled up her long leg slit to show a ragged scar high on her thigh. "I've earned my scars."

"Every one," said Marcus.

"And I will not let a one-cow girl like you take it away from me."

"Moo," said Marcus.

Josie nodded in unequivocal agreement before Meaghan could pull a shiv out of her cleavage.

"I just want to perform," said Josie. "That's the only reason I'm here. To perform."

"If Gloria sees those reviews, she'll cop a breeze," said Marcus. "And if she splits, this show is over, so behave!"

Marcus swatted her nose again with the newspaper. Then Meaghan and Marcus pivoted in unison and stalked away.

Taking a different path, Josie eased herself into the backstage, sliding between book clerks dressed in crew black. Josie's attention was pulled to the heavy stage curtain. She could sense the boiling energy of an audience on the other side. Her breath shortened with excitement and fear.

I won't fail here. There's no risk. I can do this. Just please be a musical I know, please please please . . .

In a garbage bin by a crew station, she spotted the rolled-up newspaper Marcus must have dumped. She edged over to it oh-so-casually and snatched it up. It was the arts section of the *New York Times*.

Scarlet!
Place: Broadway
Venue: Dorothy Gish Theatre
Starring: Gloria Astor, Stanley Reeves, George O'Mara
Rating: ★☆☆☆

Given the pseudo-Puritan garb, Josie figured this

must be a musical adaptation of Nathaniel Hawthorne's morose classic *The Scarlet Letter*. Because nothing screams "BROADWAY MUSICAL!" louder than a secret adulterous affair between a Puritan woman and her preacher in 1700s New England. As far as Josie knew, no such musical existed in the real world, but she'd read the novel in high school, so her subconscious must have dredged it up.

"Yay, great job, subconscious," she muttered.

The review was titled: SCARLET! BELONGS ON THE SCAFFOLD OF SHAME. Josie began to scan the article with increasing unease.

"What are you reading?"

Misty was dressed in the same white bonnet and apron as the chorus girls, though her sequined dress was hemmed even higher, and her white bib thingy was emblazoned with a red *A*.

"Nothing?" said Josie, rolling the paper back up.

Misty grabbed it out of Josie's hands.

"*The Times* reviewed the show? Gary said they skipped it. Gary said there were no reviews . . ."

Misty read. Her eyebrows were plucked thin and darkened to black. They seemed animated, the way they rose into perfect arches above her eyes.

"'. . . slutty Puritan . . .'" Misty breathed out the words.

Her pale face turned an impressive shade of scarlet(!). And she marched away.

Josie hurried after her and discovered a herd of

chorus members in the wings. She slipped in with them as Misty marched up to a man in a black suit who must be the director. Josie caught her breath as he turned. He didn't look like the community-theater director or even like Mr. Camoin—he had her father's face. Her disorientation ratcheted up till the floor seemed to lurch like a ship's deck.

"Are you illiterate?" Misty was saying. "Is that how you missed this review in the *Times*?"

At the word *review*, Josie felt the chorus girls around her shiver.

Misty cleared her throat dramatically and began to read. "'Astor's performance is perhaps too on the nose, as if she sincerely believes she's performing a great work of art—'"

"Gloria, the reviews have completely missed the—"

"*Reviews*?" Misty said, her voice rising. "Plural?"

She began to pace, crew and chorus scampering out of her path.

"'A classic!' you said. 'We're making a classic!' But you had to tramp it up, didn't you? You had to make me look like some two-bit, small-town showgirl. Like . . . them!" She gestured at the shivering pack of chorus girls.

"We only made slight changes to the book," said the director (not her dad—he was *not* her dad). "Like the ending. And a bit of artistic license with the costumes. And the addition of the talking porcupine—"

Just then Bruce, in a spiky porcupine suit, passed by, carrying the head under one arm.

"Hey," he said, waving.

"Porcupines are all the rage right now," said the director. "And every story needs comic relief! Just imagine how much better *Ben-Hur* would have been if he'd had a porcupine sidekick. Maybe with a French accent and"—he giggled—"wearing a little beret . . ."

"Fix this. Or your show doesn't have a star." Misty shoved the crumpled paper into his hands and stalked away.

The director shuffled after her. "Gloria, it's almost places. Sweetheart, this is not the time—"

Misty had gone into her dressing room and now slammed the door in his face.

The director stood there, staring at the star on her door, two inches from his nose.

She opened the door back up. His eyes lit hopefully.

"Also, my dressing room smells like ham!" She slammed the door again.

At that moment, *he* entered the scene, and just like that, the floor under Josie's feet felt more solid. That rusty hair, that nice set of shoulders. That kind mouth. In *Valentine*, his strong hands had flipped a tractor off her. In *Highwayman*, that chest had proven hard, chiseled, and hairless. Who would he be here? Not-Justin was dressed in the snazzy Puritan costume, so he must be an actor.

"What's the sitch, Gary?" Not-Justin asked the director (who was definitely not her dad).

"Gloria's going bananas," said the director, his eyes on Gloria's dressing-room door.

"Hoo-boy." Justin put a hand on the director's shoulder and waited till he looked at him. "You've got this, Gary. You're our fearless leader, and I'm here for you."

The director nodded, and a palpable calm settled backstage.

Just like real Justin, Josie thought.

At a high school party, a couple of guys had started yelling at each other, engaging in pre-fight chest shoving, and Josie had run to grab Justin so they could get out of there before someone got hurt. But instead Justin had strolled into the middle of the fray with his hands in his pockets and started to talk to one of the guys about his car. Everyone mellowed; the party went on.

Josie wished someone would say his name so she knew how to think of him, though he was already more Justin here than the others had been. He was even his actual height. If she'd wished him that way, it had been subconsciously.

"Her contract forbade me from prepping an understudy," the director was saying. "The dame is completely paranoid about being replaced."

"If only there was someone who could step into the role unrehearsed," said Justin.

There was a pause. It was like the moment in a play when an actor misses their cue, and the other actors wait, hoping that any second the actor will realize and save them all.

"Oh!" said Josie. Maybe she was the one missing her cue. But her big break? Already? She'd planned to chill in the chorus first, getting experience *out* of the spotlight before forcing herself into the lead role. "Um . . . I can do it."

"Excuse me?" said the director.

He wasn't her father, but he looked at her with those shrewd, skeptical eyes, and Josie wanted to run away. But then Meaghan whispered in her ear, "Don't you dare," and Josie's stubbornness cemented inside her. Plus, Justin was looking at her encouragingly. She had that feeling again. Like when she and Hatchet had fought back-to-back. Or when she and Justin had walked down a high school hallway side by side. So much power in knowing she was accepted by someone, that she wasn't alone.

"I can do Mist—uh, Miss Gloria's role," she said. "I know the Hester Prynne part like the back of my hand." Lies! But it was so much easier to be bold when it was all pretend.

"Are you sure you can do it?" the director asked.

I can do anything, she thought, and then spasmed with embarrassment at the memory.

"You okay, kid?" asked the director. "Your face is twitching. You're not having a seizure, are you?"

Definitely not a seizure. Or a psychotic break. Just magic glasses.

"Just a chill," she said. "Of excitement. For this incredible opportunity."

"You sure you can do it?" he asked again.

The story seemed to be demanding those four words from her. So she swallowed and did the best acting of her life. "I can do anything," she said. And then she filled herself with hope that she actually could. *Please let me sing; please let me perform; let me be a star.*

The director nodded. "What's your handle, kid?"

"Josie," she said. "Josie Pie."

And she felt it was true. This part of her, the part that played to the world, that performed to the Muses, that stepped onto a stage eager to sing, would be Josie Pie, no matter what happened with Justin.

"Josie Pie?" the director repeated.

"It's my . . . uh, stage name."

"Does that stage have a pole?" she could hear Marcus whisper. Meaghan giggled.

"What do you say, give the girl a chance?" said Justin.

"Okay, kid," said the director. "Razz my berries or it's the pavement for you."

Josie gulped. Like her throat physically made a hard swallowing motion, complete with the sound. Lady

Fontaine had "gulped" in *Highwayman*, but Josie didn't know people actually did that in real life.

"We did the five-minute call seven minutes ago," said the stage manager. "We've got to move."

"Right," said the director. "Wardrobe!"

Justin held out his hand to shake. "I'm Stanley Reeves."

According to the review, Stanley Reeves was one of the stars. But was he the eponymous "love" that she would find in the spotlight?

It didn't matter. She was here to claim her power and live out her ambition! This was no time to worry about a guy.

And then the wardrobe department descended on her. In moments she was stripped to her underwear.

Justin stood beside her, his gaze on his shoes, talking her through the first act while the dressers put her into various pieces of Misty's wardrobe: short black dress, scarlet-letter-emblazoned white collar, bonnet. She'd almost forgotten this part of theater—the quick changes, the lack of privacy, how her body was just another prop.

A dresser strapped a prop baby to a cloth sling around her chest. Josie gave its plastic head a comforting pat.

"And then it's straight into the prison scene with Chillingworth. You don't leave the stage till intermission . . ."

"Uh-huh," Josie said aloud. Inside, she said, *AAAAAAHHH!!!!*

Justin must have noticed her internal freak-out because he grabbed her hand and said, "You've got this, Josie Pie. You can do this."

"I can do anything," she mumbled.

"So I heard," he said.

There was that easy smile. In *Valentine*, his smiles had been rare and somewhat surprised to show up. In *Highwayman*, his smiles had been frequent and ripe with suggestion. Here they were straightforward, confident, and directed at her.

"I can do this," she said, wishing it to be true.

Over the audience PA system, the stage manager's voice: "Ladies and gentlemen, tonight the part of Hester Prynne will be played by Josie Pie."

The audience moaned in disappointment. Josie glanced back at the exit door, but Justin held her arm and led her onto the stage.

The lights were off. She smelled warm wood, the ozone of electricity, paint, sweat, cake makeup. Every cell of her body was buzzing.

Break a leg, Josie Pie. Break all the legs.

CHAPTER 20

Josie and Justin took their positions in front of the prison set and froze, waiting for the curtain to rise.

Muses, I perform for you, she thought with so much urgency her knees shook. *I'm ready to sing for my life. Please, Muses, please . . .*

A hum of hot energy seemed to rise up from the floorboards, burrow into her bones, heat her muscles, coat her throat. A snap of confidence. And she thought, *Maybe I really can do anything!* Now if she could just concentrate and imagine herself knowing all the words to the songs—

From the wings, Josie heard a commotion. Misty had emerged from her dressing room in her silk robe. Her body language was rigid, furious. Frisbee Guy, dressed as a rent-a-cop, was talking to her softly, his arms out as if keeping her from storming the stage.

"Stay focused," Justin whispered.

Josie looked away and took deep breaths. *I can do any-thing*, she told herself fiercely. *Besides, it's not even real!*

And . . . *curtain.*

But boy oh boy, Daddy-o, did it ever feel real.

The lights in her eyes were brilliant, masking any sight of the audience. The opening music deluged the stage, so loud Josie rocked back on her feet. The music swelled and dropped. A hushed pause. A place for some-one to sing a line.

My line, probably, she thought. Whoops.

She took a breath to sing something—anything— when the music swelled again, coming back around to pick her up. The conductor in the pit eyed her nervously.

"'It's just one small letter,'" Justin whispered.

"*It's just one small letter*," Josie sang, her voice a crackly whisper.

"*Who's that girl in fetters?*" sang a male chorus mem-ber. Josie thought it might be Blond Dreadlocks in a wig but didn't dare look closely.

"*One letter of a word.*" She made up her second line on the spot, but it felt right.

"*Oh, haven't you yet heard?*" sang Blond Trophy Wife.

The chorus of Puritan townsfolk broke into cho-reographed busy walking and small-prop action while mumble-talking and humming. So familiar and unlike actual life, Josie felt her heart squeeze with happiness. *Broadway!*

She opened her mouth to sing, and the story or her own mind or maybe the Muses themselves supplied the notes and the words.

By the end of the song, Josie was standing on the scaffold set piece, her back to the audience and her arms in the air. Her shoulders lifted and dropped with each heavy breath. And she couldn't help smiling as big as she felt.

"How *do* you know the part so well?" Justin whispered, barely moving his mouth.

"Because it's my fantasy," she whispered back.

For the next song, she just stood atop the scaffold looking meek while the chorus performed even more complicated speed walking around the stage, pointing at her in rhythm, throwing fake food whenever the cymbals clashed. Josie clutched her prop baby and felt *ignominious* indeed, a word she'd first learned from *The Scarlet Letter* in English class.

Josie was too freaked out to try to control every aspect of the musical, but her initial wish to know the songs had been like an engine that started it up, and the show just kept chugging along. Soon she was sitting on a prop rock with Bruce in a porcupine costume, stage right dark, while Cowboy as Roger Chillingworth, Hester's incognito husband, finished a dramatic solo stage left. Where was Deo in all this? she wondered.

A small twist of broken rope fell on Josie's arm. She

looked up. Misty/Gloria was standing on the lighting walkway above the stage, surrounded by heavy lights that if pulled loose would crash to the stage. Arms folded. Staring down.

Josie felt warm yellow lights drench her and she looked away. It was time for a comic-relief number, where a hilarious porcupine with an unaccountable Brooklyn accent in 1700s America would sing to her. If this had popped out of her own imagination, she really questioned her brain.

"*Any man can be rich,*" sang the porcupine. "*Wheat grows thick in every ditch. And it's been some time since we burned a witch, in New Englaaaand . . .*"

She glanced up again, but now Misty was gone, so she tried to focus on the song.

At the end of the number, standing downstage and singing out, Josie first noticed how small the audience was. Unlike Misty, they'd read the reviews.

Oh no, she thought, *my first Broadway show . . . and it's a flop!*

Perhaps because of her thoughts, a dozen audience members actually got up and walked out.

She tried to imagine it going better, but all her energy was focused on just getting through the next song. She was joined onstage by all the women in the chorus, each with her own plastic baby.

They sang to their props, "*Life's pretty good as a Puritan, if only by extensive comparison. You'll be the very definition of sexual repression, but at least you're a baby American!"*

As Josie sang a verse solo, she could hear someone in the audience snicker.

Too dramatic? She pulled back a little.

A few more laughs joined the first. *Too subtle now?*

No matter what she did, she seemed to hit it wrong. Her anxiety was frozen onto her face, probably even visible to those in the cheap seats. If there was anybody in the cheap seats.

I'm a joke, she thought. *They think this is funny. And, really, I agree.*

And then the dance break. Or, rather, the baby-tossing break. All the women tossed their babies to one another, like a complicated, syncopated game of hot potato, and Josie was a cog in the glorious, baby-tossing machine. Her forehead was wet with sweat. Her muscles ached with concentration. She couldn't think to act. She had no idea what her face was doing. She just tossed those babies like it was life or death.

This is ridiculous. This isn't serious; this is comedy, she couldn't help thinking.

Another verse followed by another round of baby tossing. But this time the Puritan women were metaphorically shunning the adulterous Hester by not catching Hester's baby, so Hester was constantly having to save her at the last minute from hitting the stage. As the music faded, the women kept tossing their babies back and forth in complicated patterns, while Hester stood center stage, tossing hers alone, lower and lower until she was just bouncing the baby in her arms as if to soothe her (perhaps from all the tossing).

A single spotlight. This was supposed to be a dramatic moment, Josie was certain, highlighting how poor, misunderstood Hester Prynne was ostracized by her community. But she couldn't help looking out at the audience with that question on her face: *I'm ridiculous, aren't I? This is silly, and I'm the silliest one.*

Snickers in the audience. And then laughter.

So much laughter. Thick, syncopated, sincere laughter.

Oh! thought Josie. *This* could *be a comedy!*

She hadn't been good at comedy in high school, preferring the deeply dramatic roles, the chances to sob and plead and feel sorry for herself. But she was dead tired of feeling sorry for herself. And, for the first time, comedy was feeling oh-so-right.

She tackled each new number with enthusiasm. *I'm ridiculous! I'm a joke! Laugh at me, I welcome it!*

And the audience did. Right up to the grand finale, where Josie was hooked up to wires to rise slowly above the stage as if ascending to heaven, an enormous *A* in battery-powered red lights blinking on her torso.

Justin and the rest of the cast were singing, *"See her there, New England's star! See her shining, a beacon from afar!"*

The cast turned and lifted hands toward her, drawing attention to the woman in the spangled gown with the blazing *A* on her chest who was rising slowly above their heads, just in case anyone hadn't noticed.

She suddenly lowered an inch. Near the top of her cable she spotted a slice. It was unraveling. Had Misty done that? The cable jolted again. It was going to snap.

The cast was still holding a forever-long final note. Josie could see crew members up there, frantically lowering a second cable with a hook. This was their backup plan? To catch her like a fish?

Be safe! she commanded herself, but before she could instruct her imagination to be more specific . . . *lurch*.

Josie fell.

The shock was like a gut punch. She didn't have time to wish. She didn't even have air to scream. The hardwood stage came in fast.

But Justin caught her. He took a couple of stumbling steps but didn't fall. For a slice of a second they stared at each other, stunned.

"I've got you," he whispered.

And then in unison they looked at the audience, each extending a *ta-da!* arm. The conductor took the cue, picking up the final measure again, to finish with a triumphant flourish.

The curtains closed. And Justin still hadn't set her down. Their faces were so close, just looking at each other was an intimate gesture. Perhaps it only lasted a second. Or less. A split second that felt like a split atom, a detonation inside her.

Theater is dangerous, she thought, *and not just from cut wires. Pretending to be in love with someone when your heart isn't free to follow through.* Sometimes imagining emotions made them real. Basic acting technique. Sense memory. Let your body do what it does when you cry and you'll feel sad. Put your body in a position of triumph and you'll feel confident. Gaze into someone's eyes, stare at his lips, wrap your arms around his neck, and your body tells your brain that you're in love.

But Justin wasn't hers anymore. And this wasn't Justin.

Not-Justin put Josie down as the cast swarmed them. Hands were on their backs, their arms, slaps of approval, hugs of relief that she hadn't been hurt. But also worried murmurs: *Why was the audience laughing? We're over—we're canceled for sure.*

So that was it. Her one night on Broadway. Imperfect and glorious and so stressful her limbs were still vibrating. Her high school fantasy had been thin and disappointing. She'd expected Broadway to feel the same, a cold reality that performing on the big stage with a big cast really couldn't be as wonderful as she dreamed.

She was wrong. It was even better.

The stage lights. The laughter and applause. The singing, and falling and catching. And especially this part, surrounded by a cast who all seemed glad to have her, even though she'd botched it. Even though her single performance as the star would shut the whole production down. Sometimes theater people could be just the best, most accepting people in the entire world.

After curtain call, Josie followed the flow of chattering chorus girls toward the stairs.

"Not down there," said a bespectacled woman in crew black, whose face Josie recognized as a bookstore clerk's. "Your dressing room is here."

She led her to the wings. And a door with a star.

Josie's insides crumpled. It was like those commercials where the lucky sixteen-year-old sees a new car in the driveway tied with a huge pink bow. Or the little girl when her grandpa walks in with a pony that has a huge bow around its neck. Basically any commercial involving gifts with huge bows. There was no bow on the dressing room, but Josie imagined one there anyway. A spiritual bow.

"For me?" she said, her voice trembling just like a commercial girl's.

"For whoever plays Hester Prynne," said the tired crew member.

"For me?" she said again.

The crew member rolled her eyes and left, so Josie let herself in.

It was the size of a hotel bathroom. A chair facing a mirror and desk. A well-used red velour love seat. She opened a door. Her own bathroom! The size of a hotel closet. But it was hers! At least temporarily, so she would temporarily revel in it.

"What's the word tonight, gals?" she heard Nina's voice say outside her dressing room door.

"Sardi's!" answered someone, maybe Blonder.

Josie put her hand on the doorknob but paused. Would she be tagging along? Asserting her own imagination over whatever Nina's character wanted to do? She didn't trust herself, wasn't even sure how to be a good friend. So she just stood there, hiding in her amazing starred dressing room till the backstage was totally quiet. When she finally emerged, she was alone. And for the first time, it was what she wanted to be.

Josie walked around the backstage, feeling all the feelings. A ghost light was already standing vigil, the only illumination on the dark set, and Josie waved to it, both in greeting and farewell. She'd promised herself: only one day, no chance to get stuck inside. But wow, even allowing for the possibility that she might be able to get into this story again, it was still hard to give up.

She closed her eyes and started pulling back. Her heart felt sticky, her whole self resisting. *No, we can't leave this story! Not this one!*

Sorry, she said to herself. And pulled harder—

"So here is our miracle!"

Josie snapped back, opened her eyes. Deo was backstage, slick in a suit but still sporting his geek-boy glasses, and looking as inviting as a dessert buffet.

"You saved the show," he said.

"Did I?" She felt pretty certain she'd doomed it. "It was entirely selfish anyway. I love being onstage."

"Do you know how rare your passion is? I can tell the moment I see someone if they have the necessary imagination and skill. You have got it, Josie Pie. You are the one. We have to keep you doing this, don't we?"

"I'd love to," said Josie, "but—"

"I fired Gloria, so don't worry about that. She defied theater's most important rule . . ."

"The show must go on," said Josie.

Deo smiled at her, and his smile said, *You get it. You're one of us.* Josie's middle melted.

"I just need you to sign the contract, and then I can put you in the playbill and start paying you a lead's salary."

He handed her a stapled stack of papers, open to the final page, pen offered. She shrugged and signed, wishing that the fantasy salary could be applied to her real-life debt.

"What else can I do for you, Josie Pie?"

"I'm just looking for the exit," she said, casting her gaze around.

"You don't need to exit. Ever. The show must go on, you know."

She laughed. He smiled, and she had the impression

that he approved of her in some way. She inhaled and smelled that sweetness again, as if he washed with sugar syrup.

"I should know this, but what do you do here?" she asked.

"I'm a producer, which means I find ways to keep the show going. You did my job tonight, and I'd love to repay you. Have dinner with me?" he asked, and suddenly looked unsure of himself.

Her hand twitched, and she realized she'd been about to lift her hand to his cheek. The instinct had felt surprisingly natural.

This was her chance, what she hadn't been able to manage in the young-adult rom-com. Date Deo in an unreal way, work through her homesickness for Justin. Be somebody else. His eyes were on her, and then they flicked to her mouth, as if he was thinking about something. And that something was smooching. So much smooching. The idea of smooching Deo felt incredibly appealing.

"I'd love to," she said sincerely.

"Yeah?" he said, his face brightening.

"Yeah," she said.

"That's swell, really swell." He took her hand and considered it. "I've been doing this a long time, Josie Pie, so believe me when I say, your talent is special. Let me just get my coat—"

"Oh, um, tomorrow night?" She'd be gone by then, but maybe she'd be ready to say yes to Deo in the real world. Tonight her imminent exit made her too melancholy to pretend-date.

Deo looked so crushed.

"I have some things to take care of tonight," she said. Like seeking closure. And getting back to her stupid real life. Adulthood really was the worst.

Josie gave Deo a little wave and went out the stage door, getting away before she changed her mind.

Outside, she stopped short. There stood the director with her father's face.

"Dad?" Josie whispered.

"Josie Pie, you were capital-*T* terrific!"

He opened his arms as if to embrace her. Josie took a step back, hands up.

"Hey!" she said. "You know, you should be nicer to your daughter. And call her back sometimes. And not only call her when you're feeling sorry for yourself. Because then it feels like you don't love her, and that can be really destabilizing to someone's self-esteem!"

His arms lowered. "I understand."

"Do you? I hope so, but honestly I doubt it." She put her hands on her hips and shook her head. "Listen, I don't want you to be a part of my story anymore, okay? I'm going to turn around and you'll be gone."

There was a time in her life when she'd ached for

his notice—a phone call, a brief visit, an approving smile. But seeing him here like this, she realized she now wanted nothing more than space. A place without him, where she could grow into herself without having to adjust around him.

She walked away without looking back, reached the sidewalk, and was honestly surprised to encounter New York City, right there waiting for her, as real as steel. 1950s Times Square was lit up in neon, advertising cars and booze and soda, Broadway and movie theaters. On the corner, Josie spied a man in raggedy clothes and a long white beard holding a sign written on cardboard: THE END IS NEAR. Behind him stood Grandma Lovey, looking equally raggedy and wearing a sandwich board that read: THERE IS NO "THE END."

Josie smiled. Did the story really have to end? A small idea: Maybe she could just stay here forever and keep being on Broadway and never face being a lousy friend to Nina or the end of her and Justin or her uncertain future.

But what would happen to *real* her if she stayed too long? Real-life time moved slower when she was in the fantasy, but it still moved. Would her body stay slumped on the bench, alive but unconscious? She shivered, the idea too gruesome to even comprehend. What would Mia think when she found her there? No, it was time to go.

I can try to come back, she assured herself. *I can start the book over.*

But she felt no reassurance. Josie sighed, put her hands in her pockets, and decided to at least walk around New York a bit to say goodbye.

This city smelled the same—exhaust, food, vapors rising from the train tunnels below (hot metal plus rats). She came upon the subway stop where she used to come in from Queens for auditions. Same train, though the signage looked decades older. Impulsively she jogged down the stairs, checking the content of the bag she'd taken from her dressing room: a coin purse, an address book, and an ID with her photo and the name Josie Pie. She paid fifteen cents to the subway attendant and hopped onto a train.

She wandered around her old neighborhood in Queens and was surprised that it looked much the same as it had in her day—laundromats and apartment buildings, row houses and bodegas, grand old trees blossoming out of tiny squares of dusty dirt and gray, weedy grass. A sign on a concrete wall that read PLEASE DO NOT URINATE HERE and a wet stain beneath it.

She didn't want this to be her last moment in this story. In New York City. In her fantasy. Not next to the urination sign. She regretted having left the theater at all. All she wanted was to stand on the empty stage with all its possibilities, friends with the ghost light, looking out at the waiting seats. She was about to hail a cab when she thought . . . maybe she could just fly there?

Josie struck a Lady Justice pose with hands on hips and really concentrated. It was easy to yearn to lift off the ground and go whooshing through the air, the power in her limbs, the delicious swooping feeling in her belly.

She put a fist in the air and said, "I can fly!"

She did not fly.

She said it again, this time taking a little hop. "I can FLY!"

She did not fly.

Apparently there were many things she could imagine, things she could change within a story—she could even turn some stories into musical versions of themselves. But she could not change the genre. People didn't fly in the *Spotlight* world unless they were on wires.

Around the corner, she heard voices speaking in a more intensely old-timey cadence.

"Ain't we tight, Daddy-o? Ain't I a keeper? So spill the beans already."

"Don't try to rattle my cage, kid."

She hurried around the corner to catch who was there, suspecting a plot point, but the narrow street was empty. She wondered if she was hearing ghosts. Book ghosts. Characters from the real story who somehow hadn't made it past her own imagination. Maybe she had changed the story too much for the normal plot engine to run. Was that possible?

What a stupid question. Anything was possible. She was in a book, for Thespis's sake.

"Hey, doll."

Josie turned. A man had entered the alley behind her. Pale, tall, thin, beard so long it seemed grown from laziness. And he was holding a knife.

"Give me your money."

"What?" said Josie. "You're mugging me?"

"I said, give me your money." He made stabby motions toward her.

"You have got to be kidding. I lived in Queens and never once even saw a mugging. And now you think—"

"Your money, kitten."

"*Excuse* me? I defeated a Zombloid army. You think I'm going to let some criminal intimidate me? This"— she waved her arms around at everything—"isn't real. I've had a bad couple of days. I lost my best friend, my dream show flopped, and I'm sad and I'm not playing along!"

"Prove it," he said. *Stabby, stabby.*

"I'm skipping this part, okay?" she said. "Flipping a few pages past. So go away. I refuse to be a part of—"

One of his stabby stabs made contact.

She felt the slide of metal against her side. He pulled back, and she saw the hole in her sweater.

Josie took two shaky breaths. With robotic detachment, she pulled her coin purse out of her bag and handed it over as if paying a fee for the service of being stabbed.

"Sing out and I'll pound you," he said. And then he ran away.

Josie stumbled out of the alley. It really was time to go. She tried to will herself out of there, but her thoughts were cloudy, shaken.

She stumbled to a pay phone and picked up. A woman's voice said, "Number, please."

Josie fumbled with her purse and took out the address book. There were only two numbers: Justin's and Deo's.

She gave the operator a number, yearning for someone to answer.

"Hello?"

"I was mugged."

"Is this . . . Josie?"

"Yeah. I was mugged. I'm in Queens and I don't have any money. I was mugged. I was . . . ."

She realized her voice was shaking.

"I'll be right there," said Justin.

She stood on the corner, frozen in shock, till a taxi pulled up and Justin jumped out. She made straight for his chest without thinking about it, curling up against him as his arms went around her. His cheek pressed against her head.

"You okay? You're all right?"

"I was mugged," she said again.

"Josie, you're bleeding."

He looked at his hand, red with blood. She lifted her sweater, expecting to see her guts pouring out of a gaping hole in her middle. So it was a pleasant surprise to find a small line. But definitely blood. With New York City honking and blaring and rattling all around her and real red blood on her hand, this story definitely didn't feel like a fantasy.

Justin walked her to the taxi.

"Take us to the nearest hospital," he said to the driver.

"Don't," she said. "I don't want to spend my—" *My final night,* she thought. "I don't want to go to a hospital or the police. I'm fine."

He inspected the cut again and agreed it didn't look bad. But he asked to take her home. Unsure where she lived, she asked him to take her to the theater instead.

Uniformed Frisbee Guy let them in backstage, and Justin bandaged her cut in her dressing room.

"It's shallow, probably doesn't need stitches," he said. "Still, it might pull when you're dancing."

"Not that I will be anymore," she said. "I'm sure *Scarlet!* isn't long for this world."

He didn't argue. She slumped down in the love seat.

"You don't want me to take you home?" he asked.

She shook her head. "I don't have long left in this theater, and I want to keep every second of it."

He sat beside her and they were quiet together, listening to the old building creak and flex. The theater felt alive and drowsy around them, a great sleeping beast, and there was nowhere else on earth or in Make-Believe Land where Josie would rather be. She closed her eyes and tried to memorize the sensation.

She didn't realize she'd fallen asleep till she woke up to the sound of the door opening.

Justin, still in his same clothes from last night, came in with a coffee mug in one hand, a newspaper in the other, and a massive grin on his face.

"Wait, is it morning?" she said, rubbing her face. "I'm not supposed to still be here—"

Without a word he dropped the newspaper on her lap. It was the Arts section of the *Village Voice*.

> Until tonight, I had studiously avoided *Scarlet!* at the Dorothy Gish Theatre, based on my esteemed colleagues' scathing reviews. When, against my will and better judgment, I reluctantly attended tonight, what a shock to discover that, just a few days after the premiere, the show's star, two-time Tony nominee Gloria Astor (*High Society, Boatshow!*) was replaced with Josie Pie, a novice chorus girl.
>
> Now, I have a gentle message to my

fellow critics. Fellas, you overlooked a crucial fact: *Scarlet!* is a comedy. This show is a rollicking, laugh-a-second, ridiculous gem that pokes fun at everything: classic literature, Puritans, modern audiences, and even Broadway itself. Hester Prynne rises up on wires for no reason other than it's Broadway and something should fly, right?

The Scarlet Letter is a classic novel best known for its egregious number of symbols. *Scarlet!* cleverly takes those symbols and blows them up till you can see their ridiculousness from the third balcony. Of particular note is the moment when Hester Prynne takes to the scaffold near the end of act three. Some of the townsfolk mock her until . . . the stage rises up on a previously hidden scaffold, higher than Hester. You see, the town itself is the *real* scaffold! The faux earnestness of the play on symbols is hilarious. In fact it was Josie Pie's perpetually bewildered Hester, amazed at all the nonsense around her, that really drew the laughs.

The reports of *Scarlet!*'s death are greatly exaggerated. And if I don't see

Josie Pie's name among the Tony nomi-
nees, I will dim Broadway's lights myself.

Josie had done this—saved the show—and she hadn't
even meant to! She stood up from the love seat and
grabbed Justin's hands. "We're in a comedy," she said.

"We're in a comedy," Justin said.

Josie squealed and hugged him and her side didn't
even hurt.

"I didn't tank the show! It's a comedy!" Josie shook
with a relieved chill. This moment was a finale worth
ending on. Now she could get back to Mia.

"We should get you some grub," said Justin. "You'll
need the energy. We have two shows today—that is, if
you're up for it."

Two shows? So she could do it all over again? It
seemed a shame to leave now, just when she felt new
hope and new possibilities.

Josie breathed in the theater scent and felt her resolve
weakening. Maybe one day more, a chance to perform
when it wasn't all new and overwhelming, when she
could really focus and imagine it perfectly—

Josie frowned.

Justin noticed. "What?" he said.

"You seem happy," she said. "You don't try to control anything; you just go along with the story, and you
still seem happy."

He shrugged. "I guess I am happy. Generally."

So was real Justin. Generally happy, at least when he was with her. Even at her height of confidence, Josie had been a bundle of anxiety: always trying to entertain everyone, sparkle, be someone worth knowing, at times assuming the persona of "fun girl" or "cool girl" or "ultrafeminine girl" or whatever people seemed to want from her. Except when she was with Justin. With him, she'd been instantly at ease.

Of course, so was everyone else. That was his superpower. Though he liked people and had loads of friends, he could get overwhelmed by everyone's needs, their pain, their hurting. His magnificent empathy could become depleted, and he needed time alone. Except when it came to Josie. He never needed time away from her. Being with her was as relaxing to him as being alone, as if she and he were already part of the same person.

She guessed that was what she'd given him. A person to be with who didn't judge him or demand things from him. They could just *be*, together.

"Okay, I'm going to do that too," she declared.

"Be generally happy?" he asked.

"Well, I'm not sure I can control that, but . . . I mean, not try to control everything. I used to believe that I could sing my 'I want' song to the universe and it would listen. But Sally Bowles didn't get what she wanted when she sang 'Maybe This Time.'"

Wait, was that musical already out in the 1950s?

303

But this Justin seemed to understand her reference anyway.

"Do the characters ever get what they want?" he said.

What did Elsa want when she sang "Let It Go"? To be left alone, probably. But that didn't work out. Instead she became queen and got saddled with a touching and sincere relationship with her sister.

In the musicals Josie really loved, the protagonists didn't get what they thought they wanted. They ended up with something entirely different and unexpected—and maybe better than before. Better, because through the course of the story, a character changes. Elphaba and Glinda. Elsa and Anna. Maria Von Trapp, Eliza Doolittle, and Annie. They changed, so what they wanted changed. Maybe there was hope for Josie, too. As long as she refused to let her life end up as a tragedy, there was always hope.

Justin was looking at her with that expression—those eyes that really saw her, that wanted to keep seeing her. And suddenly she declared, "I never wanted to be a star."

She covered her mouth, stunned that even in a fantasy, even to fake Justin, she'd confessed that truth.

"You didn't?" he said.

She shook her head. "I loved to sing, but the yearning-for-stardom part came later. After I met . . . a boy. After, uh, he looked at me like I was a star already.

It wasn't just him. My whole school—practically the whole town—expected it. But I thought, 'I have to do this for *him*, especially. I have to prove him right. Because he loves me. And if I don't become what he thinks I am—'"

"Then maybe he wouldn't love you anymore?"

"Basically."

"And did you?" asked Justin. "Become a star?"

"No," she said.

"And did he?" asked Justin. "Stop loving you?"

"Yes," she said. Her voice cracked.

Justin was silent, offering a place for the heaviness of that thought to settle.

Then he opened his arms, and she walked into them. The yearning for realness was so intense she wanted to cry.

"To tell you the truth," he said quietly, "I never wanted to be a star either."

"You didn't?"

"No," he said. "I wanted to be emperor."

She laughed, her mouth against his shoulder.

"Emperor or High Duke maybe," he said. "Grand Marquis, something along those lines."

"Dictator?"

"Yes, dictator was a reasonable option. When I was three I wanted to be a hippopotamus."

"Not all dreams come true," she said.

"I guess not." He sighed with extreme sadness. "But

if I can't be a hippopotamus, I guess a star will do, in a pinch."

She stepped back so she could see his face. And then she kissed him. It was so exhausting to fight off how she felt all the time. She had only one more day, and she would spend it grandly, loving Broadway and loving Justin. And she would let the story ride without micromanaging her imagination.

It felt a little scary, jumping into a pool without knowing how deep the water was. But she felt more confident knowing that Justin—or at least someone a lot like him—would be by her side.

Just one day more, she promised herself, and she'd get out long before she montaged.

CHAPTER 21

That day, Josie performed *Scarlet!* twice. The show was now hard-coded into her brain, as if she were a computer and the book had uploaded the information. She remembered the lines, the blocking, and the choreography, and this time she expected the laughs. Soaked them in. Sparkled for them.

She took her bow after the evening show and pretended to have every intention of leaving the story immediately—while also instantly recognizing that she had no intention of that whatsoever. A hot wire of will was rising up her back, and she would fight to stay for as long as she could—hair-pulling, fingernails out, knee in the groin, dirty and fierce and serious as literary fiction. She was going to fight for this one.

Besides, she thought, *time barely moves when I'm here. Surely I'll be fine?*

She slept in her dressing room, as content as a bunny in a warren.

The next day they performed again, and another show the day after that. Each performance she felt stronger, a better performer, a better singer. Now, this was *real* experience, far better than the workshops in New York! Every minute here mattered. She took another bow—

And suddenly it was day. Josie was no longer bowing beneath the stage lights. She was walking down Broadway in nondescript weather.

She stopped. What had just happened? Had time jumped forward? There was a word for that, but it took her a minute to remember it. *Montage* . . .

"Hiya, Josie!" Deo was coming down the sidewalk toward her. "I'm so glad I bumped into you. We never had that dinner, did we?"

"Didn't we?" Josie suddenly couldn't remember.

"Well, I'm about to have lunch with Dame Harriet Shufflebottom. She won four Tonys, you know. Come join us!"

How could Josie say no? She sat in a velvet-lined restaurant seat, ordered the soft-shell crabs, and looked around nervously, waiting for another sudden transition to strike. Nothing. Everything was fine. Dame Harriet had all the theater gossip, and Deo beamed at Josie as if she were a Dame with a capital *D*.

After lunch, Deo took her shopping for frocks. So many frocks. Just a crazy number of frocks. And hats, too, till she wondered how she'd managed to survive her whole life without them. Wearing a hat, she felt just so polished and put together. And her new heeled shoes made smart clickety-clack sounds when she strolled down Broadway. Like a boss. Like an actress.

Another performance, another standing ovation. Josie was walking out the stage door in her sassy new polka-dotted frock and hat and clickety-heeled shoes, wondering if tonight she would finally exit for good when—

She was walking back in the stage door again. She stumbled, a wave of dizziness washing over her, followed by a warm burst of euphoria like a rest after an intense exercise.

This should be alarming, Josie thought. *I think I was worried about something like this happening. Isn't this a bad thing?*

But how could it be bad? She was wearing a frock with a hat and clickety-heeled shoes. She was backstage on Broadway. She was home.

"Hey, Beth," Josie said, greeting crew members. "Hi, Marv. Hey, Stella."

She must have learned everyone's names between scenes, because there they were, ready in her brain.

Josie waved at Meaghan and Marcus, expecting the cold shoulder. They attacked her with hugs. When had this happened? In the spaces between?

"You have to come to the club with us tonight," said Meaghan.

"Yeah, we're really fun," said Marcus. "The most fun. And so are you, so now we're best friends."

And then—*snap!*—she was at a club with Meaghan and Marcus, the three of them leaning against the piano and singing "Fever." Apparently best friends.

A cast was a real family. Theater people were her people. In high school, Josie had felt that as the star she'd needed to keep herself slightly apart from the cast—and above, perhaps. She didn't feel like that anymore.

Snap. Back at the theater, Josie was watching from the wings during Justin's big solo as he ripped open his shirt to reveal a giant red *A* branded on his chest. Well, hello. His chest looked hard, chiseled, and hairless. That made her think of something else—

Snap. Speed-montage. Sold-out crowds for *Scarlet!* Laughter, applause, laughter, applause.

Josie was back on the wire at the show's finale, rising above the stage. Now that they were a comedy, the show had added more spectacle: a giant wooden *A* wrapped in Christmas lights that descended from the ceiling, and the porcupine along with a whole forest of fuzzy animals, soaring above the audience's heads on kites. Josie didn't recall kite-flying animals in Hawthorne's book, but the stage manager said, "Ever since that blasted *Peter Pan*, it ain't Broadway unless something flies!"

And then, the special release: Josie fell, and Justin

seemed to catch her, though she was really saved by the thinner wire hidden from the audience.

Another day, another number, this time the showstopper at the top of act two, "Commandments Are a Girl's Best Friend." Josie in hot-pink Puritan garb, dancing down the scaffold steps, escorted by the male chorus in sparkly Puritan black. She grabbed that solo, held that note, and belted it out for the whole world.

In high school, songs had gushed from her, passionate and thick with every tumultuous emotion roiling inside her frame. That was what she'd been trying to do in that community-theater audition—explode wide open. She'd fizzled and failed because she was no longer a ticking time bomb of passions. Time had started to temper emotions, tame the wildness. But now she found she could sing song after song, day after day, and be consistent in what she delivered. She could control the notes, the emotions, play them. No longer feral and uncharted, her singing voice was becoming a well-honed instrument. She was starting to feel like a grown-up.

She soaked in that spotlight, but it was the presence of the other actors around her that gave her the most joy. Better than solo star songs, she loved the big ensemble numbers. Reno and crew tap-dancing to "Anything Goes." "Hello, Dolly," with the entire cast loving up the stage together. "One Day More." "Stick It to the Man." "Mama Will Provide." The ensemble numbers were the showstoppers.

Snap! And Josie was dining with Justin late at a restaurant where the clientele tossed shy hellos and asked for autographs on napkins, pens shaking nervously in their hands. She didn't feel surprised, as if she'd been dealing with fans in public for ages.

Snap! Sitting in her dressing room with Justin, early for call, no hurry, nothing to do but chat.

"We'll do *The Old Man and the Sea* next," he said.

"Three entire hours of an old man singing to himself in a boat."

"And a fish. A huge, tap-dancing fish."

"And singers dressed as seagulls on wires, because it's Broadway so something must fly."

"Or *Crime and Punishment*," he said.

"But with bunnies," she said. "Everyone dressed as adorable bunnies."

"Bunnies with Russian accents."

"And angst."

In all she'd experienced—the butterfly-gnawed-belly moment before the curtain rose, the hushed breath of the audience's expectation, the wild music of the applause, the energy of the crowd's laughter pouring over her— what a surprise that this was the best moment. Sitting with Justin here in her dressing room. Alone. Casual in a robe, no makeup on. Talking nonsense.

Sometimes it occurred to her that time didn't normally move like this—skipping the sleeping bits and bathroom bits and boring bits, tap-dancing straight to the money shots, the tentpole scenes, the set pieces. But the swoop of time dulled her anxiety, boxed it away like outgrown clothes till it seemed immature to worry about it.

The forgetting and remembering went in and out like a light bulb near its end—flicker on, flicker off, flicker on—

Snap.

"Hey, Loretta."

"Hey, Lester," said Josie, entering through the stage door. "You killed it last night. Hilarious."

Bruce kissed her on the cheek in that friendly, thespian way.

"Lettie, how do I look?" asked Nina, posing in a new hat, tipped low over her forehead.

"Like trouble," said Josie.

"Who's the talent in the hat?" asked Meaghan, entering through the stage door.

"The new lead in the show at the Barrymore," said Josie.

"You don't say?"

"Lettie recommended me to the director," said Nina. "Ain't she the best pal a gal ever had?"

"Aw, I just mentioned your name," said Josie. "Your talent got you the part."

"Or something . . . ," said Meaghan.

"Now, don't get frosted," said Nina. "Your turn will come up someday."

"Who said it wouldn't?"

"What's buzzin', cousin?" said Blonder.

"Hildy's leaving us for a star role."

"You don't say? Well, brava, Hildy."

Hildy . . . Hadn't her friend had some other name once? Josie scrunched up her face, trying to recall. She almost had it . . . but Marcus entered, egging Meaghan on, and the argument escalated.

"Drop dead twice," said Meaghan.

"What, and look like you?" said Nina.

Come on, Stanley, Josie thought, staring at the stage door. He always had a way of calming down hotheads.

The door opened and in he came, almost as if she had summoned him. What a silly thought—as if she had the power to make things happen!

"Hey, cats," he said. "I just got the word from a cabbie—Mets are up two-nothing. Afternoon, Hildy, don't you look swell? Afternoon, Flossie. Your solo last night was spot-on."

He gave everyone a kiss on the cheek, smooth and cool and no rush. A minute later the group was laughing, anger forgotten.

Josie went into her dressing room, pursued by a strange feeling that something other than anger had been forgotten. She tried harder to recall, but her mind might as well have made a *pfft* sound, like a balloon leaking air.

Maybe she had amnesia . . .

From the stress, she thought automatically. It felt like a quote from some book or show, but she couldn't remember what.

Two knocks and Justin entered. He was carrying a vase of daisies.

"Happy anniversary, Lettie, honey!" said Justin, placing the vase on her dressing table.

"Anniversary?"

"Three months today since I heroically saved you from the chorus line and escorted you into the spotlight."

"I don't recall it going down exactly like that."

"I'm a fan of revisionist history."

"The flowers are beautiful."

"You're beautiful."

He smelled like witch hazel and the lemony laundry soap the theater's laundress used on their clothes. And beneath it, his smell was even more familiar than his single dimple.

He sat beside her, and she hooked her legs over his lap. He touched her feet, as if he were as comfortable with them as with his own.

"It's really been three months?" she said.

"The best three months of my life."

Has it only been three months? she wondered.

He took her hands, looked at them nervously, and she had the impression he was imagining her naked— not in an improper way, but to settle his nerves in that old and highly proper thespian way.

And then he said, "I love you."

Her heart thumped oddly, as if it were saying, *Oh!*

"I have for a long time," he said. "There was a click when we met, like we'd known each other for years. Am I wrong? Because I had this sense that we were feeling the same thing at the exact same time. And that was—"

"A miracle," said Josie. A miracle, like Montana's late spring, when the world woke up smiling, like Arizona's winter, sunny and cool and thoughtful, the blue sky a hard candy shell. Like a little-girl hug, arms around her neck as tight as life itself. Like one dimple placed just so. Like someone who wants you near as much as you want them near.

Her heart beat in her fingertips; her inhale felt as big as the whole theater.

Her smile seemed too much for him, and he leaned in. She met him halfway. They were kissing, and his hands felt so good. Like water on her. Like shower water when she was really dirty. Like, postapocalyptically dirty . . .

Don't think about it. Don't remember.

She kissed him and wanted more. The yearning was so brilliant, so hot, she was turning to ash.

They fumbled around, crashing into the wardrobe rack, kissing crazy and laughing, till they ended up on her love seat. (Love seat! What a perfect word for it!) He started to kiss her neck, and she was electric everywhere. The love seat was too small (great name, but inconvenient for making out!) and they were on their feet, cleanly knocking over the wardrobe rack this time, hangers clattering to the floor.

She couldn't stand a breath of air between them; she needed him closer, so tight they might be one person. The thinking part of her brain turned off, and she was all hunger and instinct. But that break from her thinking brain allowed a buried part of her brain to wake up.

. . . *MIA!*

The name roared inside her.

Josie pulled back and gasped. The room seemed to tilt and roll as if it were a barrel crashing down a hill. She stumbled. He caught her.

"Are you okay?" he asked.

"Mia is playing at the park! How could I forget Mia?"

"What's wrong?"

"What am I doing? I forgot what I was doing. I need to check on Mia. Mia!" she called toward the ceiling, the walls. "Mia, honey, are you okay?"

"Um . . . who are you talking to?"

"Three months, you said? Three months since I first played Hester?"

"Yeah, three months . . ."

"It didn't feel like three months. The time flew past like a . . . like a montage. It montaged me, didn't it? It did that before, but never for this long. I forgot this was a story. My plan . . . there was a plan . . . to be purely professional, mature, see that the dream wasn't so great

317

after all and let it go . . . and I wasn't going to kiss you, but I did anyway and it was like—like Persephone eating pomegranate seeds and getting stuck in the underworld. Stanley—wait, you're not Stanley; you're Justin. Justin, what's my name?"

"What's wrong?"

"My name!"

"Lettie. Loretta Sweet."

"My name's not Lettie. It's . . . it's . . . what is it?" She slapped her forehead, trying to shake it loose. The word was there, like a stuck coin in a pop machine.

"Honey," he said, taking her hand. "You've experienced some kind of trauma, haven't you? What can I—"

"Josie!"

"What?"

"Josie! I'm Josie Pie, right?"

"Of course you're Josie Pie," he said, as if he'd never called her anything else.

"I'm such a chump! I let the story keep me for too long."

She closed her eyes and pulled back. Pulled back harder. There wasn't any resistance, no stickiness trying to keep her in the story. Worse—there wasn't anything at all. No knob to turn, no place to dig in her heels, no sensation of any kind. Just . . . *nothing*. The way of exiting a story felt entirely closed to her.

"How do I get out?"

Mia, Mia, Mia . . .

Josie yanked open the door and ran into the back-stage. "Let me out!"

Stagehands scattered like startled pigeons. Josie ran for the stage door just as Nina entered.

"You okay, Lettie?"

"I'm not Lettie! I'm Josie!"

"That's what I said."

"I need out! I promised Mia I wouldn't leave her. And what if I never wake up again? Does my body just . . . just *die*?"

Nina grabbed Josie's arms and looked over her silk robe, old-timey underwear beneath, bare feet in slippers. "Baby doll, you know you're not dressed? I don't know what kind of 'sode you're having, but I won't let you go outside like this."

"Nina, I promise I'll let you go in the real world, I won't fight you when you tell me you need to move past our friendship, but you need to let me go here so I can get back to you to tell you that."

Nina nodded. "Run," she whispered.

But new hands were on Josie. Stagehand hands.

"Easy, Miss Sweet," said one. Beautiful. Blond. Wearing glasses. One of the bookstore clerks, she thought. "Let us take care of you."

So Josie relaxed and began to sing the Spice Girls' "Wannabe."

The stagehands, confused, looked around as if for help. In their confusion, their grip loosened.

Josie seized the moment to wrangle free. Nina held open the exit, Josie barreled through, and the door shut behind her.

Outside the stage door, Josie bumped into Misty, who appeared to be in the act of creeping. She was wearing a hooded cloak, large sunglasses, and carrying a bottle of chloroform. A spool of wire peeked out of her hoodie pocket.

"Oh!" said Misty, startled. "I was . . . I was just . . ."

Josie rolled her eyes. "You were about to kidnap me or tie me up or torture me or something, because you're a conflict device and the story is trying to keep me here."

"What are—"

Josie kept talking as she hurried toward the front of the theater. "Or maybe my subconscious is imagining you into this moment? Because subconsciously I want to create a conflict so I can stay? Well, forget it, subconscious! No clever plot twist or story obstacle will stop me from leaving."

Misty grabbed Josie's wrist and twisted it. Josie cried out with pain.

"Ain't that a bite?" said Misty. "Ain't that a big tickle? I'll tell you what, kid—"

Josie punched her in the face.

"Ow!" said Misty.

Josie ran.

"That hurts every time!" Josie shouted at no one,

rubbing her knuckles. She plowed down the sidewalk, bumping into pedestrians.

"Let me out! I'm done!" she yelled at the sky. "They lived happily ever after. The end. THE END!"

No bench. No park. No Mia. Josie felt so sick she doubled over. She was vaguely aware of tourists staring at her and a police officer mumbling into a walkie-talkie.

Justin was there. He took her arm and gently led her from the crowd to the shade of the theater awning.

"Josie, let's go back inside. A doctor is coming to check you."

"I don't need to be checked; I need the end." Her knees were wobbling. She felt so tired. Was her unconscious body still on the park bench? Had Mia discovered it? Or was Josie maybe already dead?

Nina came running out the front doors with the stage manager and Deo in tow. Justin turned to talk to them in hurried, anxious whispers.

Josie cast her eyes around for the best escape through the crowd and spotted Grandma Lovey. She was sitting on the curb, eating a burrito, wearing her sandwich-board sign: THERE IS NO "THE END."

"It's been too long for you," said Grandma Lovey.

"What?" asked Josie, edging nearer to her.

"And longer than long for me. You just don't get it, do you?"

"No," said Josie, because she really, really didn't.

"No going home. No getting out. I tried to warn

you," said Grandma Lovey. "Not that anyone ever listens to me. So I'll move on. I prefer tea parties. And bonnets. And men in breeches. *Tight* breeches. Don't judge me." Grandma Lovey took another big bite, green salsa spilling down her chin. "At least the food tastes real."

Josie squatted down beside her. "What did you try to warn me about?"

Grandma Lovey's mouth was still full, but she stuffed the bite into her cheek with her tongue. "I found you by your color—all bright yellow and the silveriness. You were in the camp by the fires, and again in the woodsy place."

Josie's legs felt cold. "You mean, the bandit camp? And in the . . . the Zombloid story? You remember being in those stories?"

Grandma Lovey worked the chunk of burrito between her molars. "They suck up your fantasies like milkshakes, digest them till there's nothing left of you and no way back. A lifetime of tea parties I've lived, or maybe it was several lifetimes, of drawing rooms and bonnets and balls—"

"Who's *they*?" asked Josie. "How do I fight them?"

Deo put a hand on Josie's shoulder. "Josie, we need to get you inside."

"Not yet, I need to talk to her," said Josie, but Deo, with the help of stagehands, pulled Josie away.

Josie struggled. "Let me go. I can't be trapped here!"

"Is she on the level?" the stage manager said. "Did she just pop a screw?"

A crowd was snapping photographs. They clearly recognized Justin—or Stanley Reeves, anyway. And perhaps Josie, too.

I'm a star, she thought weakly. *Everything I do is in the glow of my own spotlight.*

"You have to cool it!" Justin leaned in to whisper. "That cop called for backup, and I'm telling you they're going to come take you away. As in, wrapped in a straitjacket."

"No, I've got to get back to my kid."

Justin's arms dropped. "Your kid?"

"She's not mine, but I'm responsible for her . . ." Josie's voice cracked. "She's got no one else. I can't leave her alone. And my . . . my Justin, too."

"I'm your Justin," he said.

She touched his cheek. "You're like him, but you're not him. And I love him so much. I can't keep running away—I need to find him, even if it's just to say goodbye."

"I'm right here, Josie," he said. "And I love you, too."

Her heart ached. She shook her head. "This is a beautiful fantasy, but I haven't earned it. Please, I need to get home. Mia is just a little girl; it's not fair that she's alone. It's not fair when adults do that to kids, and I promised her I wouldn't be like that. Please."

The police officer was approaching, flanked by two

doctors in suits with white lab coats. One of them was holding a syringe. Josie turned to Nina and Justin, yearning for them to know her and love her as they once had, needing them to be on her side now, in this upside-down place.

"Justin, she needs to get out of here," Nina whispered.

Justin was studying Josie, watching her eyes. Then he whispered, "I've got you."

Justin broke out of the protective circle and into the crowd, yelling and flailing as if hysterical.

"Where is the End? Let me out! Uh, nevermore, nevermore!"

The stage manager swore and threw her hands up. Nina started to laugh.

Josie raced to the curb, frantically waving her arm at every taxi that passed. Behind her, the crowd was snapping photos of Justin. Josie could hear someone whisper, "I told you that's Stanley Reeves."

He struck a dramatic pose, knee bent, hand on hip, the other raised up.

"Life is but a walking shadow, my friends. Live it"—he lowered his eyebrows and looked out ominously—"while you have the chance." He cackled a pitch-perfect evil laugh, lifting both hands to the sky. And then he froze.

Silence. The crowd, doctors, and police officer seemed too stunned to react.

324

"And . . . scene," said Justin.

The crowd applauded hesitantly.

Justin bowed, declaring, "Thank you for participating in today's Broadway Sidewalk Theater!"

The crowd's applause notched up from confused to entertained.

On the curb, Josie's raised hand finally stopped a cab. She sneaked inside and barked at the driver, "JFK!"

"J-F-where?" said the driver.

"Um . . . the closest airport! Quick!"

As they drove away, she looked back.

Justin was bowing to the crowd, but he met her eyes. He looked gutted.

"I'm sorry," she whispered.

CHAPTER 22

The cab moved through the gridlocked streets of New York like a drop of water through a leaky faucet. Or something slower than that. A turtle in a desert. The pulse in a corpse's wrist.

Josie's leg bounced up and down, her knee restless.

She met eyes with the cab driver in the rearview mirror. Had he noticed that she was wearing a bathrobe and didn't have a purse? Never mind about paying the cab—how was she supposed to buy a plane ticket to Missoula, Montana? Did airplanes even fly from New York to Missoula in 19-whatever-year-this-was?

"Sorry, lady," said the taxi driver in a strong Brooklyn accent, "I'd love to agitate the gravel, but this city ain't moving, and that's the word from the bird."

Could she montage her way out of this? She closed her eyes, tried to visualize Missoula, but she could still smell the sweaty scent of the cab interior, hear the horns and engine sputters.

"So how you gonna be payin', Dolly? I can't make change for more than a fiver."

She shut her eyes tighter, inhaled and exhaled, and tried to imagine her way out of the dream. Was this magic? She hummed a meaningless tune and thought of all the words of power that she knew.

There's no place like home.

Sim sala bim.

Abracadabra.

Break a leg.

Macbeth!

I love you more than ice cream.

And suddenly she was no longer sitting in a cab. She was running. It was night. The air was cool, the breeze knocking open her robe and lying slick against her skin. She tripped on a crack in the sidewalk, caught herself, and sped on.

There was the Missoula condo complex, as real and normal as a heartbeat. So she was back in the right year, but why hadn't she woken up in the park?

The door of their condo was locked. Josie pounded on the door.

"Mia?" she called out. "Are you there?"

She tried the door again. It opened this time. The condo was dark. Josie tiptoed in. There was Mia's tricycle by the front door. The framed photo of one-year-old Mia on the wall. But the place didn't smell right. Dusty. Stale.

"Mia?" she whispered.

In the family room, the TV was on, crackling with static. The familiar bar stools stood at the kitchen counter. And there was the stack of books they'd checked out of the library.

"Mia?" she spoke louder.

She heard something from behind Mia's door: a thump. A scrabbling sound. Then silence.

Josie put her hand on the doorknob. And stood there, breathing. Finally she opened it.

There in the center of the room stood Mia.

Josie choked on a sob and fell to her knees. Mia ran to her, put her arms around Josie's neck, squeezed so tight it was like she'd never let go.

"I'm here!" said Josie. "I'm back! I'm so sorry, Mia. I'm so sorry."

And they just kept hugging, squeezing, Josie letting Mia know with her embrace that she was safe and wouldn't have to be alone again.

"What happened?" asked Josie. "Was I gone a long time? Did you walk home from the park all by yourself?"

Perhaps she'd been gone for months. Maybe Victoria was home; maybe Josie's photo was featured on the missing-persons page of the police website.

Mia just kept hugging Josie. Unease began to trickle down Josie's throat. She tried to swallow and coughed.

"You sure are affectionate today," said Josie. "Usually you won't let me hug you . . ."

Josie pulled back. Mia stared at her. She blinked.

"Is your mommy here?" asked Josie.

No answer.

"How long have you been alone?" asked Josie.

Mia opened her mouth. In a robotic voice, she said, "*I want to be your pal.*"

Josie laughed nervously. "Wow, you sound just like it. I mean, *exactly* like that bear toy."

Mia hugged her again. Josie patted her back.

"Are you okay, sweetie?"

"*Read to me.*"

Josie startled away. "Mia, say something normal, okay? Say something in your normal voice. I want to hear regular Mia now."

The girl didn't speak.

"Please, say Josie. Just say Josie."

"*Play with me.*"

"Aaahh . . ." Josie backed away. The Mia thing stayed in her room, staring at her, not blinking. "What are you? Where am I?"

She searched the apartment. She found her bag, the one she'd left in the theater's dressing room. Her ID said Loretta Sweet.

"This isn't real. I'm not home yet . . ."

She started for the front door.

"*Take me with you,*" said "Mia" from her room.

Josie picked her up and ran with her out into the dark night. Mia felt so light in her arms. And then she wasn't Mia anymore. Josie was carrying the creepy robot bear that had, moments ago, looked so much like a living little girl.

"CREEEPY!" Josie shouted at the night. She held the bear at arm's length but couldn't make herself drop it.

Missoula was silent, like a movie backlot between projects—no cars, no people. The few blocks rattled her lungs and hurt her knees, but she didn't slow till she got to the park.

"Mia!" she shouted.

It was empty. The moonlight picked out the bare bones of the monkey bars and the dome climber. No children, no three-headed book club. Even the trees were bare, rattling with a few dead leaves. The river was as thick and black as the Styx. Cold mist lifted off it like ghosts, drifting toward her and sliding through her, wetting her bones.

"Mia," she whispered, hugging that freaky bear toy.

She sat on the bench. Closed her eyes. Imagined it day. May. The sounds of children laughing. A book in her hands. Mia just there. Just beyond her closed lids. Mia waiting. Josie imagined so hard she trembled.

She opened her eyes. Quiet. The dead leaves rattled. The river ghosted with cold.

She closed her lids again, falling on all those years of acting classes, all that sense memory. She lifted her face toward the sunlight she could almost feel and imagined blue sky so big everything wasn't below it but rather a part of it. The river more white than blue. May in Montana, the earth's best idea since five-year-old kids.

The air warmed. The light through her eyelids went orangey. She opened them.

It was day. The leaves were yellow-green as if just blooming into spring.

And the playground was utterly empty.

Josie howled with a physical pain. She stood up and kicked the bench. She remembered it wasn't the bench that had caused this and reached for her purse to pull out the glasses. But there was no purse. No glasses.

Glasses.

She marched away from the park, the bear toy dangling from her fist. This fake echo of Missoula shimmered like a ghost town, as quiet and tight as a held breath.

The bookstore was dark. And locked. She peered in the windows and could see nothing. Less than nothing. As if the window were actually glass pressed to blackness.

"It's bad luck to see a bookstore and not go in," she said. Her voice didn't carry, as if she were speaking into a vacuum.

With an explosion of sound, she kicked in the glass pane on the door like some kind of nanny action hero. She reached through the shattered opening and unlocked it.

The bookstore was entirely empty, no bookcases or reading chairs or toy-train table. Only one light pierced the unnervingly thick darkness: a bare bulb burning a pale, twitching light atop a metal lamp stand.

"A ghost light," Josie whispered. Why did the bookstore have a ghost light as if it were a superstitious theater? And was it intended to light the space so ghosts
could perform their own revelries? Or to scare ghosts
away?

Was she herself a ghost? In a ghost world, stuck
between life and death?

Mr. Camoin used to say that theater inhabited a lim-
inal place between life and death, truth and fantasy,
ecstasy and pain. The wrestling between the opposites
was what gave theater more life than life itself.

Mr. Camoin also used to say that butter was meant
to be eaten by the spoonful, so it wasn't like Josie agreed
with him 100 percent of the time. But the liminal-place
thing was ringing true right now.

According to her grandmother's books about the
Greek myths, humans couldn't simply climb Mount
Olympus or spelunk into the underworld. In order to
commune with humans, the gods and the mythological
characters whispered to humans through oracles, listened to them in sacred temples, changed into animals
and vulnerable humans so they could walk with them on
dusty roads. A human and immortal meeting required
an in-between place and a transformation.

But a bookstore? Josie thought.

And then, *Why not a bookstore?* Like a theater, it
was a place where stories mattered, where imagination
ruled. It even smelled like a theater to Josie, fresh paint

and sawdust and the electricity of the ghost lamp burning dust.

Perform onstage as though your life depended on it, Mr. Camoin would say. *According to the oldest stories, it does.*

"We are all of us just performing for the Muses," Josie said aloud to the bookstore. And that final word made her shiver. The room shivered with her. She raised her voice. "Isn't that right? Muses? And are you amused yet? Are you enjoying my hour strutting and fretting upon the stage? Is my performance full of enough sound and fury for you?"

She didn't shiver again, but the bookstore did. They were ignoring her, whoever they were. Ignoring her need, ignoring little Mia's need too. The mama-bear nanny in her soul roared with anger.

"I summon you!" Josie yelled. "Open sesame! Break a leg! Come out, come out wherever you are! I've performed for you all my life, I've dedicated years of songs and yearning and pain and all those humiliating cattle-call auditions to you. I think that earns me a face-to-face."

The bookstore seemed to inhale.

She took up a queenly pose, feeling her body lengthen, strengthen, as she had when she'd played Queen Eleanor in *Brrr! Roar!*, the musical version of *The Lion in Winter*.

"Muses, I believe in you!" she shouted, praying that

her belief and her imagination would be enough. She couldn't fight something intangible. "I command you to appear to me!"

A mist crept along the floor. Josie took a few steps back to avoid it and then gave up and let it overtake her feet. It lapped at her ankles, chilly and dry. Her toes tingled.

The bookstore seemed darker than it should be. She looked back at the door, but there was no door. No window that she'd kicked open with her awesome fierceness. There was no more anything, except darkness and mist that stretched in every direction, seemingly for eternity. And the ghost light. It reminded her of a certain lamppost in a childhood book, a piece of modern civilization incongruous in snowy Narnia. Whether the light was intended to invite ghosts in or to scare them away, Josie felt it throb invitingly, a glowing safety circle. She stepped more firmly into its halo of light.

She caught sight of a shadow walking, just beyond the illumination the ghost light cast, and she gripped the cool metal post with one hand, the bear toy with the other.

Although she couldn't quite make out his face, she knew it was Deo, the way you know the identities of people in dreams even when they don't resemble themselves. Like the time Josie had dreamed about going to a carnival with Justin, only he'd looked like Bette Davis and she'd been a potted plant.

Deo's skin looked like pure gold in the low light. His chest was, in fact, hard, chiseled, and hairless. She knew this because he was naked. Or at least she thought he was. The mist was in constant motion around him, rising and falling, swirling like a living toga. He was not wearing his glasses.

"Josie Pie. I didn't expect to see you again so soon. Something wrong with your book?" Gone was Deo's awkward charm. He was all smooth confidence, the sliding of liquid metal.

"Something was wrong with your glasses," she said.

"Changing how someone sees the world is a powerful magic."

"But I'm not farsighted. How did you—"

"A touch is all it takes for a small magic, like cursing a girl with temporary farsightedness."

She seemed to feel again each instance when he'd touched her—bumping into his chest, his hand on her arm, his fingers grabbing hers as they sang a duet. Was it only after these encounters when she couldn't read without the glasses? "Morning eyes" had been a lie. Deo had been the cause of her seemingly random eye problems, his way to make her read with those supernatural glasses.

Other shadows moved in the mist, pacing like caged tigers. Josie hugged the bear.

"You are Muses," she said.

"We are older than that name," said Deo. "Just

because people have forgotten us doesn't mean our hunger has diminished. We survived where our cousins long ago went extinct, because we are adaptable. Like insects. Always around, unseen, hardly noticed."

"You . . . you really want to compare yourselves to insects?"

"Why? What's wrong with insects?"

"A lot of people consider them pests, and they have tiny brains—"

"Insects are cool!" he said.

"Sure, okay."

She heard him take a breath, and his voice was room-temperature mercury again.

"We notice people who notice us. We created an oracle in Missoula when you arrived, Josie Pie. The bookstore, just for you. Though you took long enough to find us, I must pose that complaint." His voice was full of smile, as if he were gently teasing an old friend. "All we managed to entice in those months were two idle daydreamers of minimal power, hardly enough for us to call a snack."

At his words, Josie could see pale tethers of light extending from Deo's middle and off into the blackness, like transparent umbilical cords.

"You had ancestors in the old land who also dreamed deeply, feeding us for centuries. But you surpassed them. At such a young age, you'd already created a fantasy version of yourself."

"Ouch," she said. That was harsh, but she couldn't argue.

"I've been doing this a long time, Josie Pie, so believe me when I say, your talent is special. You yearned to insert a fantasy version of yourself into a different story from what life offered, and for us, that yearning was both palpable and palatable."

His voice was delicious. His words seemed to lick her skin. She shivered.

And again, so did the bookstore. Or wherever she was. She blinked twice. Inside the two blinks she seemed to be in a palace hollowed out from the inside of a mountain, the mist a lake of fire up to her ankles. It was all gone again by the second blink, but she was so shocked she leaped back, disturbing the white mist. Beneath it, there was no lava lake. There was nothing. She had the stomach-sickening feeling of falling without moving. Thankfully the mist nosed its way back over the break, hiding whatever was (or wasn't) beneath her.

"I was right about her," said Deo. "She has the talent, the lineage, and the passion."

"Perhaps," said one of the other shadows. Female. Silvery voice. His sister, Bianca, Josie guessed. "I just wish this 'one' you're always looking for were a little more pliable. All her hopping in and out of stories made me queasy."

"She's here, isn't she?" he said. "I wish you'd learn to trust me."

"I wish you'd stop comparing us to bugs."

"Bugs are the most adaptable creatures on the planet," he said, his voice rising nearly to a whine. "Plus they're strong and clever and adaptable and . . . and *strong* . . ."

These were Muses. So this was a performance. Josie must play the fearless, noble heroine. She refused to be Persephone, kidnapped by Hades, helpless and lost. Instead she would be a hero like Orpheus, braving the underworld to save whoever Hades had kidnapped. And she would not look back.

She squared her shoulders, neck straight—sense memory of confidence.

"Justin is part of my true story. And Mia, too. And Missoula, Montana. Even if it's not the way I would have written it myself, it's my story and I want to finish it."

"Justin we can arrange—or at least the closest version to him that your imagination can produce. You can have anything you dream. Except Mia. Children are too volatile, even in imagination. And their own imaginations can prove catastrophically powerful. They upset the balance."

No children. How had she missed that? Even in fake New York City, everyone had been an adult. A world devoid of children. Maybe in the fake Missoula, the story had just been responding to her imagination's demand for Mia the best it could. With a creepy bear-toy substitute.

Wait—since Josie was in the fantasy, did that mean

she was no longer a child? Had she passed officially into the role of adult? When would her teenage self grow into a person who could, if she had the chance, get a credit card again and pay the bills, and struggle with something without having to run away, and make and keep long-term relationships with people? And just not be so freaked out about failing everything all the time. If she got out of here, could that be her now?

"I wouldn't have targeted you if I'd known you were so attached to a child," Deo was saying. "We avoid tapping into parents of young children, since they tend to have stronger threads tying them to real life."

"Well, I'm pulling on that thread," she said. "Send me back."

He shook his head. Or else the space shook and his head didn't.

"You signed a contract."

A contract? She was about to argue but then felt in memory her hand holding a pen, sliding over a piece of paper. "The theater contract? But that wasn't real! That was in my mind!"

"Humans!" Deo said cheerfully. "As if what happens inside your head doesn't matter. As if thoughts are meaningless, daydreams trash, ideas and understanding insubstantial."

"Well . . . ," said Josie. That was all she had.

"You signed on for the run of the show. And this show will never close."

"Always read the fine print," said Bianca, her voice singsongy, "even in dreams."

Josie glared in her direction. "Still, contracts can be challenged, ripped up—"

Deo moved in closer. The glow from the ghost light caught him. The colors of his shape solidified, his skin changing from gold to brown, the mist stiffening into clothing under his red bookstore apron. But no glasses, and his gaze bored into her with a force. She gripped the post of the ghost light with white knuckles.

"You just don't get it, do you?" he asked.

"Clearly I don't, or everybody wouldn't keep saying that!" Josie said.

Deo smiled sympathetically. "Josie, you lived *years* inside that story."

"What do you mean years? It was three months."

"Three *story* months. But many more real years. Mia is grown-up. She's forgotten you, and so have Justin and Nina."

Josie's breath froze. Her everything froze; the only way she was still standing was thanks to her cement legs and icicle spine. She recalled the spells in *Harry Potter* that could paralyze a person with a single word. Loving other people made her vulnerable. No magic required, just the words: *Justin is gone. Little Mia is gone. And everyone I know. It's my fault; I knew I shouldn't stay. I'm such a chump; I knew I shouldn't stay . . .*

Deo's eyes were soft as he said, "You've been pleading

with the Muses for years, and at last we get to grant your wishes. All I've wanted is for you to have your dream."

He put his arms around her; his face close to hers. His breath smelled like salted caramel, cinnamon bears, candy hearts. A scent that could draw Hansel and Gretel deeper into the woods.

"What do you want, Josie Pie?" he asked.

The answer came instantly, a pinpoint of pain, exact as if a thin, cold arrow had shot straight through her chest.

"Don't bother answering," said Deo. "Love, right? Acceptance?"

She shivered, ashamed to be a cliché, and yet filled with that yearning.

"In the fantasy we make for you, you'll never have to choose between being loved and being a star. You can have both. You can do *anything*."

She couldn't help snorting.

"Let me grant your wish," said Deo. His eyes were on her lower lip. She could feel his longing, as if she were the performer onstage, he in the upper balcony, yearning to join her, aching to be where she was. Her stomach hurt with the pain of his yearning. She felt certain that if she just kissed him, she could heal him. And herself, too. Just kiss him. Taste his candy mouth, allow his hands to pull her closer. His lips were right there, as close to her lips as possible without touching. She'd have to make such a small motion to reach them.

"Justin," she managed to gasp. Her heart throbbed.

"He's gone from your life forever, and you're feeling the pain of loss," he whispered. His breath was red licorice, sour cherries, chocolate pretzels. "Just kiss me, and I'll take that pain away." His thumb ran down her cheek, teased at the corner of her mouth. "A light touch for a small magic, a willing kiss for a strong magic." He touched her forehead, smoothing her hair back. "In your last fantasy, you started to forget about your other life. Remember how content you were? Just kiss me, and I can make that amnesia permanent."

"Amnesia," she whispered. Her head was spinning. "Because of the stress."

So much yearning. She felt tugged closer and closer to him, though she was already in his arms, pressed against his chest.

"That's not my yearning you're feeling," he whispered. "I'm only echoing back to you your own."

She shuddered because she instantly recognized the sensation. This was what she'd felt in the balconies of the Broadway theaters; this was the hunger she'd sent at the stage.

"I know what you want . . ."

Part of the mist rose, swirled, opened like a tunnel, and through it she could see the hallway of her high school. There was Nina, smiling, waiting for Josie to walk with her. There was Justin, leaning against the lockers, looking like all the peace in the world. And dozens of students waiting for their star to step in.

Deo slid behind her, his arms around her waist. He spoke close to her ear.

"You've proved yourself skilled at rewriting the story. Imagine what you could do with a lifetime in your fantasy! You could have your happily ever after."

"How? What would happen to . . ." She gestured to her body, meaning her actual body, sitting on a park bench. But surely it wasn't still there, years later. Here in her false body, her heart was pounding.

"The show must go on," said Deo. His breath smelled of lemon drops, nut nougat, and gummy peaches.

"Wait," she whispered. "A show is rehearsed and performed, the same lines night after night. Life is way more complicated and unexpected. There's no third act and no curtain call; it just goes on and on till it doesn't. Life's nothing like a show."

Deo's arms around her waist loosened. He exhaled sticky, rosy, perfumey Turkish delight. "For you, life *can* be a show, if you only choose."

Why candy? A tiny alarm was ringing in the back of her brain. Was he a honeypot, some creature meant to look good and smell enticing, pull in the prey? The sugary smell was giving her a headache.

She heard a bell and saw Justin and Nina headed to class. Justin looked over his shoulder, as if expecting Josie to join him. The edges of the school hallway flickered, and as she squinted at it, she could just make out a different image. She gasped. It was Grandma Lovey wearing a bonnet and having tea with a man in breeches. That drawing room faded into a castle, where a figure in silver armor was currently fighting a dragon, and beyond that she caught a glimpse of a black-haired woman on the bow of a ship on the sea. Other people inside their fantasies? Deo was telling the truth—there was a way for her to just stay, perhaps forever.

Josie took a last look at Justin and Nina and the perfect high school life that had never really existed, and she turned her back, stepping out of Deo's arms and faced the dark nothingness. The knot inside her chest loosened again, loops of rope falling free, and the sensation came with an astounding thought: *I've lost Justin, and Nina, and Mia, too, and everyone I love has outgrown me, but I'm still me. Somehow, I still survive.*

She put her fists on her hips and declared, "You just don't get it, do you? I'm not going to play your game. Give me back my real life, or I will go full Spice Girls."

CHAPTER 23

Deo stared at her, that burrowing gaze. She tried not to flinch but couldn't help rapid blinking, and for a nanosecond between the blinks she saw it again: marble palace hacked into a mountain, red lava lake swirling around her ankles, and Deo and his family all golden, luminous beings.

"I can't do that, Josie." Now Deo's voice had an edge like grating steel. "We've already invested so much in your story. Losing you would set us back years. Besides, there aren't many dreamers like you. As long as I keep you dreaming, your fantasies alone can feed my entire family."

The shadows moved forward into the silver ring the ghost light cast. No longer shadows, they were the clerks from the bookstore in red aprons, six seemingly young men and women. Without their glasses on, she could feel their hunger tug at her, gnaw on her. It was the flavor of her own hunger, amplified and played back at her like a weapon. She fell to her knees, cowering at the nakedness of her own desires.

You are not only this moment. What would Nina say? To not fight the yearning but own it. Flow with it. Have compassion for it, and for herself. Accept it lovingly.

She exhaled, relaxing into the sensation, and the yearning arced and fell on her like a wave.

"Oh," she said, feeling it clearly now. Her years of yearning for Broadway weren't a purely selfish desire to become a star—her yearning was for the song, and the communion between audience and performer, and the unity of a cast that felt more like family than her own, and the lights and sounds and the words so she always knew what to say, and character shoes that fit just right and the costume that transported her.

And also the yearning was for Justin, because she'd believed that becoming a star was what she needed to keep him. After her quick ticket to Broadway failed, she'd curled up tighter, mourning the loss of him, even when he'd probably still been in love with her.

She climbed back to her feet.

"Return to your fantasy, Josie Pie," said Deo.

"No!" she said. She thrummed with memories of rehearsals and shows, of Justin and Nina, and Mia, too, of the realness of life, even the mundane pieces of being an adult—laundry and grocery shopping and making mac and cheese, the way life smelled and felt in her hands, like a library book, like steeping mint tea, like a worn-in sweatshirt. She smiled. "No," she said again.

Deo scoffed. "You can't defeat us. You yourself helped shape our power."

Two of the book clerks were suddenly dressed as the police officer and the white-coated doctor with his syringe. Bianca and another became bandits with swords. The last two combined into a gray, bubbling Zombloid.

"You mean I did that?" said Josie. "So my imagination affected how even you all appeared in the stories?"

Deo didn't respond.

"Are we still in the story?" She gestured around. "This isn't really a bookstore in Missoula. We're inside a book, right? Some weird empty pocket of the imaginary world I helped develop with Old Betsy here." She tapped the side of her head, as if Old Betsy were a common nickname for a brain.

Deo flinched. At first Josie thought it was because of her weird Old Betsy comment. But there was a trace of fear in his eyes.

"Oh, for a Muse of fire!" he declared, lifting his hands high. Fire erupted around him. Bright, twisting, heatless fire.

Josie laughed. She knew a show when she saw one. Why so much spectacle? Why not just *make* her do what he wanted her to?

Because he couldn't. He must not be able to force her into a fantasy. She had to choose it herself.

"Hey, Muses, I do *not* perform for you anymore," she said. "The. End."

The creepy book clerks in their various incarnations rushed her.

"You shall not pass!" Josie shouted, surprising herself. It was always alarming what would come flying out of her mouth in high-stress situations. This was why she'd never done improv.

But as the words came out, a wizard staff appeared in her hands. She swung it at the oncoming book clerks, who dodged away.

"Ha-ha! Looky what I did!" said Josie. "I made a staff! *With my mind!* That's right, Old Betsy is back."

"We have feasted on the dreams of thousands before you," said Deo, perhaps stunned by her second attempt at referring to her brain as Old Betsy. "You can't think to defeat us alone."

Alone. Wait . . . she didn't have to be alone.

"Then good thing I've been developing my imagination, jackwad."

To her right appeared Bruce as the Doctor with Cowboy and the Frisbee players as ragged survival fighters, hefting hatchets, pipes, and shovels.

To her left, Nina, Meaghan, and Marcus, outfitted like Puritans going clubbing, struck a fight pose, backed by the chorus-girl Trophy Wives.

Filling in the space was a high school hallway's worth of teenagers carrying backpacks like lethal weapons.

348

And then, pushing Josie aside so she could take center stage, came Misty as seventeenth-century Lady Fontaine, fan out and hard at work.

"Pardon my French, but who the devil are these riffraff?" said Misty.

After that, it didn't take much imagination to turn Mia's creepy toy into a ten-foot killer robot bear.

"I WANT TO BE YOUR PAL!" Its creaking jaw opened and closed as it stalked toward Deo.

Josie laughed with joy. Here, at the end, she didn't need to go solo. It was time to finish the show, and that called for a big finale. Bring on the ensemble.

Josie looked down at herself, still in costume underwear and robe, and she imagined the crap out of a new outfit for herself: black combat boots, black stretchy pants, black T-shirt with black leather jacket.

"You guys ready to fight?" asked Josie.

"Oh yes," said chorus-girl Nina.

Perform as if your life depended on it, Josie seemed to hear Mr. Camoin call to her through memory.

I rather think it does, Josie thought back.

Deo shouted something in another language, his voice metal against stone. The changed book clerks charged.

"Die, creepy fake booksellers! Die!" Josie shouted, and her army attacked. The two groups clashed in the ghost light's glow.

Instantly, something struck Josie, and she was thrown away from the ghost light. She rolled into the shadows, where the mist was sticky thick with raw yearning. It clawed at her skin, crawling over her head and arms, stinging like nettles. She scrambled to her feet and ran back toward the ghost light.

Deo got in her way. She swung her staff, clocked him on the head, but he didn't flinch. His eyes were like fire, and he put his hands out as if to push her deeper into the shadows, when a robot bear hand picked him up.

"READ ME A STORY!"

While Deo was occupied with the kaiju bear, Josie hurled herself back into the safety of the light. She breathed hard, rubbed her arms and legs, checking to make sure she was still intact. Only here felt safe. Surely Deo wouldn't allow anything that gave her an advantage if he could help it, which meant there were rules in this place that bound even the Muses. She had no idea what those rules were, but hopefully they would give her some advantage. Deo was so strong; fighting him felt impossible.

Her army was in the thick of battle: *Valentine* survivors fought back-to-back, the *Scarlet!* contingent had formed a lethal kick line, and Misty was liberally smacking book clerks with her fan. But even as Josie watched, a third of her crew were knocked down and disappeared before her eyes.

With a *BOOM* and a shudder, the giant bear fell, whining mournfully, "I WANT TO BE YOUR PAAAAAAALLL . . ."

If the bear failed, then where was Deo? Terrified, Josie spun around to find him right behind her. Instinctively, she jumped in the air, and he punched the space where she'd just been. She hung there for a moment, out of his reach. She couldn't see the stage wires, but they were probably where she'd imagined them, holding her up.

Pausing to look around and try to form some kind of a plan, Josie again spotted those pale, glowing tethers. Three of them, leading from Deo into the shadows.

As she squinted down at herself, a fourth tether slowly brightened into visibility. It led from her middle to Deo's.

Josie came back down. Deo's eyes were wide with panic, as if he realized what she'd seen.

"There are other victims like me, aren't there?" she said. "Feeding you."

Suddenly Deo was holding a long, silver sword. He swung it at her neck, and she ducked barely in time. Sword? What genre was this story? Any genre worked here, it seemed.

In a blink she was Lady Justice, her sword of justice in hand.

She swung at him, and he parried, twice, three times. He was so fast, she could see no hope to get past his defenses. She looked down.

"No," said Deo.

"Yes," said Josie.

She swiped her sword—not at him but at the tether between them. It snapped like rope.

"NO!" said Deo.

"Not only do I have a cool sword too," she said, "but I can *fly*!"

And she flew around him, trying to get at his other tethers, but he was too fast, always keeping them behind him and driving her off with his whirling silver weapon. For the briefest moment, the toe of Josie's boot brushed one of the tethers. An image flashed in her mind: Grandma Lovey, lying unconscious in a hospital bed.

Josie glanced out toward the scary, clawing darkness and took a breath.

"Okay, Josie Pie," said Josie, "you're a hero. This is what heroes do."

So she flew, not at Deo but away, following the tethers into the darkness. At once he was chasing after her, leaping like a golden tiger. She swooped down toward the other end of the tethers, and the shadows clawed up, reaching. She screamed and slashed at them with her sword, and then finally made contact with something solid. A tether. She sliced through it.

Deo leaped at her, but Josie flew out of his way, dove again toward the clawing shadows and slashed at the remaining tethers.

Deo howled.

Josie jetted full speed above the grasping mists and back into the safety circle of the ghost light, landing hard and rolling. She crashed into the fallen robot bear. Her skin felt raw and painful where the shadows had grazed her, and her chest squeezed tight with panic. She gasped, trying to catch her breath.

"ATTACK!" yelled Bruce the Doctor. Her imagined army was fighting the rest of the Muses with renewed strength—or else the Muses were weakened, now that she'd cut off the energy source that had been feeding their leader.

Deo emerged from the shadows back into the light, and Josie scrambled to her feet. He juggled his sword from hand to hand.

"If you think you've won, you are very wrong. You *will* go back into your fantasy."

"You can't make me," she said, taunting.

"I can make your existence in this void unending misery till you beg to return!"

Josie swung her sword, but he caught it easily by its sharp tip, yanked it from her hand, and threw it back into the shadowy mists. He was about to pounce, but a herd of cows trampled him, led by Nina dressed as Anne of Green Gables. He tried to stand up, but Mr. Camoin as Boring Lecture Guy dropped a podium on his head. Then a mechasaur opened its screeching jaws and swallowed him whole.

Josie tried to take stock of the rest of the battle, but she barely had time to see that most of the other book clerks were gone when Bianca was at her back, her perfectly toned arm around Josie's neck. Josie fell to her knees, her mouth open but no air going in.

"You . . . will . . . PAY!" said Bianca.

Deo cut his way out of the mechasaur and landed by Josie, pushing his hand into her face.

"Give up," said Deo. "We are older than sand. You can't win."

Two daggers suddenly pierced Deo's hands, and he let go with a yipe. Two more into Bianca's arm, and she let go of Josie's neck.

"Princess," Justin said with a nod. He was dressed all in ninja black, two more throwing knives in hand. He threw them toward Bianca's perfect face, and she fell backward into the mist.

Josie shot Deo with magenta magical energy from her fingertips and crowed, "I AM SECRETLY THE MOST POWERFUL OF ALL!"

Deo rolled through the mist, pushed by the energy blast. "How . . . are you . . . doing this?"

"You said it yourself," she said. "I can do *anything*!"

Deo attacked them again and again—with swords, with guns, with cartoony cannons. He even pulled out his "danger sticks." But whatever his attack, Josie and Justin met it: with highwaymen ropes and arrows, with Broadway high kicks and high school backpacks, and finally ending back-to-back with hatchet and crossbow.

Deo was on his knees, angry, exhausted, but still there.

"You can't defeat me!" he said.

"I think you might be mistaken," said Josie.

Justin put down his hatchet and nodded at Josie. "You've got this."

"Wait—" she said, but he bowed his head and faded away.

Standing there alone, facing her personal demon, Josie was surprised to feel an unfamiliar peace. Deo was rising to his feet. He lifted a sword with a wicked-looking jagged blade and began to swing it toward her neck. She aimed her crossbow and shot him in the eye.

Again the space seemed to blink. To flicker. For a hundredth of a second, the mist was lava, and it seared her feet. The empty space was a marble palace, the walls crumbling. Before she had time to scream, the mist and darkness were back.

Instead of blood, nothingness dripped from Deo's eye. Where the blackness leaked, she could see right through to the crawling mist behind him.

"I'm older . . . than sand!" he said.

"So what?" she said. "I'm Josie Pie."

Deo roared, and the space roared too, a massive, crumbling roar as if she were inside his mouth. He came at her. She shot him in the other eye.

"The end," she said.

There was a swoosh, as if this place were indeed a mouth, exhaling a final breath. The mist went with it.

And the floor, as she'd feared, wasn't real after all. She was falling. She only knew she was falling because her stomach told her so, from somewhere up above her where she'd apparently left it. She tried to fly, and when that failed, she tried to imagine a parachute, but nothing appeared.

All was darkness and falling and nothing, and Josie hugged her arms around herself and shut her eyes so she didn't have to see the nothing. *Justin is gone . . . everyone is gone . . .*

Behind her lids, Josie saw a glow. She peeked. The ghost light! Falling at her same speed. She leaned into the nothing, aiming for the post. She grabbed hold and hugged it, falling now with the light, down, down, seemingly without speed or destination. Perhaps she'd just fall forever.

Realistic transubstantiation, she chanted at herself. *That's what I need. Right now. I don't care what I'll find, what year it is, what I've lost. I don't want the fantasy. I'm ready to claim my life, whatever it is. I just want to be real again. Now. Now. Now—*

CHAPTER 24

Josie gasped. Air thundered into her lungs.

Someone said, "Whoa!"

She didn't know who spoke because she couldn't see. Her hearing also wasn't gold-medal quality. It was like her head had been underwater and her ears were still draining.

"Josie? Can you hear me?"

"Mia?" Josie's lips tried to say, but only managed "Mehh?"

A few more minutes, a firm scolding at her brain, and Josie managed to force her eyes open and focus on who, what, when, and where.

Hospital room. And she was in the bed. A nurse was bustling around, shining a light in Josie's eyes, sticking her finger and arm into things that squeezed, asking her questions that Josie began to understand.

How much time had passed? She examined her hands, looking for signs of aging. They looked kinda normal.

She looked around for a mirror and noticed that besides the nurse, there were other people in the room.

It was Meaghan and Marcus. Not dressed like spangled Puritans or Zombloids or French servants but in their normal *shall we step into a Patagonia photo shoot* attire.

"Mehh?" Josie said.

"You're going to be okay, honey," said Marcus. His eyes were wobbly with tears. He sniffed and held her hand. "You're going to be okay, you hear me?"

Why was Marcus crying over her? And why didn't he look any older?

Josie double-blinked. No lava lake in the space between. She tried to sit up but immediately lay back down. Her head felt like a carnival goldfish prize carried home in a baggie of water.

"Of course she's going to be okay," said Meaghan. "Your cousin is tough as nails."

Cousin? Josie's eyes widened, terrified that she'd gotten sucked into another book, like maybe a kidnapper horror story.

"Your vitals are good, Ms. . . ." The nurse checked her chart. "Ms., um . . ."

"Pie," said Meaghan. "Josie Pie."

"I'll be back with the doctor."

When the nurse left, Meaghan shut the door behind her. She and Marcus exhaled in unison, and then laughed.

"I've never lied so much in my life!" said Marcus. "Good thing you're alive and okay or I don't know what I'd do."

"Mia?" Josie finally managed.

"She's fine," said Meaghan. "Misty is watching all our kids."

Now it was Josie's turn to cry.

"Don't you start!" said Marcus, starting back up again himself with a sniff.

"What—"

"You fainted or something," said Meaghan, leaning over the bed, her hands on the bar at the foot. "On the park bench. Just went unconscious. We called 911, and they brought you here."

"Did anyone call—" Josie started.

"Your mom?" said Meaghan. "Your cell has a pass code."

Josie had been about to ask, *Did anyone call Justin?* But why would they? She leaned back on the stiff hospital pillow.

"We didn't want to leave you till we were sure . . ." Marcus's lower lip trembled. "Sure that you'd be . . ."

"Marcus, for real, you've got to stop," said Meaghan.

"I know," he said, fanning his eyes with his hands. "You see? This is why I never start crying, because once the floodgates open—"

"I know, sweetie," said Meaghan. She rested her head on his shoulder.

Marcus raised his hand. "I'm now your first cousin, by the way. They needed a relative to sign the forms. I hope impersonating a cousin isn't a felony. Oh no, what if it's a felony . . ."

"They did blood tests and CT scans and all that dramatic medical show stuff," said Meaghan. "Couldn't find anything wrong. Said you just randomly went comatose and maybe you'd come out of it and maybe you wouldn't. But I *knew*."

"For real, ladies, is it a felony?" asked Marcus. He held his phone to his mouth. "Siri, is forging a signature on hospital documents a felony?"

"It'll be fine," said Meaghan. She leaned over his phone. "Never mind, Siri!"

"How long was I in there?" asked Josie. "I mean, asleep?"

Meaghan looked at her watch. "About three hours?"

Josie exhaled. Then shook her head. Then smiled.

"So, today is . . ." Josie held her breath.

"May fifteenth," said Meaghan.

The same day she went to the park to read *Spotlight*. A relief . . . though part of her was disappointed that she hadn't been simmering in a coma since *Highwayman*. That meant she'd *actually* had the audition from hell, "I can do anything" and all.

"Thanks," said Josie. "Really, thanks for looking out for me. And for Mia." Perhaps she still had some of that otherworldly boldness, because normal Josie never would have added, "I feel like we could have been friends in a different place."

Meaghan's mouth opened. Marcus hiccuped. And then his tears returned.

"Marcus . . . ," said Meaghan.

"I'm sorry," he said. "That was just so kind. You know I get awkward around blatant expressions of kindness. Besides, Meaghan and I read those books you were reading, the *Highwayman* one and the Zombloid one. They were really *fun*, and you know, I had the exact same thought about *you*."

"Hey," said Josie, "is it weird that all three of you have M-names?"

"Um . . ." Meaghan looked to the side. "My name is actually Vera? But Misty started calling me Meaghan so we could match or something, the way all our kids had A-names. That's weird that she did that, right? And that I let her? I don't know why I let her."

"It's okay," said Josie. "My last name isn't really Pie."

"Do you like being Josie Pie?"

"Yeah. Do you like being Meaghan?"

"No."

Josie and Vera laughed.

"We're already to the confessions stage of our friendship!" said Marcus. "This is getting real."

He got Josie's number and immediately sent a group text:

The hospital could find nothing wrong with Josie and discharged her into her cousin's Dodge Charger.

"Most of the neighborhood is still empty this time of year," said Marcus as they passed million-dollar houses overlooking a golf course. His lip curled up as he said, "They're second homes of *Californians*."

"I'm originally from Arizona," Josie said, to distance herself a whole state away from California. She was scanning the world for children and proof she wasn't still *there*.

Marcus had just pulled into the driveway of a brown-brick, two-story home, nearly identical to the other brown-brick, two-story homes on the block, when Mia ran out the front door. Josie flung herself out of the car, and nanny and kid met on the front lawn.

"I'm so sorry, Mia. I'm so sorry," Josie said, hugging her tight.

"It's okay, Josie," said Mia, nothing robotic or creepy or remotely bearlike in her voice. "I didn't interrupt you on the bench. I wanted you to finish your book."

Josie could feel Mia's frantic heart thumping against her chest. That pounding seemed to jump-start her own heart, and she became painfully aware of the warm blood rushing through her veins, the tension of her bones, every ache, every itch, every crick and thump and cramp. This was what real life felt like. And still Mia let Josie hold her. The hug felt like a blessing.

"You smell weird," said Mia.

"Like a hospital," said Josie.

"And burned things. You didn't wake up, Josie. Were you still in your story?"

Josie pulled Mia back to look her in the eye. "How did you know?"

"Bleh, I don't like your smell. You should shower." Mia squirmed free, done with hugging.

Misty stood on the front steps, watching them with folded arms.

"So . . . drugs?"

"What?" said Josie.

"You're on drugs, right?"

Josie sighed. "Thanks for looking out for Mia."

Marcus offered her a ride home, but Josie wanted to keep the real sky overhead, the open air circulating around her. They were a ten-minute walk from the condo and took it slow.

Mia named every dog they passed—Itchy, Gravy, Crackers, Poop—and Josie went through her purse.

"Sweetie, do you know where my glasses are?"

"You don't need them anymore."

"But . . . well, you're right; how did you know that?"

"They looked wrong on you. They looked like bad luck."

"Oh. Did you see them anywhere? At the park?"

"I took them off your face when you wouldn't wake up," said Mia. "I gave them to Ahab's nanny."

Ahab's nanny . . . "Misty? You gave them to Misty?"

Mia nodded. "She talked mean to me so I put the bad-luck glasses in her purse."

Josie's frame tensed—panic mode!—but she exhaled and said, "Oh well." Unlikely that Misty would put on reading glasses. Unlikely that the glasses were still magicked, or that the Muses were still in shape to do whatever it was they'd done to Josie. If they even still existed.

But if the unlikely happened, and Misty was currently reading something like *This Slow, Miserable Death Called Life* . . .

Josie giggled. Just a little bit.

"What's funny?" asked Mia.

"Life," said Josie. "Me. I don't know, I'm just happy."

"My good luck hopping worked," said Mia. "It just took a little long."

They walked down Main Street, the afternoon light all buttery yellow, the air crisp as apples and just as flowery. Josie breathed in. The air was richer, here in the real world. Not just her brain believed it but her body knew it. She inhaled and felt herself expand.

They turned a corner and she stumbled, caught unsuspecting by a jolt of fear at the sight of the bookstore.

"Josie, it's bad luck—" Mia started.

"To see a bookstore and not go in. I know."

She touched the glass pane that she had recently kicked in, but it was unbroken. Cautiously, she opened the door.

Mia ran to the train table like always. But this time, she had no other child to shove aside in order to claim the lone remaining engine.

The bookstore was deserted. Dark. Not even a ghost light illuminating the abandoned bookcases.

"Hello?" Josie asked the void.

A figure came in from the back, just putting on a red apron. Josie struck a fight pose but quickly relaxed. It wasn't a red-eyed shadow. It was a middle-aged man with a very familiar face.

"Bruce!" she said.

He seemed to barely hear her, gazing around. "Strangest thing happened . . . I'm working my shop this morning when customers start running out of here, all spooked. One stops to tell me all the bookstore clerks vanished. I'm sure she meant figuratively."

"I'm sure . . ."

"And I think, well, if those college kids who work here got lazy and quit all at once, people might shoplift. I never should have leased this property to them. Funny, I don't even remember doing it . . ."

Bruce touched a book display. "I always liked a bookstore. Ever hear that saying, that it's bad luck to see a bookstore and not go in?"

"Yeah, I have, actually. You know, if you knocked

down that wall, you could combine the bookstore and the coffee shop."

"I was just thinking that!" he said.

Josie spun the reading glasses display. All the glasses were gone, empty plastic holes where the frames used to sit.

"Promise you won't sell creepy magic reading glasses, and I'll be your best customer." Once she was out of debt, that is. And if she stayed in Missoula. And if, and if . . .

Bruce was staring off as if imagining how to rearrange the cases, create a flow from the bookstore into the coffee shop. His imagination was so strong, Josie could almost see it herself.

On the walk home, Josie and Mia passed Blond Dreadlocks and Frisbee Girl. They didn't seem to know her, but she waved and shouted hello as if they were old friends. As if they'd been through life and death together.

"Hey, we're going to play Frisbee in the park," said the girl. "Wanna join us?"

"Not now, but another time!" Josie called back.

For dinner, they ate peanut butter sandwiches by the river, throwing rocks into the water. When Mia got busy collecting three-leaf clovers, which she deemed "lucky," Josie reached for her phone.

The aftertaste of her yearning for Justin—that palpable, exquisite sensation the Muses had echoed back at her—still lingered on her tongue. It was sweet. And heartbreaking. She was still bracing herself to say goodbye.

But first, Nina. Her heart thumped so hard it hurt, but she wrote an email:

> Nina,
> High school was my high, but I realize now
> that it was your low, and I keep dragging
> you back into your low. I think when you
> came to Missoula, you were trying to break
> up with me. Or whatever best friends do to
> not be best friends anymore. And I haven't
> let you. But I'm ready now. Thank you for
> being willing to give up Chicago for me, even
> though I never should have asked. Thank you
> for all the years. I'm sorry I was so selfish.
> You have every right to need time away from
> me. I'm here if you're ever ready to try again,
> and I'll try to be better.

Send.

And then, without thinking twice, she sent a text to her sister Lila, the first one since a generic "Merry Christmas."

JOSIE
Hey

Well, it was a start. Who knew what might change in the future.

Josie didn't have time to sit refreshing her inbox

for any potential Nina replies because Mia was bored of three-leaf clovers and suddenly needed to wash her hands now, now, now, Josie, I feel bugs all over me, now!

They hurried home, but after a block, Mia just collapsed onto the sidewalk, holding her hands in the air and crying. Crying so hard her chest trembled without a sound.

"Mia, sweetie," said Josie.

"I want my mama," she said.

"She'll be back soon, Mia."

"I want . . . I want her . . . *now*!"

Josie sighed and rubbed Mia's back.

"You said you wouldn't leave me," said Mia. "But you did, Josie, you did!"

And Josie was eight again, pouring cereal for dinner, watching TV all weekend—cartoons, reruns, old movies, infomercials—looking out the window, watching for anyone to come home.

She picked up Mia and carried her the rest of the way. She weighed much more than a stuffed bear toy.

While Mia was in the bathroom, Josie sent another email.

Hey Victoria,

Everything is fine here. Mia is the best. I love her so much. But she really misses you. She's in the bathroom washing her hands over and over again. Her obsession with good luck is getting worse. Today she cried for you. And you know she's not a big crier.

I didn't really have hands-on parents. I know what it's like growing up lonely. I love Mia and give her all the attention, but it's not the same as having her parents around. I really, really know all about this. I hope you'll listen to me. I don't know what you should do, but I think something's got to change.

And I can't keep running away from my own life either. So I'm giving you my one month's notice. I hope you'll figure out what's right for you and Mia.

Take care,
Josie

Josie's heart was pounding; her finger hovered; she took a breath and clicked send. And immediately started to cry.

Even if change was right, it still hurt.

She tapped her browser to check what time it was in Nairobi, and it opened directly to the local news page.

COMA PATIENTS WAKE UP THE SAME DAY

Josie clicked the link at lightning speed. According to the article, the two Missoulians who had both succumbed to sudden and unexplained comas had just woken up in perfect health. The article's writer also cited a peculiar coincidence: a seventy-eight-year-old woman in Boston had also just woken up from a mysterious coma, though hers had lasted for nearly two decades. She'd fallen unconscious at age fifty-nine while sitting on her sofa at home.

Bet she was reading a book, Josie thought. *And had recently acquired new reading glasses. And really prefers stories about teatime and men in tight breeches.*

The end of the article made Josie gasp.

According to Janae Stephenson, RN, the patient's first words after waking were, "She did it."

"I asked her what she meant, but she seemed confused," said Stephenson. "And later she couldn't remember saying anything. I think she was reacting to whatever dream she'd just woken up from. A dream that she quickly forgot."

I won't forget, Grandma Lovey, thought Josie. *I'll remember for both of us.*

CHAPTER 25

Josie slept that night as if she hadn't slept in months, deep and dreamless. The next day, Mia should have gone to preschool, but she was acting so anxious at the thought of leaving Josie, they scrapped that plan and walked instead to a park—a different park. Josie felt so aware of everything: the elegant way the leaves on the trees were uncurling, the *ffftt* of the dragonflies, and the hushing sound of shoes walking on grass. She noticed the pleasant bubbling of gas in her intestines, which she had never thought to appreciate before her fantasy self had been gas-free.

While Mia played, Josie stood nearby, assuring Mia every couple of minutes that she wasn't going anywhere. After a while, she pulled out her phone.

"Hey, Mom, if you want to be an energy worker or whatever, I fully support you."

"What?"

"I fully support your being an energy—"

"What are you talking about?"

"Remember when you said I had like a yellow energy? With silver lining or something? I was thinking—"

"Like in that video? It was so boring!"

"I'm just trying to—"

"I don't have time for stuff like that."

"I'm trying—"

"All that meditation? Who can sit still for that long? And the humming tickles my nose."

"Mom, I'm trying to, you know, take a step back from myself and be more mindful of others. More supportive of my friends and family, take an objective picture of my faults and—"

"What faults? You're my little girl. You're perfect."

"Aw, thanks—"

"You just need to get over yourself, quit moping, forget your dreams, and become a hairdresser, maybe."

"Yeah. Thanks."

"Anyway, I'm thinking of becoming a yoga instructor."

"Oh! Well, I fully support—"

"I'm kidding."

"You're kidding? Oh good, because you're like the last person I could see as a yoga instructor."

"I'm not kidding. You should try yoga. You had terrible posture when you were little. I bet you did permanent damage to your spinal column. I have to go. There's a dog parade downtown. Listen, don't call your sister with this feel-good support stuff. She's in a worse mood than normal. I called Rafi's phone thinking it was her phone and a woman answered, and Lila is losing her mind over it."

"Wait—that was me. You called Justin instead of me and a girl answered—"

"Is that what happened? Why would a girl have Justin's phone? Sounds suspicious to me."

"Mom . . ."

"You jump into relationships too fast, if you ask me."

"I know. I'm impulsive, I don't think things through. But I wish now that you didn't let me go to New York so soon."

"I tried to talk you out of it."

"You did? I don't remember."

"You were so set on going. What could I do? Lock you in a closet?"

"I don't know. But . . . the credit card you cosigned for me? I ran up the limit and I had to shred it, and I'm in a lot of debt—"

"Yeah, yeah, I know."

"You know?"

"Of course I know. I get your statements every month."

"Oh."

"Debt is a mistake. There it is. You made it, you're sorry, but it's still there. I'm proud of you for never missing a monthly payment."

"Thanks."

"So just pay it off. And don't come home."

"Thanks a lot."

"I mean it. Don't be like me. I've done everything wrong. But you've changed out there, grown up some. It's doing you good. You'll figure it out."

"Oh. Actually, that's really nice to—"

"Stop worrying all the time, Josie. Breathe. It's dog-parade time. Namaste."

Josie hung up and took a deep, cleansing breath. Lorna hadn't taken a big role in her dream sequences, but maybe in the future, that might change too.

Before bed last night, Josie had scanned the rest of *Spotlight*. The big secret "written right into her features" that Loretta Sweet was hiding? She was biracial: white and Japanese.

Josie supposed that in the 1950s, after World War II, that was a thing? Openly hating on Japanese-Americans even though they'd had nothing to do with the war? "Gross," she'd said at the book.

She remembered a time when Mr. Camoin had praised her for looking "unspecified ethnic," able to "pass as all sorts of races, in a pinch."

At the time, she hadn't really understood that what he'd said was hugely problematic. Absorbing that now for the first time felt like drinking sewer water. Not that she'd ever actually drunk sewer water. But she could imagine, because, it turned out, she had an epically good imagination.

The rest of the book had been pretty uninspired. Chorus girl shines, falls in love with star, while the ousted star, Gloria, cuts her wires, rigs trapdoors, hires some riffraff to mug her at knifepoint, and, when she fails to kill Loretta, finds out about and exposes her racial heritage. By then Loretta has earned enough goodwill that the cast stands with her and the star loves her "even though."

My version was better, Josie thought. *Even though it didn't have an ending.*

"Josie! Josie!" said Mia.

"Yes, Mia, love?"

"You're still here?"

"Yep. I'm still here." And she felt guilt settle all over her. Here for now. In a month, where would she be?

Her phone rang. Her heart startled and sang out, *Justin!*

She checked the number. Victoria.

"Josie! Is everything okay?"

"Hi, yeah, Mia is fine."

"Josie, please don't leave us. Please, please, I'm begging you. At least not till end of summer."

"I can't nanny forever. Mia is getting so attached to me, but I'm not her mom. And I've got . . . stuff to figure out."

"I know. Believe me, Josie, I know. And you're right. I had to jump back into work so quickly, I didn't have a good plan in place. That wasn't fair to Mia. But a great company here I've consulted for just offered me a permanent position, so starting in August, I'm moving to Nairobi and bringing Mia with me."

"Oh! That's . . . that's good. I mean, that'll be really good for Mia."

"Yes! I think so. There's a great international school here; she'll love it. But I'd also love to bring you here too. You could live in Kenya! Travel! And still take care of Mia."

"Wow. That's amazing, but I already decided to leave in June." To go where? That she hadn't decided yet.

"Please stay a little longer. I'll be traveling back and forth till August, and I need to know Mia is in good hands till she can join me full-time. Listen, if you stay, for the next three months I'll pay you double salary."

Josie did a quick calculation. That would pay off over half her debt!

"You don't have to decide about Nairobi now. Just tell me you'll stay for the summer and we can work out what comes next."

"Yes. Okay, I'll stay for the summer. Wow, seriously, thank you."

"Don't mention it. If women don't take care of each other, then what's the point?"

Mia talked to her mom for a while, but the moment she hung up, Josie made another call without thinking twice about it: to the Missoula Repertory Theatre to sign up for a callback slot.

"Who needs New York City?" Josie said to Mia as they ate mac and cheese that evening. "If I can make it in Missoula, Montana, I can make it anywhere."

"Josie, will you sing me a song?" Mia asked.

It was one of the nicest things anyone had ever asked her. Josie jumped up and gave her an exclusive one-woman show, ending with a rousing rendition of "There's No Business Like Show Business," replete with jazz hands. And Mia rewarded her with some mildly sincere applause and a yawn.

A small theater. A small town. If Mia could love Josie more than the whole world, wasn't it scientifically possible that Josie could love a community theater as much as Broadway? Finding an ensemble where she could belong didn't feel impossible. A theater family would definitely be in her future—maybe here, maybe in New York, maybe in . . . Kenya?

But for the moment, she felt no need to decide everything. For the moment, this was enough. The world felt like a better place for having Josie in it, whether or not she was at her peak.

After Mia went to bed, Josie cleaned up slowly and, for the first time since returning, let herself think directly about Justin.

The idea of him had been baking there in the back of her mind. Rising, getting fluffier and fluffier, like a muffin. A delicious thought muffin. She no longer felt stressed at the idea of him, out there in the world without her. She was just left with a lingering kindness—compassion toward their years together and all their love and talk and kisses and stomach-cramping laughter and caring for and about each other like she hadn't known was humanly possible. It was okay if they'd fizzled out and drifted away. Well, it wasn't great, but she would manage. What a wondrous thing that, even if only for a time, he'd been hers and she'd been his.

Now that she'd let the thought of him back in, she felt again that yearning—her own yearning, which the fake book clerks had echoed back at her like a weapon. It hadn't crushed her. It had made her feel stronger. Powerful was the girl who could feel things like that.

Powerful. She felt possible. She allowed herself to feel hope instead of fear of failure. And she picked up her phone.

JOSIE
I want to fight for you. I want to fight to keep us

The words felt lifeless. She deleted the text without sending. These feelings didn't work on a phone. She needed to see him, make eye contact, hear his voice.

She started toward the front door but turned back. She couldn't go hop on a plane to Arizona. Mia was asleep in the next room. Maybe when Victoria returned? But Josie didn't have enough cash for a plane ticket. She wouldn't mind a fast horse-drawn carriage right now. Maybe she could walk there, living off the land. She felt almost capable of it, if she could get ahold of a crossbow. Or she could jump in a taxi and montage herself there.

No, it was impossible. Justin would have to come to her.

She stared at the front door and willed him to come. What if she had some leftover magic in her? That humming energy she'd felt in the mist-infested fake bookstore when she willed her imaginary army into existence.

"Sim sala bim!" she shouted at the door.

"Bubble, bubble, toil and trouble . . ."

"Open sesame!"

"You *shall* pass!"

Show up, Justin. I believe that you can. So show up—
Knock knock knock.

Josie startled. She tore open the door.

"Oh! Hey, Marcus."

"Hey, sorry, I know it's late, just wanted to drop these off." Marcus handed her a stack of books. "Maybe look through them, see if there's anything you want to read for our book club. There's at least one tawdry romance, FYI. I can't wait!" He waved as he jogged off.

Passing Marcus as he left, walking up the driveway, was Justin.

"There you are," she said with an exhale.

He wore a University of Arizona sweatshirt—dusted with what were probably Doritos crumbs—and loose-fitting jeans, his hands in his pockets.

"Surprise!" he said.

"You . . . you drove here? From Arizona?"

"Yeah, it, uh, took longer than I was expecting. I had some car trouble, spent a couple days at my cousin's in Utah—"

"I've called you," she said. "I've texted you."

"I didn't want to talk to you much till I got here, so I could surprise you."

"I hate surprises."

"You do?" he said. The side of his mouth quirked. "Are you serious?"

"Yes. Hate. Hate surprises."

"But all those surprise birthday parties—"

"Sorry, you were being nice. I didn't want to hurt you."

"Yeah . . ." He looked down at his feet. "I know you don't want to hurt me, and I don't want to hurt you, but we keep doing it anyway."

His red hair seemed dark brown in the night, his pale skin golden. He looked tired and pale, and so achingly familiar. She began to shiver.

"Oh, let me . . ." He came in and shut the door behind him, as if she were shivering from the chilly night and not from the effort of holding herself still, resisting a burst forward, a tackle-embrace, to stuff him back into her life.

In the indoor light, he was *such* a ginger. Pale as cream, hair like strands of copper, and freckles that deepened whenever he got into the sun. His people really never should have migrated to sunny Arizona. Why was she wasting this moment thinking about geographically challenged gingers? Justin was standing there, looking like yearning in a bottle, and she couldn't stop shivering.

"You came a long way just to surprise me," she said.

"That was an excuse," he said. "I just wanted to talk to you. And not on the phone. I borrowed my brother's car and I drove, Josie. I just drove." He shrugged, and she saw a little of Hatchet in there: the loneliness, the vulnerability.

She went to the kitchen sink. Too much stuff was whirling in her head and pumping through her veins for her to stand still. He followed her. She started washing the dishes. He stood beside her with a towel, ready to dry. Justin came from a family of eleven. He was used to a lot of dish washing.

"You haven't been happy," he said at last.

A hot cord of anger tightened inside her. *Don't blame everything on me!* But she bit her lip and listened.

"I guess I thought you weren't just depressed about Broadway but that you also missed me, and that once I got to New York, we'd be okay again. Like that stereotypical guy who thinks he can fix everything?" He laughed. "I'm a cliché."

"You kinda are."

"Right?"

That intonation was all Stanley Reeves. His easiness

with his own imperfection gave everyone around him the permission to be at ease with theirs, too. The cord inside Josie relaxed like a dangling rope. He was so much like his *Spotlight* incarnation, and even like Hatchet and the Bandit King too, yet in her imagination she hadn't been able to conjure up the exact Justin, the real Justin. He was always just a little unpredictable.

"Doing something was easier than talking to you about it." Justin took another wet dish from her hand and started to dry. "I got to wondering if maybe you were in love with someone else."

"Me?"

"Well, you moved to Montana. I mean, that was strange, right? Out of the blue? And then you talked to me less and less these past few weeks."

"You barely ever called me!" she said.

He raised an eyebrow at her.

"Yeah, I know. I went silent and weird too, when I moved here," she admitted.

"I was busy with school . . . and honestly, not sure you wanted me to call. I tried to be cool about transferring to New York City, but I feel like such a fraud. Who do I think I am, some big shot?"

Josie laughed. "Well, what was I, then?"

"Josie, you left home when you were seventeen and moved to New York, and lived in a hostel, and found an apartment, and survived on your own. You were the fierce one. While I feel like I've been pretending to be grown enough to match you."

"And any day the fraud police would come and take you away?" she said.

"That's it," he said.

She'd been washing the final dish slowly, in no rush to end the talking. Reluctantly she handed it to him. He took his time drying. His silence was like Hatchet's, easy and thoughtful.

"I've been wrong—a lot," said Josie. "Living in a fantasyland, basically. First believing that I was so much more than I am and then believing I'd lost everything. All or nothing. I assumed my life was a tragedy—full of suffering and lost potential and bad luck. And as a tragedy, my life was a flop. I think the only people left in the audience were you and Nina, and I kept expecting you to walk out at intermission. But it turns out I'd just misunderstood the material. My life isn't a flop. It was just a comedy."

Josie giggled, which made Justin giggle too.

"What?" he asked.

"'I was kind of a big deal in high school,'" said Josie. "I actually said that to people. Like, that was my standard of worth."

"You told people that? Recently?"

"Yes! And think about"—she couldn't stop giggling—"think about those awful workshop shows in New York

I paid to be in because I was so desperate to be in anything."

Justin was laughing too. "The fly-heap one? When that director decided to reenvision *A Midsummer Night's Dream* on a pile of dung and the fairies were all maggots and flies?"

"And the lovers were dung beetles. So magical! Or the one we performed in the kitchen of a tapas restaurant the health department had shut down."

"Was that the one when the whole cast was robots?"

"We were people but we were supposed to sing in monotone and occasionally beep. Because dependence on modern technology."

"And the—" Justin had to stop, he was laughing so hard. Josie just nodded, because she knew which one he meant but couldn't speak either. He mimed the stop-sign hat. They wiped their tears and caught their breaths.

He was looking at her, so close beside her that a kiss would be as easy as a lean, and though she'd kissed him thousands of times, she felt icy-scaredy-shivery. She strolled to the other side of the counter.

"I've been reading a lot of books lately," she said, "and the guy lead, it's always you. Well, they look like you, anyway. You know, in my mind. They have your body, your face, your hard, chiseled, hairless chest."

He frowned and rubbed his chest. "Is it?"

"They weren't you *exactly*, but they did have pieces of you, as if your personality splintered and bits of it went into each of them. I felt like I was experiencing your youness in small offerings."

"That's . . . kinda great."

"Well, me through the main character. It's a long story; I'll explain later." She was actually looking forward to it, because she was suddenly certain that Justin would believe her. "But the point is, when Old Betsy"—she tapped her temple—"searched for the face of the guy my main character should fall in love with, I always chose you."

"Wait . . . Old Betsy?"

"My new nickname for my brain."

"Got it."

"But the important part is, even when you were ignoring all my calls and texts for days . . ." She looked hard at him. He cringed. "Even when I thought you might be in love with someone else, I pictured you in these stories not as the villain but as the love interest. *My* love interest."

"That's pretty amazing."

"Yeah, it was." She frowned. "Well, one time you were the villain, but you also built an awesome mechasaur, so you weren't entirely unredeemable."

He leaned against the counter, hands out. "And now I'm here. So . . . what do we do next?"

"I told Victoria I'd stay the summer. I have a callback for the chorus in a community theater production and . . . I kinda want to do it."

"Cool," said Justin.

"I guess. And then . . ." She looked up at him, needing to read his expression. "I could stay here, get my GED, and study theater at the university. Or I could move to Nairobi with Victoria and Mia. Or I could work till I pay off my debt and try New York again."

"Or?" he said.

He looked at her plaintively, pleadingly. She laughed.

"I love your laugh," he said, a little hoarse.

She felt at once so comfortable and yet also timid, as if this was building to their first kiss again. The one they'd shared on the back porch of Nina's house during a drama-club party.

"Lately I realized I *could* lose you and survive. I'd be okay. But I'd rather not have to. I'd rather keep you."

He smiled, and that one dimple came out. The sight of it made her smile, which in turn made him smile bigger.

"What?" he asked, but still smiling. "Did I miss something?"

"Yeah," she said. "Me."

She could see it take a second for him to get it, and then he groaned.

"You are so cheesy, and I love the cheesy so much, I can't help it."

All over again, Josie felt that peculiar thumping in her chest, as if a bird were trapped, wings flapping, trying to free itself of her rib cage. She felt those lines of cold travel up her legs from her feet, threatening that the ground was unstable, that she shouldn't trust any foundation no matter how strong it seemed. And then the push of emotion in her throat, all that feeling boiling up, uncontainable. Her hands gripped together, shy, afraid of rejection. Yet her eyes watched his, asking him to see her.

He'd been coming closer. The counter was no longer between them. He held out his arms, and she moved in. He pulled her in closer, she hummed, and he led. They danced.

"Missoula seems nice," he said into her hair.

"Winter is cozy until it's not. I hear summer is transcendental. There's a great bookstore under new ownership and more yoga studios and pubs than you can shake a stick at. Also I'm joining a book club. I could stay here, but I don't know."

"I don't know either," said Justin. "Why is it as soon as we turn eighteen suddenly we're supposed to know everything?"

"I don't know," she said.

"Exactly."

She wanted Justin to put his arm around her waist and pull her suddenly up a rope and into a tree house. She wanted to make out with him in the back of a hay wagon. She wanted to spoon beneath a shared blanket under the stars in a ruthless, uncivilized landscape. She wanted to share a stage with him, pull him into the spotlight with her, and kiss him for all the world to see, surrounded by glorious woodland creatures flying on kites.

"I missed you so much," she said. "The real, surprising, imperfect you."

Justin dipped her, just as the Bandit King had in his treetop lovers' lair.

"You just missed my smooth skills on the dance floor," he said.

He brought her back up. Her hand was in his ruffled, rust-colored hair. He took that hand and kissed her fingers.

There were, Josie considered, any number of things worse than peaking in high school. Chronic toothache. Being eaten alive by ants. Genocide. Somewhere further down Josie's list—but still on the list—was giving up what you loved because you were afraid of failing, whether it was a stage or a person. Or both.

So she kissed her person.

He picked her up, an arm under her shoulders, another beneath her knees, the way Stanley Reeves had caught her when the wire broke. She squealed with surprise.

"I've got you," Justin said.

"You've been working out," she said.

"Push-ups, baby. Every morning."

He carried her to the couch and made to toss her onto it, but she wouldn't let go, and pulled him down with her.

They kissed, and though his body was so familiar to her, she felt as if she were discovering it anew. She bit his chin and kissed his neck, felt his stomach and entwined her legs with his.

Josie leaned back, her shoulders pressing against something too bulky to be a throw pillow. There was a click, and a robotic voice said, *"Read me a story."*

ACKNOWLEDGMENTS

This book spent years in workshops and rehearsals before it was finally ready for its opening night. Many thanks to the supporting cast who offered feedback and encouragement, including Samantha Richardson, Patrice Caldwell, Justine Larbalestier, Dean Hale, Jodi Reamer, Jessica "Yatzee" Sheridan, Max Hale, Victoria Wells Arms, Jerusha Hess, Barry Goldblatt, Eddie Gamarra, Zac Chandler, Karen Sherman, Jennifer Healey, Megan Abbate, Alice Gorelick, and Anah Tillar.

A standing ovation for my editor Connie Hsu and her tireless devotion to the story. A spotlight on the Trevor Project for their life-saving work. And an encore for my kids, who waited patiently while their mama got lost in this story again and again and again. Bravo, readers. Now let's go out for cheese fries.

Josie Pie's Bookshelf

FEMURS IN THE ATTIC
This is book fourteen in the series. At what point is someone going to say, "Hey, Emma, there sure are a lot of murders happening in your high school."

THE TREMBLING
WHAT IS THE MATTER WITH YOU— DO NOT READ THIS!!! (note to my past self after three sleepless nights)

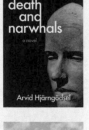

DEPRESSION, DEATH, AND NARWALS
DNF*

VALENTINE'S DAY
So romantic! I want to live in this book! JK. You'd have to be some kind of dark-minded non-human to want to live in this. I mean, it is a really good read, but it's not going to be what you'd expect, unless you're expecting bleak survivalist horror with a splash of romance and a lot of post-mortem goo.

*DNF = did not finish

THE HIGHWAYMAN CAME RIDING

I didn't know I was a tawdry romance kind of a gal, but this book proved me wrong. I read it aloud to my BF and he also enjoyed. :)

GREEK MYTHOLOGY

Informative. This book is definitely for you if you like droughts, towels, firewood, fossils, and cereal without milk.

ANNE OF GREEN GABLES

I loved it when I was in middle school, and I love it now too, though in a different way because I'm a different person. It's so cool how books grow up with us.

LAVENDER GARCÍA AND THE UNEXPECTED CANADIAN SEMESTER

I really liked this book—great characters, great dialogue—but it has way more medical drama than the cover let on. SPOILER: Am I the only one who didn't know that "Canadian Semester" is a kind of necrotic fungus???

THE NAUSEOUS LIFE

DNF

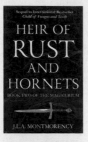

HEIR OF RUST AND HORNETS

So enchanting and exciting and fun! Also, the second book in a trilogy apparently! Hey, Josie, maybe read book jackets more carefully before jumping in!

LADY JUSTICE (Issue #318)

I've read this entire series from the beginning, but this issue remains my favorite. For personal reasons.

BLEEDING FROM OUR EYEBALLS

DNF. TBH, DNStart.

LOVE IN THE SPOTLIGHT

It may look bland and old-fashioned, but this is honestly a book I could live in. At least, if I could reimagine a few parts . . .